Also available from

LINDA LAEL
MILLER

and HQN Books

And don't miss

Forever a Hero

LINDA LAEL MILLER

Always a Cowboy

HQN™

HQN™

ISBN-13: 978-0-373-80284-5

Always a Cowboy

This edition published by arrangement with Harlequin Books S.A.

For questions and comments about the quality of this book, please contact us at CustomerService@Harlequin.com.

www.HQNBooks.com

Printed in U.S.A.

Dear Reader,

Welcome back to Mustang Creek, Wyoming, home of hot cowboys and the smart, beautiful women who love them.

Always a Cowboy is the story of Drake Carson, the second of the three Carson brothers, and Lucinda "Luce" Hale. Drake is a true cowboy with a ranch to run, plus stallion trouble and a mountain lion trying to wipe out his whole herd of cattle. He certainly has no time, or so he thinks, for the likes of Luce, a stranger and a trespasser to boot.

Luce is doing a postgraduate study, and her subject is wild mustangs and their interactions with livestock. She is one determined city woman, willing to climb over fences and hike for miles, rain or shine. Luce wants to know all about ranching, and ranchers—one in particular.

If you read the first book in this new trilogy, *Once a Rancher*, you'll recognize a lot of the characters, and I hope you'll feel right at home in their midst.

The third book in the series, *Forever a Hero*, features the youngest Carson brother, Mace, a combination cowboy/winemaker, and the woman whose life he once saved.

Ranch life runs deep with me; I live on my own modest little spread, called the Triple L, and we've got critters aplenty: five horses, two dogs and two cats. And those are just the official ones—we share the land with wild turkeys, deer and the occasional moose, and I wouldn't live any other way.

My love of animals shows in my stories, and I never miss a chance to speak for the silent, furry ones who have no voices and no choices. So please support your local animal shelters, have your pets spayed and neutered and, if you're feeling a mite lonely, why not rescue a four-legged somebody waiting to love you with the purest of devotion.

Thank you for bending an ear my way, and enjoy the story.

With all best,

Linda Lael Miller

For Doug and Teresa, with love

CHAPTER ONE

THE WEATHER JUST plain sucked, but that was okay with Drake Carson. In his opinion, rain was better than snow any day of the week, and as for sleet...well, that was wicked, especially in the wide-open spaces, coming at a person in stinging blasts like a barrage of buckshot. Yep, give him a slow, gentle rainfall every time, the kind that generally meant spring was in the works. Anyhow, he could stand to get a little wet.

Here in Wyoming, this close to the mountains, the month of May might bring sunshine and pastures blanketed with wildflowers—or a freak blizzard, wild enough to bury cattle and people alike.

Raising his coat collar around his ears, he nudged his horse into motion with his heels. Starburst obeyed, although he seemed hesitant about it, unusually jumpy, in fact, and when that happened, Drake paid attention. Horses were prey animals and, as such, their instincts and senses were fine-tuned to their surroundings in ways a human being couldn't equal.

Something was going on, that was for sure.

For nearly a year now, they'd been coming up short, Drake and his crew, when they tallied the livestock. Some losses were inevitable, of course, but too many calves, along with the occasional steer or heifer, had gone missing over the past twelve months.

Sometimes, they found a carcass. Other times, not.

Like all ranchers, Drake took every decrease in the herd seriously, and he wanted reasons.

The Carson spread was big, and while Drake couldn't keep an eye on the whole place at once, he sure as hell tried.

"Stay with me," he told his dogs, Harold and Violet, a pair of German shepherds from the same litter and two of the best friends he'd ever had.

Then, tightening the reins slightly, in case Starburst took a notion to bolt instead of skittering and sidestepping like he was doing now, Drake looked around, squinting against the downpour. Whatever he'd expected to see—a grizzly or a wildcat or even a band of modern-day rustlers—he *hadn't* expected to lay eyes on a lone female. She was just up ahead, crouched behind a small tree and clearly drenched, despite the dark rain slicker covering her slender form.

She was peering through a pair of binoculars, having taken no apparent notice of Drake, his dogs or his horse. Even with the rain pounding down, they should have been hard to miss, being only fifty yards away.

Whoever the lady turned out to be, he wasn't giving her points for alertness.

He studied her as he approached, but there was nothing familiar about her. Drake would have recognized a local woman. Mustang Creek was a small community, and strangers stood out.

Anyway, the whole ranch was posted against trespassers, mainly to keep tourists on the far side of the fences. A lot of visiting sightseers had seen a few too many G-rated animal movies and thought they could cozy up to a bear, a bison or a wolf and snap a selfie to post on social media.

Some greenhorns were simply naive or heedless, but others were entitled know-it-alls, disregarding the warnings of park rangers, professional wilderness guides and concerned locals. It galled Drake, the risks people took, camping and hiking in areas that were off-limits, walking right up to the wildlife, as if the place were a petting zoo. The lucky ones got away alive, but they were often missing the family pet or a few body parts when it was over.

Drake had been on more than one search-and-rescue mission, organized by the Bliss County Sheriff's Department, and he'd seen things that kept him awake nights, if he thought about them too much.

He shook off the gruesome images and concentrated on the problem at hand—the woman in the rain slicker. Wondered which category—naive, thoughtless or arrogant—she fell into.

She didn't appear to be in any danger at the moment but, then again, she seemed oblivious to everything around her, with the exception of whatever it was she was looking at through those binoculars of hers.

Presently, it dawned on Drake that whatever else she might be, she *wasn't* the reason his big Appaloosa gelding was so worked up.

The woman seemed fixated on the wide meadow, actually a shallow valley, just beyond the copse of cottonwood.

Starburst pranced and tossed his head, and Drake tightened the reins slightly, gave a gruff command.

The horse calmed down a little.

Once Drake cleared the stand of cottonwoods, he stood in the stirrups, adjusted his hat and followed the woman's gaze. Briefly, he couldn't believe what he was seeing, after days, weeks and months of searching, with only a rare and always distant sighting.

But there they were, big as life; the stallion, his band of wild mustangs—and half a dozen mares lured from his own pastures.

Forgetting the rain-slicked trespasser for a few moments, his breath trapped in his throat, Drake stared, taking a quick count in his head, temporarily immobilized by the sheer grandeur of the sight.

The stallion was magnificence on the hoof, lean but with every muscle as clearly defined as if he'd been sculpted by a master. His coat was a ghostly gray, darkened by the rain, and his mane and tail were blacker than black.

The animal, well aware that he had an audience and plainly unconcerned, lifted his head slowly from the creek where he'd been drinking and made no move to run. With no more than a hundred yards between them, he regarded Drake for what seemed like a long while, as though sizing him up.

The rest of the band, mares included, went still, heads high, ears pricked forward, hindquarters tensed as they awaited some signal from the stallion.

Drake couldn't help admiring that four-footed devil, even as he silently cursed the critter, consigning him to seven kinds of hell. The instant he pressed his boot heels to Starburst's quivering sides, a motion so subtle that Drake himself was barely aware of it, the stallion went into action.

Nostrils flared, eyes rolling, the cocky son of a bitch snorted, then threw back his head and whinnied, the sound piercing the moisture-thickened air.

The band whirled toward the hillside and scattered.

The stallion stood watching as Drake, rope in hand and ready to throw, drove Starburst from a dead stop to a full run.

Before Starburst reached the creek, though, the big gray spun on his hind legs and damn near took wing as he raced across the clearing and up the slope.

Drake and his gelding splashed through the narrow stream, and up the opposite bank, the dogs loping alongside.

But hard as he rode, the whole experience felt like a slow-motion sequence from one of his brother Slater's documentaries. He and Starburst might as well have been standing still for all the progress they made closing the gap.

The stallion paused at the top of the ridge, he and his band sketched against the stormy sky. Time seemed to stop, just for an instant, before the spell was broken and the whole bunch of them vanished as swiftly as if they'd melted into the clouds.

Drake knew he'd lost this round.

He reined Starburst to a halt, grabbed his hat by the brim and slapped it hard against his left thigh before jamming it back on his head. Then, still breathing hard, his jaw clamped down so hard that his ears ached from the strain, he recoiled his rope and fastened it to his saddle.

Harold and Violet were at the foot of the ridge by then, panting visibly and looking back at Drake in confusion.

He summoned them back with a shrill whistle, and they trotted toward him, tongues lolling, sides heaving.

Only when he'd ridden across the creek again did Drake remember the woman. Coupled with the fact that he'd just been outwitted by that damn stallion—again—her presence stuck in his hide like a burr.

She stood watching him as he rode toward her, her face a pale oval within the hood of her slicker.

With bitter amusement, he noticed that her feet were set a little apart, as in a fighter's stance, and her elbows jutted out at her sides. Her hands, no doubt bunched into fists, were pressing hard into her hips.

As he drew nearer, he noted the spark of fury in her eyes and the tight line of her mouth.

Under other circumstances, he might have thrown back his head and laughed out loud at her sheer audacity, but at the moment his pride was giving him too much grief for that.

He hadn't managed to get this close to the stallion—or his prize mares—for longer than he cared to remember. While he hated letting them get away so easily, he knew the dogs would be run ragged if he gave chase, and might even end up getting their heads kicked in. They'd been bred for herding cattle, not wild horses.

They were disappointed just the same and whimpered in baleful protest at being called off, which only made Drake feel like more of a loser than he already did.

Harold and Violet, named for two of his favorite elementary school teachers, ambled over to him, tails wagging. They were drenched to the skin and getting wetter by the minute, but they were quick to forgive, unlike their human counterparts, himself included.

Just then, Drake's chestnut quarter horse, a two-year-old mare with impeccable bloodlines, caught his eye, appearing on the crest of the ridge. Hope stirred briefly, and he drew in his breath to whistle for her, but before he could make a sound, the stallion came back, crowding the mare, nipping at her flanks and butting her with his head.

And then she was gone again.

Damn it all to hell.

"Thanks for nothing, mister!"

It was the intruder, the trespasser. The woman stormed toward Drake through the rain-bent grass, waving the binoculars like a maestro raising a baton at the symphony. He'd forgotten about her until that moment, and the reminder did nothing for his mood.

He was overreacting, he knew that, but he couldn't seem to change course.

She was a sight, he'd say that, plowing through the grass the way she was, all fuss and fury and wet through and through.

Drake waited a few moments before he spoke, just watching her advance on him like a one-woman army.

Miraculously, he felt his equanimity returning. In fact, he was mildly curious about her, now that the rush of adrenaline from his lame-ass confrontation with the stallion was starting to subside.

Drake waited with what was, for him, uncommon patience. He hoped the approaching tornado, pint-size but definitely category five, wouldn't step in a gopher hole and break a leg, or get bitten by a snake before she completed the charge.

Born and raised on this land, where there were perils aplenty, Drake understood the importance of practical caution. Out here, experience wasn't just the best teacher, it was often a harsh one, too.

As the lady got closer, he made out her face, still framed by the hood of her coat, and a pair of amber eyes that flashed as she demanded, "Do you have any idea how long it took me to get that close to those horses? Days!" She paused to suck in a furious breath. "And what happens when I finally catch up to them? *You* come along and scare them off!"

Drake resettled his hat, tugging hard at the brim, and waited.

The woman all but stamped her feet. "Days!" she repeated wildly.

Drake felt his mouth stretch in the direction of a grin, but he suppressed it. "Excuse me, ma'am, but the fact is, I'm a bit confused. You're here because…?"

"Because of the horses!" The tone and pitch of her voice said he was an idiot for even asking such a question. Apparently, she thought he ought to be able to read her mind—ahead of time, and from a convenient distance. Just like a woman.

Silently, he congratulated himself on his restraint—and for managing a reasonable tone. "I see," he said, although of course he didn't see at all. This was his land, and she was on it, and he still didn't have any idea why.

"The least you could do is apologize," she informed him, glaring. Her hands were resting on her slim hips, like before, causing her breasts to rise in a very attractive way.

Still mounted, Drake adjusted his hat again. The dogs sat on either side of him, looking on with calm and bedraggled interest. Starburst, on the other hand, nickered and sidestepped and tossed his head, as startled as if the woman had sprung up from the ground like a magic bean stalk.

When Drake replied, he sounded downright amiable, his tone designed to piss her off even more, if that was possible. If there was one thing an angry woman hated, he figured, it was exaggerated politeness. "Now, why would I apologize? Given that I *live* here, I mean. This is private property, Ms.—"

She wasn't at all fazed by this information. Nor did she offer her name.

"It took me hours to track those horses down," she ranted on, flinging her arms out wide for emphasis. "In this weather, no less! I finally get close enough to observe them in their natural habitat, and you…you…" She paused, but only to take in a breath so she could go right on strafing him with words. "*You* try hiding behind a tree for hours without moving a muscle, with water dripping down your neck!"

Drake might have pointed out that he was no stranger to inclement weather, since he rode fence lines and worked under any and all conditions, white-hot heat and blinding snowstorms and everything in between, but he felt no need to explain that to this woman or anyone else on the planet.

Zeke Carson, his late father, had lived by a creed, and he'd drilled it into his sons early on: never complain, never explain. Let your actions tell the story.

"What were you doing there, anyhow, lurking behind my tree?" he asked moderately.

She bristled. "*Your* tree? No one owns a tree. And I wasn't *lurking*!"

"You were," he contradicted cheerfully. "And maybe you're right about the tree. But people can sure as hell own the ground it grows out of, and that's the case here, I'm afraid."

She rolled her eyes.

Great, he thought, half amused and half annoyed, a tree hugger, of the holier-than-thou variety, it seemed.

The woman probably drove one of those little hybrid cars, not that there was anything wrong with them, but he'd bet she was self-righteous about it, cruising along at the speed of a lawn mower in the fast lane.

Impatient with the trail his thoughts were taking, Drake made an effort to draw in his horns a bit. He was assuming a lot here.

Still, he made every effort to protect and honor the environment, trees included, and if she was implying otherwise, he meant to set her straight. Nobody loved the natural world more than he did and, furthermore, he had a right to ask questions. The Carsons had held the deed to this ranch since homestead days, and in case she hadn't noticed, he wasn't running a public campground. Nor was this a state or national park.

He leaned forward in the saddle. "Do the words *no trespassing* mean anything to you?" he asked mildly.

Although he didn't want it to show, he was still enjoying this encounter, and way more than he should have at that.

She merely glowered up at him, arms folded now, chin set at an obstinate angle.

Suddenly, Drake was tired to the bone. "All right. Let's see if we can clarify matters. That tree—" he gestured to the one she'd taken refuge behind earlier and spoke very slowly so she could follow "—is on my ranch." He paused. "I'm Drake Carson. And you are?"

The look of surprise on her face was gratifying. "*You're* Drake Carson?"

"I was when I woke up this morning," he drawled. "I don't imagine that's changed since then." He let a moment pass. "Now, how about answering my original question? What are you doing here?"

She seemed to wilt, and Drake supposed that was a victory, however small, but he wasn't inclined to celebrate. Her attitude got on his last nerve, but there was something delicate about her. A kind of fragility that made him want to protect her. "I'm studying the horses."

The brim of Drake's hat spilled water down his front as he nodded. "Well, yeah, I kind of figured that. It's really not the point, though, is it? Like I said before, and more than once, this is private property. And if you'd asked permission to be here, I'd know it."

She blushed, but no explanation was forthcoming. Her mouth opened, then closed again, and her eyes went wide. "You're *him*."

"And you would be...?"

The next moment, she was blustering again. Ignoring his question, too. "Tall man on a tall horse," she remarked, her tone scathing. "Very intimidating."

A few seconds earlier, he'd been in charge here. Now he felt defensive, which was ridiculous on all counts.

He drew a deep breath, released it slowly and spoke with quiet authority. He hoped. "Believe me, I'm not trying to intimidate you," he said. "My point—once again—is that you don't have the right to be here, much less yell at me."

"Yes, I do." Her tone was testy. "Well, the being here part, anyway. And I don't think I was yelling."

Of all the freaking gall. Drake glowered at the young

woman, who was standing next to his horse by then, un-afraid, giving as good as she got.

"Say what?" he asked.

"I *do* have the right to be on this ranch," she insisted. "I asked your mother's permission to come out and study the wild horses, and she said yes, fine, no problem at all. She was very supportive, as it happens."

Well, shit.

Why hadn't she said that in the first place?

Moreover, why hadn't his mother bothered to mention any of this to him?

For some reason, even in light of this development, he couldn't back off, or not completely, anyway. Maybe it was his stubborn pride. "Okay," he said evenly. "*Why* do you want to study wild horses? Considering that they're...*wild* and everything."

She was undaunted. No real surprise there, although it was frustrating as hell. "I'm getting my PhD, and my dissertation is about the way wildlife, particularly horses, co-exist with the animals on working ranches." She added, "And how ranchers deal with them. Ranchers like you."

Ranchers like him. Right.

"Let's get something straight, here and now," he said, feeling cornered for some reason, and wondering why he liked it. "My mother might have given you the go-ahead to bedevil all the horses you can rustle up on this spread, but that's as far as it goes. You aren't going to study *me*."

"Are you saying you don't obey your mother?" she asked sweetly.

"That's it," he answered, without a trace of goodwill. By then, Drake's mood was back on a downhill slide. What was he doing out here in the damn rain, bantering with some self-proclaimed intellectual? He wasn't just cold, tired and wet, he was hungry, since all he'd had before leaving the house this morning was a slice of toast and a cup of coffee. He'd been in a hurry to get started, and now his blood sugar had dropped to the soles of his boots, and the effect on his disposition was not pretty.

The saddle leather creaked as he bent toward her. "Listen, Ms. Whoever-you-are, I don't give a rat's ass about your thesis, or your theories about ranchers and wild horses, either. Do whatever it is you do, stay out of my way and try not to get yourself killed while you're at it."

She didn't bat an eye. "Hale," she announced brightly, as though he hadn't spoken. "My name is Lucinda Hale, but everybody calls me Luce."

He inhaled a long, deep breath. If he'd ever had that much trouble learning a woman's name before, he didn't recall the occasion. "Ms. Hale, then," he began, tugging at the brim of his hat in a gesture that was more automatic than cordial. "I'll leave you to it. While I'm sure your work is absolutely fascinating, not to mention vital to the future of the planet, I have plenty of my own to do. In short, while I've enjoyed shadowboxing with you, I'm fresh out of leisure time."

He might've been talking to the barn wall. "Oh, don't worry," she said cheerfully. "I wouldn't *dream* of interfering. I'll be an observer, that's all. Watching, figuring out how things work, making a few notes. You won't even know I'm around."

Drake bit back a terse reply and reined his horse away, although he didn't use his heels. The dogs, still fascinated by the whole scenario, sat tight. "You're right, Ms. Hale.

I won't know you're around, because you won't be. Not around *me*, that is."

"You really are a very difficult man," she observed almost sadly. "Surely you can see the value of my project. Interactions between wild animals, domesticated ones and human beings?"

LUCE WAS COLD, wet, a little amused and *very* intrigued.

Drake Carson was gawking at her as though she'd just popped in from a neighboring dimension, wearing a tutu and waving a wand. His two beautiful dogs, waiting obediently for some word or gesture from their master, seemed equally curious.

The consternation on the man's face was absolutely priceless.

And a very handsome face it was, at least what she could see of it, shadowed by the brim of his hat the way it was. If he resembled his younger brother, Mace, whom she'd met earlier that day, he was one very impressive man.

She decided to push him a bit, just to see what happened. "You run this ranch, don't you?"

"I do my best."

She liked his voice, which was a deep, slow drawl now, not mocking like before. "Then you're the one I want."

Open mouth, she thought, insert foot.

"For my project, I mean," she added hastily.

His strong jawline tightened visibly. "I don't have time to babysit you," he said. "This is a working ranch, not a resort."

"As I've said repeatedly, Mr. Carson, you won't have to do any such thing. I can take care of myself, and I promise you, I won't be underfoot."

He seemed unconvinced. And still irritated in the extreme.

But he didn't ride away.

Luce had already been warned that Drake wouldn't take to her project, but somehow she hadn't expected this much resistance. She was normally a persuasive person, and reasonable, too.

Of course, it helped if the other person was somewhat agreeable.

Mentally, she cataloged the things she'd learned about Drake Carson.

He was in charge of the ranch, which spanned thousands of acres and was home to lots of cattle and horses, as well as wildlife. The Carsons had very deep roots in Bliss County, Wyoming, going back several generations. He loved the outdoors, and he was good with animals, particularly horses.

He was, in fact, a true cowboy.

He was also on the quiet side, solitary by nature, slow to anger—but when he did get mad, he could be formidable. At thirty-two, Drake had never been married; he was college-educated, and once he'd gotten his degree—land management and animal husbandry—he'd come straight back to the ranch, having no desire to live anywhere else. He worked from sunrise to sunset and often longer.

Harry, the Carsons' housekeeper, whose real name was Harriet Armstrong, had dished up some sort of heavenly pie when Luce had arrived at the main ranch house fairly early in the day. As soon as Harry understood who Luce was and why she was there, she'd proceeded to spill information about Drake at a steady clip.

Luce had encountered Mace Carson, Drake's younger

brother, very briefly, when he'd come in from the family vineyard expressly for a piece of pie. Harry had introduced them and explained Luce's mission—i.e., to gather material for her dissertation and interview Drake in depth, thus getting the rancher's perspective.

Mace had smiled slightly and shaken his head in response to Harry's briefing. "I'm glad you're here, Ms. Hale, but I'm afraid my brother isn't going to be a whole lot of use as a research subject. He's into his work and not much else, and he doesn't like to be distracted from whatever he's got scheduled for the day. Makes him testy."

A quick glance in Harry's direction had confirmed the sinking sensation Mace's words produced. The older woman had given a small, reluctant nod of agreement.

Well, Luce thought now, standing face-to-horse with Drake, they'd certainly known what they were talking about, Mace and Harry both.

Drake was *definitely* testy.

He stared grimly into the rainy distance for a long moment, then muttered, "As if that damn stallion wasn't enough to get under my hide like a nasty itch."

"Cheer up," Luce said. She loved a challenge. "I'm here to help."

Drake gave her a long, level look. "Why didn't you say so in the first place?" he asked very slowly, and without a hint of humor. He flung out his free hand, making his point, the reins resting easily in the other one. "My problems are over."

"Didn't you say you were leaving?" Luce asked.

He opened his mouth, closed it again, evidently reconsidering whatever he'd been about to say. Finally, with a hoarse note in his voice, he went on. "I planned to," he said. "But if I did, you'd be out here alone." He looked around. "Where's your horse? You won't be getting close to those critters again today. The stallion will see to that."

Luce's interest was genuine. "You sound as if you know him pretty well."

"We understand each other, all right," Drake said. "We should. We've been playing this game for a while now."

That was going in her notes.

She shook her head in belated answer to his question about her means of transportation. "I don't have a horse," she explained. "I parked my car at your place and hiked out here."

The day had been breathtakingly beautiful, before the clouds lowered and thickened and began dumping rain. She'd hiked in all the western states and in Europe, and this was some gorgeous country. The Grand Tetons were just that. Grand.

"The house is a long way from here. You came all this way *on foot*?" Drake frowned at her. "Did my mother know you were crazy when she agreed to let you do your study here?"

"I actually enjoy hiking. A little rain doesn't bother me. I'll take a hot shower when I get back to the house, change clothes and—"

"When you get back to the house?" he repeated warily. "You're staying there?"

This was where she could tell him that Blythe Carson was an old friend of her mother's, and she'd already been installed in one of the guest rooms, but she decided not to mention that just yet, in case he thought she was taking advantage. She was determined not to inconvenience the family, and if she felt she was imposing, she would move to a hotel. She'd planned to do just that, actually, but Blythe, hospitable woman that she was, wouldn't hear of it. Lord knew there was plenty of room, she'd said, and it wouldn't make any sense to drive back and forth from town when Luce's work was right here on the ranch.

"You live in a beautiful house, by the way," she said, trying to smooth things over a little. "Not what I expected to find out here in the wide-open spaces. All those chandeliers and oil paintings and gorgeous antiques." Was she jabbering? Yes. She definitely was, and she couldn't seem to stop. "I mean, it's hardly the Ponderosa." She beamed a smile at Drake. "I was planning to check into a hotel, or pitch a tent at one of the campgrounds, but your mother wanted no part of that idea, so…well, here I am." Why couldn't she just shut up? "My room has a fabulous view. It'll be incredible, waking up to those mountains every morning."

Drake, understandably, was still a few beats behind, and little wonder, the way she'd been prattling. "You're *staying* with us?"

Hadn't she just said that?

She smiled her most ingenuous smile. "How else can I observe you in your native habitat?" The truth was, she intended to camp at least part of the time, provided the weather improved, simply because she wanted to enjoy the outdoors.

Drake himself was one of the reasons she'd chosen the area for her research work, but he didn't know that. He was well respected, a rancher's rancher, with a reputation for hard work, integrity and intelligence.

She'd known, even before Harry filled her in on the more personal aspects of Drake's life, that he was an animal advocate, as well as a prominent rancher, that he'd minored in ecology. She'd first seen his name in print when she was still an undergrad, just a quote in an article, expressing his belief that running a large cattle operation could and should be done without endangering wildlife or the environment. Knowing that her mother and Blythe Carson were close had been a deciding factor, too, of course—a way of gaining access.

She allowed herself a few minutes to study the man. He sat his horse confidently, relaxed and comfortable in the saddle, the reins loosely held. The well-trained animal stood there calmly, clipping grass but not moving otherwise during their discussion.

Drake broke into her reverie by saying, "Guess I'd better take you back before something happens to you." He leaned toward her, reaching down. "Climb on."

She looked at the proffered hand and bit her lip, hesitant to explain that, despite her consuming interest in horses, she wasn't an experienced rider—the last time she'd been in the saddle, at summer camp when she was twelve, something had spooked her mount. She'd been thrown, breaking her collarbone and her right arm, and nearly trampled in the process.

Passion for horses or not, she was anything but confident.

She couldn't tell him that, not after the exchange they'd just had. He would no doubt laugh or make some cutting remark, or both, and her pride smarted at the very idea.

Besides, she wouldn't be holding the reins, handling the huge gelding; Drake would. And there was no denying the difficulties the weather presented, in terms of trailing the stallion and his mares from place to place.

She'd gotten some great footage during the afternoon,

though, and made some useful notes, which meant the day wasn't a total loss.

"My backpack's heavy," she pointed out, her drummed-up courage already faltering a little. The top of that horse was pretty far off the ground. She could climb mountains, for Pete's sake, but that was small consolation; she'd been standing on her own two feet the whole time.

At last, Drake smiled, and the impact of that smile was palpable. He was still leaning toward her, still holding out his hand. "Starburst's knees won't buckle under the weight of a backpack," he told her. "Or yours, either."

The logic was sound, if not particularly comforting.

Drake slipped his booted foot out from the stirrup to make room for hers. "Come on. I'll haul you up behind me."

She handed up the backpack, sighed heavily. "Okay," she said. Then, gamely, she took Drake's hand. His grip was strong, and he swung her up behind him with no apparent effort.

It was easy to imagine this man working with horses, delivering breach calves and digging postholes for fences.

Settled on the animal's broad back, Luce had no choice but to put her arms around Drake's cowboy-lean waist and grip him like the jaws of life.

The rain was coming down harder, and conversation was impossible.

Gradually, Luce relaxed enough to loosen her hold on Drake's middle.

A little, anyway.

Now that she was fairly sure she wasn't facing certain death, Luce allowed herself to enjoy the ride. Intrepid hiker though she was, the thought of trudging back in the driving rain made her wince.

She hadn't missed the irony of the situation, either. She wanted to study wild horses, but she was a rank greenhorn with a slew of sweaty-palmed phobias. Drake had surely noticed, skilled as he was, and he would have been well within his rights to comment.

He didn't, though.

When they finally reached the ranch house, he was considerate enough not to grin when she slid clumsily off the horse and almost landed on her rear in a giant puddle. No, he simply tugged at the brim of his hat, suppressing a smile, and rode away without looking back.

CHAPTER TWO

WHEN DRAKE CAME in for supper that night, he was half-starved, chilled to the bone and feeling as though he'd worked like an old cow pony and still achieved next to nothing.

He'd seen the mare he'd bought for a small fortune and personally trained, out there on the range that day, but he sure hadn't won her back. Which only added insult to injury. That whistle had always brought her right to the pasture fence at a full run for an apple or a carrot and a nose rub. It had almost worked today, but not quite, not with that young stallion keeping watch.

Drake hadn't found the latest missing calf, either. He'd repaired one of the gates on the north pasture—and discovered he had exactly the same problem with the one just east of it. Then he had to call the vet to come out because he had a cow dropping a calf and she was in obvious trouble...

Every single minute of the day had brought new problems.

Add to that the young graduate student who, for some

reason he couldn't understand, was now living in the same house. *His* house. He'd deposited her near the porch when they got back, and he'd ridden away. Surely that was polite enough. Especially since he wasn't interested in being part of her "study."

He remembered to take off his boots in the nick of time, leaving them on the porch. Harry would lynch him if he mucked up her floors, after delivering a loud lecture of the how-many-times-do-I-have-to-tell-you variety. In his sock feet, he hung up his coat and headed for his room. A long shower and a hot meal would solve *some* of his problems.

But not all of them.

He met Luce Hale as soon as he'd rounded the corner and stepped into the hallway. Actually, he practically body-slammed the woman and would have sent her sprawling if he hadn't been so quick to grab her by the shoulders.

Getting another look at her, he realized she was a hell of a lot prettier than he'd thought at first, now that she'd shed her rain gear. In fact, she was *very* pretty, with her long chestnut hair and incredible tawny eyes, and that tall, toned and athletic body of hers. Seeing her in the formfitting jeans and pink shirt she'd changed into, he could believe she'd done plenty of hiking.

He, on the other hand, probably looked as if he'd been hog-tied and dragged through a mudhole. He might've had to do some hiking himself earlier, come to think of it, when a bolt of lightning spooked his horse while he was checking out a broken gate. On foot, he'd managed to catch hold of the reins just before Starburst lit out for the barn and left him behind—no matter how loudly he whistled.

"S-sorry," she stammered as she hastily stepped back.

"This place is the size of a hotel—I keep getting turned around."

This part of the house did involve quite a few hallways and bedrooms. The plantation-style setup was hardly a cozy bungalow. The size of the place meant it was easy for Drake and both his brothers—and now Slater's wife, Grace, plus her stepson—to continue living there without colliding at every turn. Each brother had his separate space.

Slater was out of town half the time, anyway, filming on location. Mace sometimes slept at the winery in his comfortable office, and Drake was out all day. So while they lived in the same house, they often didn't see one another except at dinner. The situation was a little different now, since Slater and Grace had a baby on the way, but Grace and his mother got along well and spent a lot of time together.

"Dining room is that way." He pointed.

Luce, evidently, was in no hurry to get to the table, and her project was very much on her mind. "Do you normally get home this time of day? Will you be going back out?"

Oh, great. So it begins. The "study" of his movements and the inquisition that would undoubtedly follow.

"Yes."

She nodded, obviously making a note of his answer.

Drake had an urge to sigh, but didn't. This was *not* what he needed right now.

Or ever.

He was going to have a word with his mother about this situation and her failure to discuss it with him.

Still, he made an effort to be civil, if not cordial, grumpy mood notwithstanding. "I sometimes eat with the ranch hands—they have their own kitchen, off the bunkhouse— and I have to go out and see to the livestock after supper, close the gate to the main drive, check the stables." That was enough information for one evening, as far as he was concerned. Under normal circumstances, he didn't say that many words in a whole day. "Please excuse me, I really need a shower. Sorry. I didn't do your formerly clean shirt any favors when I, ah, ran into you."

It didn't help when Ms. Hale grinned as she surveyed his disheveled appearance. "Can't disagree with that."

"It's been a long day and it's far from over," he said as he walked away. Drake wasn't usually self-conscious, but he was aware that he wasn't at his charming best, either. If he ever *was* charming.

Slater could be charming. Mace was smooth, when he wanted to be. But Drake was no talker, smooth or otherwise. He tended to be distracted and was always either busy or tired, or both.

Meeting a beautiful woman in the hall while covered in dirt didn't exactly boost his confidence.

And judging by Luce's teasing smile, she thought the situation was funny.

Well, that was just great. On top of everything else, he was stuck with a city girl who planned on following him around day and night, asking dumb questions and making notes.

The uncivilized cowboy in his natural habitat.

He flat out wasn't interested. Not in the role of lab rat. The woman, unfortunately, was another story.

And that just made things worse.

Once he'd reached his room, he shut the door hard, kicked off his boots, peeled off his shirt, which stuck to his skin.

At least he didn't have a farmer's tan going, he observed,

after a glance in the mirror; what he had was a *rancher's* tan. He was brown from elbow to wrist, since he had a habit of rolling up his sleeves when the weather was decent, and the brim of his hat saved him from the famous red neck.

Tanned or not, he felt about as sexy as a tractor—and why the hell he was thinking along such lines in the first place was beyond him. Luce made for some mighty fine scenery all on her own, but that wasn't reason enough to put up with her, or have her stuck to his heels 24/7.

Besides, she was a know-it-all.

He moved to a window, looked out, drank in what he saw. Even in the rain, the scenery was beautiful.

Drake's bedroom was on the eastern side of the house, which was convenient for someone who got up at sunrise, his favorite time of day. He never got tired of watching the first dawn light brightening the peaks of the mountains, of anticipating the smell of damp grass and the fresh breeze. He liked to absorb the vast quietness, draw it into his very cells, where it sustained him in ways that were almost spiritual.

He loved the sights and sounds of twilight, too. The lowering indigo of the sky, the stars popping out, clear and bright—unsullied by the false glow of crowded communities—the lonely howl of a wolf, the yipping cries of coyotes.

Drake had little use for cities.

Sure, he traveled now and then, for meetings and a few social functions his mother dragged him to, but Mustang Creek suited him just fine. It was small, an unpretentious place, full of decent, hardworking people who voted and went to church and were always ready with a howdy or a helping hand.

Crowds were rare in those parts, except during tourist seasons—summer, when vacationers came to marvel at Yellowstone or the Grand Tetons, and winter, when the skiers and snowboarders converged. But a person got used to things like that.

Drake left the window, went into his bathroom, finished undressing and took a steaming shower, letting the hard spray pound the soreness out of his muscles and thaw the chill in his bones.

Afterward, he chose a white shirt and a pair of jeans, got dressed, combed his hair. He considered shaving, but he was blond, so his light stubble didn't show too much, and anyway, there was a limit to how much fuss he was willing to undergo. He was starting to feel like a high school kid getting ready for a hot date, not a tired man fixing to have supper in his own house.

Shaking his head at his own musings, he looked at the clock—Harry served supper right on schedule, devil take the hindmost—and then he made for the dining room, which was downstairs and on the other side of the house.

As far as Harry was concerned, showing up late for a meal was the eighth deadly sin. If he was delayed by an unexpected problem, she understood and saved him a plate—as long as he let her know ahead of time.

If he didn't, he was out of luck.

And he was so ravenous, he felt hollow.

He had one minute to spare when he slid into his seat. The dogs, Harold and Violet, immediately headed for the kitchen, since it was suppertime for them, too. They had it cushy for ranch dogs, sleeping in the house and all, but they weren't allowed to beg at the table and they knew it. Plus, they both adored Harry, who probably slipped them a scrap or two, on the sly, just to add a little zip to their kibble.

Tonight, the beef stew smelled better than good. Harry knew how to hit that particular culinary note. Stew was one of her specialties—great on a rainy day—and he was starved, so when she brought in the crockery tureen and set it in the middle of the table, he favored her with a winning smile.

Harry didn't respond, except to wave off his grin with a motion of one hand.

So far, Drake thought, he had the whole table to himself—not a bad thing, when you considered the extent of his brothers' appetites.

Harry left the room, returned momentarily with a platter of fresh-baked biscuits and the familiar butter dish.

Things were looking up, until Mace ambled in and took his place across from Drake. Slater soon appeared, along with Grace, smiling and sitting down in their customary chairs, side by side. Drake and Mace, having risen to their feet when their sister-in-law entered, sat again.

If their mother, Blythe, was around, she was occupied elsewhere.

Once settled, everybody eyed the soup tureen, but nobody reached for the spoon. In the Carson house, you waited until all expected diners were present and accounted for, or you suffered the consequences.

"Where's Ryder?" Mace asked. They all liked Grace's teenage stepson and considered him part of the family.

"Basketball practice," Grace replied, arranging her cloth napkin on her lap. Drake and his brothers would have been all right with the throwaway kind, or even a sheet of paper towel, but Blythe and Harry took a dim view of both, except at barbecues and picnics.

Luce trailed in then, looking a little shy.

Slater, Mace and Drake stood up again, and she blushed slightly and glanced down at her jeans and shirt—blue this time—as though she thought there might be a dress code.

Drake drew back the chair next to his, since there was a place setting there and his mother always sat at the head of the table.

Luce hesitated, then seated herself.

Harry bustled in, carrying a salad bowl brimming with greens.

"Go ahead and eat," she ordered good-naturedly. "Your mother's having supper in her office again. She'll see all of you later, she said."

Having delivered the salad, the housekeeper deftly cleared away the dishes and silverware at Blythe's place and vanished into the kitchen.

For a while, nobody said anything, which was fine with Drake. He was hungry, fresh out of conversation and so aware of the woman sitting beside him that his ears felt hot.

He helped himself to stew and salad and three biscuits when his turn came and hoped Luce wouldn't whip out a notebook and a pen and make a record of what he ate and the way he ate it.

There was some chitchat, Grace and Slater and Mace all trying to put Luce at ease and make her feel welcome.

Relieved, Drake ate his supper and kept his thoughts to himself.

Then, from across the table, his younger brother dragged him into the discussion.

"So," Mace began, "have you warned Luce here that she ought to be careful because you like to swim naked in the creek some mornings?" He paused, ignoring Drake's scowl. "I'm just saying, if she's going to follow you around and all, certain precautions ought to be taken."

Drake narrowed his eyes and glared at his brother, before stealing a sidelong look at Luce to gauge her reaction.

There wasn't one, nothing visible, anyway. Luce seemed intent on enjoying Harry's beef stew, but something in the way she held herself told Drake she was listening, all right. She'd have had to be deaf not to hear, of course.

Drake summoned up a smile, strictly for Luce's benefit, and said, "Don't pay any attention to my brother. He's challenged when it comes to table manners, and he's been known to dip into his own wine vats a little too often. Must have pickled his brain."

"Now, boys," Grace said with a pleasant sigh. "Let's give Luce a little time to get used to your warped senses of humor, shall we?"

Slater met Drake's gaze, saying nothing, but there was a twinkle in his eyes.

Mace pretended to be aggrieved, not by Grace's attempt to change the course of the conversation, but by Drake's earlier remark. "My wine," he said, "is the finest available. It won't pickle anything."

"That so?" Drake asked. In the Carson household, bickering was a tradition, like touch football was with the Kennedys. He was beginning to enjoy himself, and not be so worried about the impression all this might make on Luce. "I seem to remember a science project—the one that almost got Ryder kicked out of school last term? Something about dissolving a tenpenny nail in a jar of your best Cabernet."

"Stop," Grace said, closing her eyes for a moment.

Luce giggled, although the sound was nearly inaudible.

"Why?" Mace asked reasonably. Like Drake, he loved Grace.

"Because it wasn't a tenpenny nail," Grace replied, looking to Slater for help, which wasn't forthcoming. Her husband was buttering his second biscuit and grinning to himself.

"Your problem," Mace told Drake, "is that you are totally unsophisticated. To you, warm generic beer from a can is the height of elegance."

Let the games begin.

"*I'm* unsophisticated?" Drake raised his brows. "This from a man who wore different colored socks just the other day? That was sophisticated, all right."

Mace looked and sounded pained. "Hey, it was dark when I got dressed, and I was in a hurry."

"I bet you were," Drake shot back. "Come to think of it, little brother, those might not have been your socks in the first place. Guess it all depends on whose bedroom floor you found them on."

"Oh, for heaven's sake," Grace said, tossing a sympathetic glance Luce's way.

"Are they always like this?" Luce asked.

"Unfortunately," Grace answered, "yes."

Just then, Blythe Carson breezed in, carrying a place setting and closely followed by Ryder.

"We've decided to join you," Blythe announced cheerfully.

"Thank God," Grace murmured.

Ryder, holding a bowl and silverware of his own, sat down next to his mother. "Basketball practice got out early," he said. He nodded a greeting to Luce and reached for the stew.

Blythe Carson, more commonly known as "Mom," sat down with a flourish and beamed a smile at Luce. "How nice to see you again," she said. "I hope my sons have been behaving themselves."

"Not so much," Grace said.

"Hey," Slater objected, elbowing his wife lightly. "I have been a complete gentleman."

"You've been a spectator," Grace countered, hiding a smile.

"All I did," Mace said, "was warn Luce about Drake's tendency to skinny-dip at every opportunity. Seemed like the least I could do, considering that she's a stranger here, and a guest."

"Hush," said Blythe.

Harry reappeared with a coffeepot in one hand and a freshly baked pie in the other.

Once she'd set them down, she started whisking stew bowls out from under spoons. When she decided a course was over, and that folks had had enough, she took it away and served the next one.

Blythe sparkled.

The coffee was poured and the pie was served.

Ryder excused himself, saying he had homework to do, and left, taking his slice of apple pie with him.

The others lingered.

Grace, yawning, said she thought she'd make it an early night and promptly left the table, carrying her cup and saucer and her barely touched pie to the kitchen before heading upstairs.

Blythe remained, watching her sons thoughtfully, each in turn, before focusing on Mace. "Seriously?" she said. "You brought up skinny-dipping?"

Luce, who had been soaking up the conversation all evening, and probably taking mental notes, finally spoke up.

She smiled brightly at Slater, then Mace, and then Drake. "I enjoy skinny-dipping myself, once in a while." She paused, obviously for effect. "Who knows, maybe I'll join you sometime."

Blythe laughed, delighted.

Mace and Slater picked up their dishes, murmured politely and fled.

"I'd better help Harry with the dishes," Blythe said, and in another moment, she was gone, too.

LUCE TURNED TO DRAKE, all business. "Now, then," she said, "the wild herd has almost doubled in size since you first reported their presence to the Bureau of Land Management several years ago. What accounts for the increase, in your opinion?"

The change of subject, from skinny-dipping to the BLM, had thrown Drake a little, and Luce took a certain satisfaction in the victory, however small and unimportant.

The room was empty, except for them, and Luce was of two minds about that. On the one hand, she liked having Drake Carson all to herself. On the other, she was nervous to the point of discomfort.

Drake, she noticed, had recovered quickly, and with no discernible brain split. He'd probably never been "of two minds" about anything in his life, Luce thought, with some ruefulness. Unless she missed her guess, he was a one-track kind of guy.

Now he leaned back in his chair, his expression giving nothing away. And, after due deliberation, he finally replied to her question.

"What accounts for the increase? Well, Ms. Hale, that's simple. Good grazing land and plenty of water—the two main reasons my family settled here in the first place, over a hundred years ago."

She wondered if he might be holding back a sarcastic comment, something in the category of any-idiot-ought-to-be-able-to-figure-that-out.

She had, in fact, taken note of the obvious; she'd put in long hours mapping out the details of her dissertation. She wanted his take on the subject, since that was the whole point of this or any other conversational exchange between them.

Okay, so she wasn't an expert, but she was eager to learn. Wasn't that what education was all about, from kindergarten right on up through postgraduate work?

She decided to shut down the little voice in her head, the one that presumed to speak for both her and Drake, before it got her into trouble.

"What makes it so good?" she asked with genuine interest. "The type of grass?"

His gaze was level. "There's a wide variety, actually, but quantity matters almost as much as quality in this case." A pause. "By the way, there are a lot more wild horses in Utah than here in Wyoming."

Zap.

"Yes, I know that," Luce replied coolly, determined to stay the course. She hadn't gotten this far by running for shelter every time she encountered a challenge. "And I realize you would prefer I went there to do my research," she countered, keeping her tone even and, she hoped, professional. "Bottom line, Mr. Carson, I'm not going anywhere."

"Why here? Why me?" For the first time, he sounded plaintive, rather than irritated.

"Fair questions," Luce conceded. "I chose the Carson ranch because it meets all the qualifications and, I admit, because my mother knows your mother. I guess that sort of answers your second inquiry, too—you're here, and you run the place. One thing, as they say, led to another." She let her answer sink in for a moment, before the windup. "And, I will admit, your commitment to animal rights intrigues me."

That was all Drake needed to know, for the time being. If she had a weakness for tall, blond cowboys with world-class bodies and eyes so blue it almost hurt to look into them, well, that was her business.

He surprised her with a slanted grin. "I know when I'm licked," he drawled.

The remark was anything but innocent, Luce knew that, but she also knew that if she called him on it, she'd be the one who looked foolish, not Drake.

Bad enough that she blushed, hot and pink, betrayed by her own biology.

He watched the whole process, clearly pleased by her involuntary reaction.

She had to look away, just briefly, to recover her composure. Such as it was.

"This can be easy," she said when she thought she could trust her voice, "or it can be har—difficult."

Wicked mischief danced in his eyes. "The harder—more difficult—things are," he said, "the better I like it."

Luce wanted to yell at him to stop with the double entendres, just stop, but she wasn't quite that rattled. Yet.

Instead, she breathed a sigh. "Okay," she said. "Fine. We understand each other, it would seem."

"So it would seem," he agreed placidly, and with a smile in his eyes.

Luce would've liked to call it a day and return to her well-appointed guest room, which was really more of a suite, with its spacious private bathroom, sitting area and gorgeous antique furnishings, but she didn't. Not only would Drake have the last word if she bailed now, she'd feel like a coward—and leave herself open to more teasing.

"We have one thing in common," she said.

"And what would that be, Ms. Hale?"

Damn him. Would it kill the man to cut her a break?

"Animals," she answered. Surely he wouldn't—couldn't—disagree with that.

He looked wary, although Luce took no satisfaction in that. "If I didn't like them," he said, his tone guarded now, and a little gruff, "I wouldn't do what I do."

Like all ranchers, he'd probably taken his share of flack over the apparent dichotomy between loving animals and raising them for food, but Luce had no intention of taking that approach. Would have considered it dishonorable.

She enjoyed a good steak now and then herself, after all, and she understood the reality—everything on the planet survives by eating something else.

"I'm sure you wouldn't," she said.

Drake relaxed noticeably, and it seemed to Luce that something had changed between them, something basic and powerful. They weren't going to be BFFs or anything like that—the gibes would surely continue—but they'd set some important boundaries.

They were not enemies.

In time, they might even become friends.

While Luce was still weighing this insight in her head, Drake stood, rested his strong, rancher's hands on the back of her chair.

"It's been a long day, Ms. Hale," he said. "I reckon you're ready to turn in."

At her nod, Drake waited to draw back her chair. As she rose, she watched his face.

"Thank you," she said. Then she smiled. "And please, call me Luce."

Drake inclined his head. "All right, then," he replied, very quietly. "Shall I walk you to your room, or can you find your way back there on your own?"

Luce laughed. "I memorized the route," she answered. Then, pulling her smartphone from the pocket of her jeans, she held it up. "And if that fails, there's always GPS."

Drake smiled. "You'll get used to the layout," he told her.

"Here's hoping," Luce said, wondering why she was hesitating, making small talk, of all things, when most of her exchanges with this man had felt more like swordplay than conversation.

"Good night—Luce." Drake looked thoughtful now, and his gaze seemed to rest on her mouth.

Was he deciding whether or not to kiss her?

And if he was, how did she feel about it?

She didn't want to know.

"Good night," she said.

She left the dining room, left Drake Carson and was almost at the door of her suite before the realization struck her.

She'd gotten the last word after all.

CHAPTER THREE

Drake rolled out of bed at his usual time, ignored the clock—since his inner one was the real guide—and pulled on his jeans.

Harold and Violet both got up, tails wagging.

Boots next, hat planted on his head and, seconds later, he was out the door. He'd grab coffee at the bunkhouse. Red, the foreman, was always up and ready, and that seasoned old cowboy could herd cattle with the best of them. Drake drove his truck over just as dawn hit the edge of sunrise and, sure enough, he could smell coffee.

Red, who did a mean scrambled egg dish and some terrific hash browns, was already done eating, elbows on the farmhouse-style table, something he never did when he ate up at the house. He nodded good morning and went back to his book, which happened to be *Shogun* by James Clavell. Drake wasn't surprised at his choice. Red looked like a classic, weathered Wyoming ranch hand, which he was, but he also fancied himself a gourmet cook—he could give Harry a run for her money now and then—and he listened more often than not to classical music. The package wasn't all that sophisticated, but there was a keen intellect inside.

Drake fed the dogs, helped himself to a plate of eggs and potatoes, ate with his usual lightning speed and got up to wash the dishes. That was the arrangement and it was fine with him. He'd had to cook for himself in college and discovered he didn't have the patience for it. He'd survived on hamburgers fried in a pan, sandwiches and spaghetti prepared with jarred sauce. Coming back to Harry's or Red's cooking made all those winter morning rides to feed the stock, with the wind tossing snow in his face and biting through his gloves, worth it. If Red cooked breakfast, he would wash up, no problem.

"How's the horse lady?" Red put a bookmark between the pages and shut the novel, setting it aside.

Drake braced himself for a sip of coffee—Red was a great cook, but his coffee could strip the hide off a steer—before he answered. "Enthusiastic college girl. Bright, but has no idea what she's getting into. I have the impression that she likes to be outdoors, since she hiked all the way to the north ridge, can you believe that? But I don't think she really knows anything about horses, wild *or* domesticated."

"The north ridge?" It wasn't easy to surprise Red, but he just had.

"Yup. I gave her a lift home on Starburst, but she was planning to walk it. Go figure."

"Can't."

"Me, neither." Drake spent nearly all his time outdoors, and if he had the right weather, he sometimes canoed and did some fishing in the Bliss River, but he wasn't a hiker.

"The outdoorsy type. That's good. You need a dainty debutante like you need a big hole in your John B. Stetson."

Such a Red thing to say. Drake didn't need another female in his life right now, period. He had his mother, Harry, his niece, Daisy—Slater's daughter by an earlier relationship—and, now that Slater had finally settled down, his sister-in-law, Grace. The men were getting outnumbered even before the arrival of Ms. Hale.

Drake shrugged. "She's pretty, I'll give her that."

"That so?" Red grinned. "Easy on the eyes, huh? And you've noticed."

"I'm not blind, but that doesn't mean I want her here." That was the truth. "I just plain don't want the complication."

"Women complicate just about everything, son."

That he agreed with, at least based on his own observations—and experience. So he changed the subject. "Move the bull to the high pasture for a few days? I think he needs new grazing. After that, we'll get feed out and tackle the faulty gate."

"You're the boss."

Technically, he thought, but Red was the one who really ran the show. Drake was born and raised on this land, but Red had more ranching experience. Drake always asked for his advice and ended up regretting the few times he hadn't followed it. "He's getting old."

"Sherman? That he is."

"So…what do you suggest?"

"We need a new bull." Red got up and refilled his cup. "Been meaning to say it, but I know you don't want to part with that critter. Don't move him. He's getting touchy in his old age. Just retire him. Sherman has more gray on his snout than I do in my hair. Out to pasture will work fine. We have the land to keep him in comfort."

"My father raised that bull." Drake's throat tightened.

"I know. I was there. I'm hurting, too. Think of it this way—he's done his job. If I thought a recliner and a remote would make him happy, I'd give him both. Sherman is a tired old man."

He'd asked, after all. Drake ran his fingers through his hair. It wasn't as if he hadn't thought about it. He exhaled. "I don't disagree. Not from a practical point of view, anyway. Auctions, then? Or do you have another bull in mind?"

Red scratched his chin. "I might go into town and ask Jim Galloway. Been meaning to stop by and see him and Pauline, anyway. He knows most of the livestock breeders in the state."

Jim was the father of one of Slater's best friends, Tripp Galloway, a pilot who'd returned to his roots and, like Drake, had taken over the family ranch near Mustang Creek after Jim remarried and retired. "Good call." Drake managed to down the last of his coffee—not easy, since it was particularly make-your-hair-stand-on-end this morning— and set down his cup. "I'm going to help you with the horses and then ride out."

"Sorry I'm late."

The breathless interruption made him swivel toward the plain wooden doorway. He saw with dismay that Luce Hale stood there, hair pulled back in a no-nonsense ponytail, wearing a baggy sweatshirt with well-worn jeans, backpack in hand. She added, "That is one very comfortable bed, so I slept longer than I intended. Your mother should run a hotel. Where are we headed?"

We? First of all, *he* hadn't invited her to the party. Second, the woman couldn't even ride a horse.

And damned if Red wasn't snickering. Not openly, he'd never be that rude, but there was laughter in his eyes and he'd had to clear his throat—several times.

He should be at least as polite. Grudgingly, he said, "Red, meet Ms. Lucinda Hale. Ms. Hale, Red here runs the operation but likes to pretend I do."

Red naturally shuffled over to take her hand, playing it up. "Pleased to meet you, ma'am. So you're here to study that worthless cowpoke?" He leveled a finger in Drake's direction. "Hmm, prepare to be disappointed. Kinda boring would be my take on him. I've tried to take the boy in hand, but it hasn't worked. Nary a shoot-out, no saloons and he has yet to rescue a damsel in distress, unless you count the time Harry had a flat tire and he had to run into town to change it, but I swear that's just 'cause he's more afraid of her than he is of an angry hornet. Would you like a cup of coffee, darlin'?"

Red was ever hopeful that someone might like his coffee—he called it Wyoming coffee, which was quite a stretch, since he seemed to be the only one in the entire state who liked it.

Okay, she was an annoyance in his already busy life, but Drake was about to rescue a damsel who'd be in true distress if she agreed to that coffee.

He said coolly, "I'm off to the glamorous world of feeding the horses and then fixing a gate. I also need to look for a missing calf and am fairly sure it's a goner. Please don't let the excitement of my day overwhelm you, but come along if you want. You'll have to skip the coffee."

She tilted her head to one side, considering him, obviously undeterred. "I need to see if the wild horses affect how you run your business. Therefore, I need to know how you run it in the first place. I want to find what you do day-to-day."

Why hadn't she picked a topic she actually knew something about before deciding on this venture? Like buying shoes, for instance.

Not fair, he corrected himself. She *had* trekked all the way to that ridge—in hiking boots, no less, nothing fashionable about those—and she'd found the horses. Maybe he was underestimating Ms. Hale. She was certainly determined, no doubt about that. "Follow along. Be my guest. If you enjoy the smell of manure and hay, I'm more than happy to escort you to the stables."

For that condescending statement he received a derisive look. "I can find the stables on my own. I promise I won't get in your way. This project is important to me, and as far as I can tell, it's important to you."

He failed to see the logic there. "How so?"

"What if I can help you figure out what to do?"

Drake was honest, but he was also diplomatic—or so he hoped. He fought back a response that included *How the heck could you help me?* and substituted, "I look forward to your suggestions."

LUCE COULDN'T DECIDE if he was just being sarcastic, but at least he was courteous.

She'd meant it.

"You don't think I can help?"

He walked next to her, toward a weathered structure bordered by a fenced enclosure. Several sleek horses were grazing and lifted their heads to watch as they approached, curious but unafraid. Some of them nickered, wanting his attention. "You don't know horses."

"Wrong."

She was above average height for a woman and still reached only his shoulder. He was one tall man. She'd mostly seen him on horseback or sitting at the dinner table with his brothers, who were also tall, so she hadn't realized.

He looked skeptical. "How am I wrong?"

"I don't know them the same way you do. I've worked on a lot of studies, read the literature, done my homework, so to speak, but that doesn't mean I completely understand their behavior. I do, however, understand the situation."

She'd describe his expression as unconvinced.

"That's fine," he said. "You go about your business and I'll go about mine."

"Suit yourself."

You are *my business*. She didn't say it out loud, but it was true. She found it disconcerting to recognize that he might be more interesting than those beautiful horses. When her thesis topic had first come to her, she'd wondered abstractly how wild horses impacted the environment.

Here she was now, and she had a Zen-like feeling that maybe fate was toying with her. At first he'd caught her attention because, from what she'd read, they shared similar views on ecological issues, but there was more to it.

Drake opened the stable door. "After you."

The place smelled earthy, lined with rows of neat stalls, and Drake was greeted with soft whinnies as the animals poked their heads over the stall doors. He was gently companionable with each one, unhurried in his attentions. Luce was moved by this, but not really surprised; the way the dogs followed him around, quiet and devoted, had told her a lot about the man. In her experience animals had more insight than people normally did, so that said something very positive about Drake Carson.

"Anything I can do?"

"I doubt it." He carried a bucket of water into a stall and softened that by adding, "By the time I told you what to do, I could probably have done it myself."

"Probably," she conceded, "but keep in mind, I'm a fast learner."

He turned, empty bucket in hand, and gave her a measured look. "Good to know."

She caught on quickly that they were no longer talking about feeding a barn full of horses. Her response was tart. "Isn't it a little early in the morning for sexual innuendos, Mr. Carson?"

"I figure all twenty-four hours of the day are good for those." He led out his big horse and she scooted aside. "I'm going to saddle up and ride out now. You do whatever you want to, but I have a gate to fix and that has nothing to do with wild horses and everything to do with keeping the cattle in that pasture."

"I can't ride along?"

He went into a small room and emerged with a well-worn saddle. "Grace's horse, Molly, is in that stall." He pointed. "Saddle her and follow me if you like. For now, I need to move along. Have a nice morning."

It took him about three minutes to saddle his horse, slip on the bridle and mount up. Then he was heading out, the beautiful dogs trotting alongside. She'd yet to even hear them bark.

Learn to saddle a horse—that was item number one on her to-do list. But first she hurried to the doorway to see which direction Drake had gone. Maybe she couldn't ride or fling saddles around with any confidence, but she was wearing her hiking boots, had a bottle of water in her pack and a sack lunch Harry had handed her as she'd hurried out the door. If dinner the night before was any indication, there could be something magical in there.

Perfect day for a walk.

That obnoxious cowboy wasn't getting rid of her as easily as he thought.

Besides, she was hoping to take more pictures of the horses. She'd gotten some good shots, but she hoped to do that each and every time she was close enough to manage it. She'd already caught an excellent image of the stallion; she knew more about horses than Drake gave her credit for. It was obvious to her that the magnificent animal was the one in charge of the herd—even before she'd listened to the conversation at dinner. He was beautiful, too, with clean lines and fluid grace.

If she could find Drake, she'd photograph him at work, whether he liked it or not. Better to ask forgiveness, as the saying went, than permission. Besides, it wasn't as if she was going to publish them or anything. They were purely for research purposes. Having a physical record would help her organize her notes when she began the process of writing the actual paper. As she hefted her pack and left the barn, the sun-gilded Tetons felt like familiar friends, the glory of the setting an undeniable perk. There was still snow on the peaks, and the air was crisp and fresh.

Lovely, lovely day.

CHAPTER FOUR

It had already been one hell of a day, and there was still a long trail ahead.

Drake tried to concentrate on fixing yet another gate hinge so rusted it was next to impossible to remove the screws without help. Red had sacrificed some of his considerable pride by turning the job over to a younger man. Luckily, the old bull in the pasture beyond hadn't figured out how easy it would've been to bust the thing and make a run for it.

Slater was lending him a hand by holding the gate steady.

As he worked, Drake mulled over a more complex problem.

He felt guilty for ditching Lucinda Hale on a daily basis this past week. It wasn't as if he didn't understand her zeal for the animals. It was just that at the beginning, middle and end of the day, or *any time* he really didn't need a shadow, she seemed to appear. And what made it worse was the fact that he couldn't stop himself from worrying about her.

Drake totally understood her objectives, but this was his land, so every creature on it was his to take care of, with the exception of his brothers, who could handle themselves. He even worried about Red, since he was showing his age but refused to slow down. In his entire life Drake had never known the man to go to a doctor. Once, Red had fractured his arm breaking a colt and the vet had been handy, since he was taking care of one of the horses. So Red had asked him to set it and wrap it in an Ace bandage, then used a makeshift sling made from an old halter and lead. They'd all shaken their heads over that one, especially the vet.

With a motion of his hand, Drake indicated the bull grazing nearby. "Red's going to ask Jim Galloway to recommend the best stock breeder he knows, not just in Bliss County, but in the state. We could use some new blood." He dropped a crowbar into his tool kit and wiped his brow. "Damn hot out here. Shades of summer, I guess."

"Not much of a breeze, either," Slater observed, using a cordless drill to put the first screw into the new hinge. "That sure isn't usual in Wyoming."

Drake grimaced. "I swear it only happens if you're repairing a fence. That'll make the breeze die down every single time. I'll do the dirty work and hold it in place."

The gate was heavy, but his older brother knew his stuff and the hinge was done in a matter of minutes. Slater leaned against the fence and crossed his arms. "So, still no missing calf?"

"Nope." Drake had searched as far as anyone could in country this size and hadn't found anything; that was predictable. "Not a trace."

"Too bad—but here comes trouble of a different kind."

Slater's grin was wide. "I think your campaign of avoidance is about to go south, brother. I have to give you credit. Up until now, you've been fairly successful."

Damned if his brother wasn't right. Drake saw the unmistakable outline of the female figure walking toward them, the sun catching the chestnut glints in her hair. Any trace of guilt was wiped clean by his irritation. He muttered, "I know you find this just hilarious, but how would *you* like it if some eager film student wanted to follow your every movement?"

"Hmm." Slater nodded with exaggerated introspection. "Grace might not approve of this answer, but between you and me, if the nonexistent film student looked like Ms. Hale and I wasn't happily married, I would have no objections at all."

"She knows nothing about running a ranch."

Slater burst out laughing. "So maybe you should teach her? I think that's why she's here."

Starburst had the gall to lift his head and whinny in greeting as she walked up. Her cheeks held a slight flush, but otherwise the hike apparently hadn't been that much of a challenge. Slater was watching in obvious amusement, so Drake tried to respond with equanimity. "You found us, I see."

"And I did it without a horse," she shot back defiantly.

He let the gibe pass. "Red will teach you to saddle one if you give him a sweet smile. Grace's mare is gentle enough." *For a greenhorn.*

"Why do I feel I'm being patronized?" So much for his attempt at subtlety. "Plus, you've been avoiding me."

That was true. Slater was clearly enjoying the exchange. From the corner of his eye, Drake could see his brother grinning like a damn fool. "I'd say you *are* being patron-ized," Slater said.

Luce seemed to be as annoyed by that as Drake was, so at least they had one thing in common.

"The wild horses are back on that ridge," she said curtly.

Drake's attention sharpened. "The entire herd?"

Luce nodded. "I spotted them as I walked up here. The stallion was standing at the top, watching me. A hundred feet away is my estimate."

Drake felt a prickle of alarm. That was *way* too close. "A hundred feet?"

"Yes. That's what I said." In the next moment, she turned breezy. "I go looking for them every day, and when I'm lucky enough to be in the right place at the right time, I sit there as quietly as I can and try not to spook them. The big guy's starting to get curious about what I might be up to." A pause. "Should we go over and take a look if you're done here?"

They could. Why not? Slater was still smiling to himself as he gathered up the tools, not even bothering to pretend he wasn't taking in every word.

Drake considered Luce's invitation. He had plenty of other things to do, but he wouldn't mind an opportunity to recover at least some of those mares. There were other considerations, of course. Starburst was not a small horse, and he might spook the herd. Size-wise, he and the stallion could stand shoulder to shoulder; they were both males, but Star was gelded.

If the stallion got aggressive, Starburst would come out the loser.

More likely, though, the wild horse would turn his mares and head for the hills, as he'd done all the other times.

Another part of Drake's brain was caught upstream in the conversation. A hundred feet? She *had* gotten awfully close to those horses, and she didn't seem to have the first clue how dangerous they could be.

"I'll walk up there with you," he said reluctantly. He asked his brother, "Mind unsaddling Starburst for me and letting him graze with the cattle?"

"Nope." There was still a wicked glint in Slate's eyes. "Have fun hiking in those boots."

"I *live* in these boots," Drake retorted. "I'll be fine, big brother."

"Just sayin'."

"Thanks for your concern," Drake responded drily. "You can put salve on my blisters and rub my feet when we get back."

"I think you'll have to find someone else for that." Slater raised his brows and turned to Luce.

"No way." She smiled. "If anyone's entitled to a foot massage, it's me. I'll have walked up there *twice* today."

"I learn something new about you every day." Drake took his rope from Starburst's saddle, in case it came in handy. He doubted he'd get close enough to use it, but stranger things had happened.

"You don't know as much about me as you think you do. We only met eight days ago."

He couldn't possibly ignore that one. "Maybe it just seems longer. Let's go."

He received a well-deserved lethal look for that comment. "If you're ready, cowboy."

She led the way, sticking to the open areas, which told him she really wasn't a greenhorn when it came to this sort of country.

She provided him with a very nice back view. Following her was no hardship.

He knew the trail to the ridge as well as anyone and better than most. Certainly better than she did. But she walked with a sense of purpose and he climbed behind her. Slater had a point about his cowboy boots, but he could cope. Those mares had cost the ranch a small fortune.

Sure enough, Luce was right. The group of horses was at the top, quietly cropping the grass, half-hidden by a line of aspen. Ever vigilant, the stallion noticed their approach, lifted his head and allowed them to get decently close, with little more than a warning snort. They stopped obediently behind a small group of bushes, fairly well hidden, but the stallion made clear that he knew they were there.

Luce whispered, crouching next to him, "Smoke's in a good mood today."

She'd named the horse. *That figures.*

Those mares were valuable, he reminded himself again, and losing them permanently would have an effect on the bottom line. "Smoke? That's original," he said sarcastically.

"Hey, he's gray and black. Pet names are not my forte."

Drake sighed. "That's no pet, that's more than half a ton of testosterone and muscle. I couldn't take him, even in a fair fight. Think teeth and hooves."

He might have come across as peevish; he was used to riding, not walking, and he'd broken a light sweat on their impromptu stroll. His companion, on the other hand, looked as if they'd been cruising some city park, throwing bread at ducks in ponds or whatever people did in places like that.

She gave him an assessing stare. "Yet I feel you *are* about to beat him—but not on a physical level."

That was absolutely correct. "Yup. I'm going to win this one. I want my horses back, and he needs to go somewhere else."

Easier said than done, of course. That horse had no respect for fences at all. He'd kicked his way through more than one to get at the mares. Drake had thought about building an enclosure like the ones they used for bull riding at rodeos. But getting him into it was quite the challenge. Although he and Luce had barely met, he sensed that she wasn't going to agree with what he had to say next. "A tranquilizer dart is probably my best bet at this point. I'm going to hire someone to do it because that horse knows me. He's smart. He knows exactly who runs this ranch. I'm a good shot, but this is about as close as I've ever gotten to him and I doubt I could do it from here."

As predicted, she turned to scowl at him and said firmly, as if she had some authority over the situation, "No. You aren't shooting him with anything."

She'd gotten some pretty good snaps of Drake Carson, shirtless, as he fixed that gate. He had impressive muscles and a six-pack stomach. Cowboy poster-boy material. Maybe someone needed to do a calendar with ranchers, like they did with firemen and athletes. She'd be happy to put him in it and leave it turned to that month forever. She had his grudging permission to shoot a few pictures of him if she wanted, but he hadn't been very enthusiastic.

That was nothing compared to what was about to happen, though. They were about to get in a really big argument. She could feel it coming. Whenever she had a strong opinion, she couldn't help expressing it, as her entire family would point out.

She stood up. "Smoke isn't going to understand. He'll hate it. Suddenly going to sleep and waking up somewhere else? How would you like that? Come up with some other idea."

All the horses lifted their heads at the raised voice.

Drake straightened, too. "You have a better one?"

"Not yet." She shook her head. "I just don't want that."

"Hell, neither do I. *You* come up with something else and I'll listen."

"I'm thinking on it." She wasn't thinking about anything else. Well, except him.

Here, among the horses, the mountains, the blue sky, he looked like the real deal, a cowboy all the way. Of course, that was probably because he *was* the real deal—and his authenticity wasn't compromised by the exasperated expression on his face. She liked how he habitually tipped back his hat and then drew it forward.

"As I told you, I'll ponder it," she couldn't resist saying.

"*Ponder?* Really? Is that how you think we talk out here?"

"It's a perfectly good word." She stood her ground. "People from California say it all the time."

"Yeah, maybe a hundred years ago." He gestured at the horses. "Smoke—if that's what we're going to call him—would be fine after the trank. But the point is, he has to go. He's wreaking havoc with the ranch's working horses. Get it? Put that in your thesis."

"What if I could coax him into coming close enough so you could just catch him?"

"What?" He looked incredulous. "You can't. He's a wild stallion."

"I think I could."

He let out a long, slow breath. "You can't even *saddle* a horse."

"That's a skill I intend to learn. Can I give it a try? By the way, I'm well aware that we aren't talking about a domesticated animal. If we were, I wouldn't be here."

Drake threw up his hands. "This is the most ridiculous conversation I've ever had. He isn't going to do it."

"Let me try before you shoot him."

That riled him. "I'm not going to shoot that horse or any other horse, for heaven's sake! I'll sedate him and have him moved to federal land set aside for wild horses. *Not* the same thing."

It wasn't as if she didn't know that, but still…it was fun to tease him. She couldn't believe she was about to ask this, but she'd been pretty brazen already. "Can you wait two more weeks? I need that much time for my study, and you've had this herd around for a while, anyway. Then I promise I'll get out of your hair. I was planning on staying a month."

A bribe of sorts, and a shameless one.

His cooperation in exchange for getting rid of her. She figured he might go for it.

"A month!" He seemed properly horrified.

"You'd have one less week with me—if you'll just hold off a bit."

He took the deal. He smiled grimly and jerked off his glove, then thrust out his hand. "Let's shake on it."

Solid grip. He didn't try to break her fingers or anything, which she appreciated, since she could tell he'd reached the end of his patience.

He had the bluest eyes she'd ever seen.

Was there any chance he'd actually pose for a formal

photograph? Maybe next to that giant horse of his... Uh-uh, she thought wisely. This would *not* be the right moment to ask more of Mr. Drake Carson.

Instead, she said simply, "Thanks."

"Don't mention it," he muttered as he stalked away. "All I ask is that you be a man of your word."

"I'm not a man," she called out to his retreating back.

"I've noticed that," he said.

He didn't turn around.

CHAPTER FIVE

THE WEEKLY POKER GAME was set up at Bad Billy's Biker Bar and Burger Palace. Drake could use a cold one, so he approved of the choice. He spotted two of his friends already at the table, then sauntered up to the bar and nodded at Billy in greeting. "Who's waiting tonight? Thelma?"

"Sure is. Full of piss and vinegar, too. Got into a fender bender on her way to work. You know how she loves that old car. You boys be on your best behavior."

"Thanks for the warning." Thelma was a crusty older lady who, like Harry, tolerated no nonsense. Billy didn't need a bouncer; if anybody dared misbehave, Thelma effectively booted him out, although how she managed it when she was only about five feet high—and that was on a tall day—was a mystery. She never had a problem getting her point across, either. "Tell her I'll have my usual, and be polite about it, okay? Especially if she's in a no-bullshit mood." The place seemed busier than ever that night.

Billy laughed, a low rumble in his wide chest. "You are

a wise man, my friend. Our Thelma has a soft spot for you, but she's about reached her cowboy quotient for the day, so I'll go ahead and draw your beer myself."

Tripp Galloway and Tate Calder were halfway through their first mugs of beer, elbows resting comfortably on the nicked wooden table. Tripp hooked a foot around a chair and tugged it out so Drake could sit. "You're late, but Spence texted and said he was tied up, so you don't get the slow prize this time. He figures maybe twenty minutes."

Drake took the chair. In the background a jukebox was playing Willie Nelson and the place was loud, but never so loud that you couldn't talk to the people at your table. One of the many reasons he disliked big cities was the noise— restaurants where you couldn't hear yourself think, much less converse with the person next to you. Traffic snarls, horns honking, sirens blaring. The skyscrapers and office buildings made him feel hemmed in, and the smell of exhaust fumes followed you everywhere. Give him the sweet scent of long grass in a clean breeze.

Tate said, "I need to warn you that Thelma's on the warpath and she's headed this way."

"Billy mentioned that she was in some kind of snit," Drake muttered under his breath, just before she plonked down his beer.

"Carson, you're always running late. And where's that worthless Spence Hogan, anyway? I spent some quality time with him earlier."

Spence was the chief of police, and whatever else she might be, Thelma was no criminal. Drake wondered what she meant, although he wasn't stupid enough to ask.

Thelma had ringlets of gray hair, pale blue eyes, and wore her glasses on the end of her nose. As far as Drake could tell, she didn't actually need them; they seemed to be mainly for effect, probably so she could glare at people over the top.

Then he abruptly remembered and said, "Oh, the accident. Yeah, I heard. Sorry about Frankie."

She'd named her 1966 bright yellow Impala Frankie, and since this was Mustang Creek, he knew that car well. "That out-of-town asshole had no insurance. It's going to cost me seven hundred bucks to fix the car. I can take that idiot to small claims court, and Spence is going to make sure his license is suspended, but that won't do Frankie any good, will it?" She blew out a loud breath. "I'm *really* pissed off."

Now, there was breaking news.

"As soon as Spence gets here, your food will be out."

Tripp made the mistake of saying, "We haven't ordered yet."

Thelma sent him a look that would've scared the average grizzly bear. "All of you will have the special."

Every one of them wanted to ask what the special might be, but none had the guts to do so.

"Get it?" she demanded, just in case they didn't know what was good for them, which was whatever Thelma *thought* was good for them.

They sure did. Not one of them said a thing as Thelma walked away, ignoring a table full of customers madly waving to get her attention.

"I was kind of hoping for the bacon cheeseburger, but I'll take whatever she sets in front of me," Tate said. "Whew. I wouldn't want to be the guy who made that grave error in judgment and hit her car. That had to be one hell of a conversation."

"If I was Spence, I'd throw him in jail for his own protection." Tripp drained what was left of his beer.

Drake didn't disagree. "Now, back to the menu... I'm praying for chicken-fried steak, but I'll roll with whatever happens to come my way. Did Red have a chance to talk to your dad?"

"About the bull, Sherman? Yeah, Jim will handle it—does him good to get involved. He misses that sort of thing."

Jim, Tripp's stepfather, had run the ranch for a long time before Tripp took over. Drake nodded. "I feel regretful about it. Sherman was great in his prime, but he's not doing real well right now. Slowing down, you might say."

Tripp got that faint grin on his face. "So, tell us about the student. The one who's cuter than a pup in a little red wagon. That's Red talking as you might've guessed, via Jim."

"I already figured that out." Drake took a long cool drink. It tasted great. "She's fine. She's *trying*—in more ways than one." Tripp rolled his eyes at the pun, but Drake ignored him. "She's a pretty graduate student who has no idea what she's doing."

"How pretty?" That was Tate, also grinning.

"Very," he admitted, remembering the gold highlights in her hair.

"That's what we heard." Tripp was clearly teasing, but before Drake could respond, he lifted a hand. "I actually think that what she's doing is important. I'll bet most of America isn't even aware we have wild horses, much less that they can be a problem. My two cents' worth."

Spence's arrival stopped the discussion. He slid into the fourth chair at their table. Tall, with a natural air of command that wasn't overstated, he was both confident and good at his job. "Thelma's still mad, I take it."

"She's steaming," Drake informed him. "Don't try to order off the menu, my friend. She's decided we're all having the special, whatever that might be."

"Gotcha." Spence grimaced. "You should've been there when Junie got the call. She's a seasoned dispatcher and even she was shaking her head. When Thelma asked that I personally respond, Junie threw me under the bus and said I would. Both of my deputies were laughing their asses off."

They were all laughing, too, but instantly sobered when Thelma showed up with Spence's beer, glowered at him and asked, "That noninsured yahoo in prison yet?"

"Took him there myself. Straight to the dungeon section. He's chained to the wall." Spence said it with a straight face.

Thelma did have a sense of humor and it finally surfaced. "See that he gets no food or water."

"Yes, ma'am."

"Your food will be right up. I'll bring another round when you start your game. But then I'm cutting you off. Y'all have to drive home." She stalked back toward the kitchen.

Spence said mildly, "I could point out that I walked from the station and Melody's having dinner with Hadleigh and Bex, so she's picking me up. But I think I'm just going to keep my mouth shut."

"Good idea." Tripp nodded. Since Hadleigh was his wife and Bex was married to Tate, they were undoubtedly doing the same thing. Drake had planned on having only two beers, anyway, so the decree didn't bother him at all.

Their weekly poker game usually took a couple of hours. He'd be completely sober when he drove back to the ranch.

The special ended up being chicken-fried steak, mashed potatoes and garden-fresh green beans, which meant it was his lucky night. Until he saw who was walking through the front door...

Ms. Lucinda Hale.

Drake couldn't believe it. She spotted him and waved. She looked different with all that long hair in loose curls and a denim skirt that reached only midthigh, with some sort of frothy pink top that left her slender arms bare. Didn't matter how she looked, though. She was still his nemesis. Or, if that was too fancy, he could just call her a pain in the butt. *Focus.* Poker night.

He waved back. What could he do but be polite? Tate narrowed his eyes. "That's her? The graduate student? *Pretty*'s an understatement, I'd say."

"Whatever." He finished his first beer in a gulp and grumbled, "What she's doing here, I don't have a clue."

"Maybe she heard that Billy serves the best burgers in town and decided to try one." Tripp looked amused at Drake's discomfort, especially when Luce started to walk toward them. "Here she comes. No offense, but I've never thought you were all that irresistible myself."

That was *not* worth responding to.

They all stood when she walked in their direction.

"Hello." Luce smiled at them, leaving Drake no choice but to introduce everyone. Once that was done, she said, "Please sit down and eat. I didn't mean to interrupt. Mace is parking the car. Nice to meet all of you."

About two seconds later, his brother strolled through the door, the slightest hint of a smirk on his face, as if he knew their arrival would annoy the hell out of him. Mace waved a casual hello and Luce went off to join him at a table in the corner, near the antique jukebox.

As if they were on a date or something. It definitely got to him, which he'd have to think about later.

"I guess you're not the irresistible one, after all." Tripp was joking, but his gaze was speculative. "You might want to adjust your expression, Carson, because Mace knows you even better than we do and he'll be able to read it loud and clear."

"What expression?" He caught the hint of defensiveness in his voice. Damn.

Spence said to Tate, "Two brothers after the same girl. Not a good scenario, is it?"

Tate took a bite and chewed for a minute as though he was thinking it over. "Especially if they live in the same house. Nope, not good at all."

"I'm not 'after' her," Drake snapped. He knew they were ribbing him, but he was afraid his current level of annoyance wasn't solely because Mace had deliberately brought her to Billy's to irritate him. They were best friends, yet they had fought like two male bighorn sheep their entire lives, arguing so much that even Slater had given up trying to tone them down. Unless it got physical, which it had once or twice when they were teens.

"Why aren't you?" Tripp asked that as if it were a legitimate question. "Attractive and obviously smart. Gorgeous eyes. Does she snore or something?"

"You've known Hadleigh since she was six. I just met Luce. She's only been around for about a week. Our arrangement, if you can call it that, is strictly business." He paused. "So I couldn't tell you if she snores. I haven't slept with her."

"He's always been the bashful type." Spence was doing a lousy job of hiding his glee. "Tripp has a point, though. A woman like that, following you around, living in the same house—seems like an opportunity not to be missed."

Tate had to throw in his opinion, too, of course. "Bex told me she's going to be here all summer. That's plenty of time to win her over. Unless Mace beats you to it."

"You three are worse than my mother. All I want to win at the moment is our poker game. Can we change the subject?" The chicken-fried steak was delicious, he was hungry and he rarely took a night off except for their poker game, so he wanted to enjoy it. If Luce felt like having dinner with his brother, that was her choice.

It didn't upset him.

Not at all.

Well…not much.

A reasonable voice inside him said he resented the intrusion she'd brought into his life, but another nagged that maybe he wasn't as indifferent as he wanted to be.

Thelma used the same tray to deliver their second round and stack up their empty plates. She cocked a brow in challenge. "Food's good?"

"Great," they answered in unison.

"I'll tell Billy. Deal the cards. Hard to believe, but the four of you are the only customers I've seen tonight who didn't make me say to myself, *Damn, it's them.* Hey, Carson, what's your girlfriend doing here with your brother, anyway?"

He would've explained that Luce wasn't his girlfriend, but Thelma sashayed away before he could comment, moving toward another table, muttering, "Keep your panties on, dammit. I've only got two hands."

They probably all looked shell-shocked. "Did we just get a compliment? From *Thelma*?" Spence whispered when she was far enough away to be out of earshot.

Tate said, "Can't be."

Tripp sat immobile. "I think we did."

Drake said, "Maybe she likes us. Let's not ruin it. You heard the lady. Hurry up and deal the cards."

MACE CARSON WAS entirely too pleased with himself. "Told you so," he said smugly.

Luce was torn between tossing her glass of wine at him—Mountain Vineyards, of course—and just laughing. She decided the waitress was too scary and she didn't dare make a mess, so he won the lottery. "I don't know what you think you're going to accomplish," she said. "Drake and his buddies are playing cards, and you and I are only here because Harry's cousin came to town unexpectedly and she took the night off."

"My mom is friends with Cindy, too, so coming here seemed like a good plan. The three of them will sit and gossip on the veranda all evening. Did you notice that Slater and Grace went off with Raine and Daisy? And Ryder's hanging out with Red."

She wasn't fooled. "But *you* chose when and where we'd go—just to be sure I'd intrude on your brother's evening with his friends."

His mouth twitched. "Not a ton of restaurant choices in Mustang Creek."

"Whatever lucky woman's out there waiting for you, she should be warned that you're a smooth liar."

He didn't even pretend to dissemble. "You think she's lucky, huh? I'm honored."

Luce watched him over the rim of her wineglass. Of the three Carson men, he was perhaps the most complicated. Slater was brilliant and driven. Drake was the pragmatic, down-to-earth type who dealt with life head-on. Mace was harder to figure out. All she knew with certainty was that he liked to needle his older brothers and would've been disappointed if they hadn't returned the favor.

Luce liked him. There wasn't the same pull she felt with Drake, but chemistry was an unpredictable thing. "Hmm. She'd need to be sassy. Sophisticated. Smart. And she has to be able to handle you."

"You fit the bill." His smile was flirtatious.

"I'm not sophisticated." She wasn't particularly; she'd always been more of an academic than the polished type she pictured at his side. He was equally aware that they weren't well suited in a romantic sense. And he obviously had some intuition about her and Drake—or at least her attraction to Drake—since he was pressuring his brother. She liked him all the better for his matchmaking because she found it both funny and touching. "I'm all about hiking boots and skinny-dipping in the river. You want someone who can pick up a wine list and recognize every single label."

"I don't like snooty women."

"That's not what I said, is it?"

"No." Mace was drinking one of his own red wines, and apparently enjoying the conversation. "I'll wait for her to come along. In the meantime, you and my brother?"

She had no idea what to say. She raised her shoulders in a helpless shrug. "I don't think he even likes me."

"Think again. I recognized that scowl on his face when I walked through the door. It wasn't because you were here. It was because you were here with *me*."

She regarded him dubiously.

With a cheeky grin, he added, "Trust me on this one, Ms. Hale. He just doesn't know what to do with you. Whoops, badly put. He knows what he'd *like* to do with you, but the thought of being part of a research project affronts his desire for solitude. You could put Drake in a time machine and take him back about a hundred and fifty years, drop him anywhere in the American West, and he'd fit right in. Even when we were younger, he hardly ever watched TV or played any video games. When we got home from school, he did his homework as fast as possible so he could saddle his horse and ride out. Harry used to get on him because he missed supper so often."

As Luce took another sip of wine, she was tucking this information away for reasons that weren't really connected to her graduate thesis. The hum of the restaurant had faded into the background. "Yet he went to college, even played a collegiate sport."

Mace leaned his forearms on the edge of the old wooden table, which had seen years of use. "Not going to college wasn't an option. Our father made that clear very early in our lives. What we did after college was our decision, but we were going to college, all three of us. And yeah, Drake is one hell of a tennis player. Think about it, though. Unless you play doubles, that's not a team sport. Slater played football and I ran track, but you should see Drake rope a calf. He's got incredible aim, so that's why he chose tennis. If I was drowning and needed someone to toss me a flotation device, I'd sure hope he was around."

Fascinating. And not what she needed. She was a bit too fascinated already.

"Do you suppose he'd ever let me film him doing that? The calf roping, I mean?"

"Doubtful." Mace shook his head. "Slater might be Mr. Showbiz, but Drake is camera shy. I remember that he had to be bribed with this vintage pickup truck he wanted before he agreed to have his senior pictures taken. He just wanted to skip the whole thing. Some sort of compromise was reached because he said yes to the pictures and he got the truck. He and Red restored it. They're kindred souls."

She'd met Red and could agree with that. "Hard to reach. Softhearted, but they hide it well."

"See, you're observant. What else have you picked up on? Have you decided he's worth the effort?"

Luce kept her cool. "I've decided you're jumping to a few conclusions here."

"I doubt it."

The reappearance of the grouchy waitress ended that conversation. Luce couldn't recall ordering, but she got a plate of fried walleye with homemade coleslaw and thick-cut fries, and Mace got a burger loaded with all the extras. Mystified, she asked, "How did she know what I was going to order? That's impossible."

"There are some questions better left unasked." He gestured at his plate. "Usually, I arrive, she brings me a drink, then she delivers the food. Maybe she's a witch or something, but like my brother, she tends to hit the mark."

The fish was delicious, crispy and paired with tartar sauce made from scratch. She'd barely finished the last bite when the poker party broke up and the players headed for the door, probably eager to get home to their wives and kids. Drake, the only bachelor in the bunch, didn't keep late hours, either, since he got up before dawn.

Speak of the devil... He stopped by their table. "How was your dinner?" he asked.

"Delicious." She waited; he seemed to have something to say.

"Good." He planted a hand, palm down, on the table, looking at her intently. "Finish your wine. You're coming with me. Mace can find his own way home."

When the ultimate cowboy gave you an ultimatum, it was kind of hard to ignore.

Mace was grinning behind his wineglass and his eyes twinkled. "Sure. Home. The place where we grew up. Sure, I can find it on my own."

"Don't even try to be funny. It's never worked for you before. I just want to show Luce something—not that it's any of your business."

"Wonder what that might be," Mace speculated, his tone easy and unhurried.

A muscle tensed in Drake's jaw. "Your tactless comments are getting on my nerves, little brother."

Time to run interference.

Luce finished her wine in an inelegant gulp and smiled apologetically at Mace. If she hadn't known what Mace was up to, she would never have agreed to leave one brother, who'd treated her to dinner, for the other. But he was the one who'd set everything in motion, so she interrupted whatever he was going to say next. "Thanks for dinner. So...what's your advice?"

He gave Drake a once-over. "He's harmless enough."

Drake didn't look flattered. "Don't be so sure."

Luce stood up hastily, aware that Mace could be right and Drake hadn't liked her coming to Bad Billy's with him. Even though it was none of his business. Her reaction to this was both positive and negative. So far, all her interactions with the Carson family had run that way. Three very different brothers who got along well, but there was some head-butting now and then. And she just happened to be the reason for this latest bout.

Drake steered her toward the bar. "I'll be a second. I need to talk to Billy."

Billy—a former biker, or so she'd heard—was busy pouring drinks. Smiling, he paused when Drake walked up. "You boys seemed to like the food okay. I see you stole Mace's woman. That didn't take long. Ain't you slick, cowboy."

"She isn't Mace's woman." Drake sounded emphatic. "Anyway, here's Thelma's tip. I didn't want to leave it on the table. Tell her it's from all of us."

Billy's eyebrows rose as he took the thick wad of bills. "Let me guess. Seven hundred dollars—enough to take care of the car repairs. That's real thoughtful of you."

Drake shrugged. "She brought us chicken-fried steak and beer. The least we could do is help her fix Frankie."

"Dammit, son, don't make me tear up in front of a pretty girl. It'd ruin my reputation. I'll see that Thelma gets this."

Luce would give a lot to see Bad Billy all misty-eyed, but Drake was already leading her toward the door, his fingers firmly around her wrist. Outside, the night was clear and, according to the weather report she'd heard earlier, unseasonably warm. "Do you mind telling me what I need to see so badly that I rudely abandoned your brother?"

He opened the passenger's-side door of his truck for her. "Explaining would defeat the purpose. *See* is the operative word here. Hop in."

CHAPTER SIX

THE MOON ROSE slowly above the mountains, right on cue, spreading its silvery light, and while he certainly knew she'd seen a full moon before, he was convinced she'd never seen one quite like this. Drake thought it was spectacular and he never tired of it.

Since he was going to watch it, anyway, she might as well come along.

Okay, the truth was he *needed* her to see it. If she wanted to have a true Wyoming experience, this was one of the best. He pointed. "This way."

He'd driven his truck as far as possible, but it was still a considerable walk, although he knew she wouldn't mind that part. Luce gave him an inquiring look and he just shook his head. "Worth it. Trust me."

"I am, obviously," she said drily.

He led her over the rustic pass, since he was the one who knew where they were going, and because there might be snakes. Rattlers usually left the vicinity as fast as possible when human beings showed up, but if they were startled, it was a different story. He'd been raised to pay attention, and he did.

The sound of rushing water told him they were getting close. When they got to the stream, he eyed her impractical open-toed shoes and without a word picked her up, ignoring her sudden gasp of protest, then waded across. Once he'd set her down on the other side, she straightened her skirt and glared at him. "I could've carried my shoes."

She did have the world's prettiest eyes, even when they were staring at him indignantly.

"That was easier, wasn't it? Look around. I think this might be the most beautiful place on earth."

In the twilight, a small waterfall that fed into the stream from a rocky outcrop glimmered. There was a natural bench in the form of a flat stone about six feet wide. He gestured toward it. They were in a small theater of aspens and ponderosa pine, and the air smelled like fresh water and meadow grass. "Have a seat and let the show begin. We're right on time."

"On time for what?"

"Wait for it. Watch the tree line."

The sunset was even *more* spectacular than usual—or at least he felt as if it was. The rows of trees were illuminated in a glow that intensified as the moon came up. With the mountains behind, and a starry sky above, the veil of the waterfall reflected the light.

Luce's eyes widened, and Drake heard her catch her breath as she took it all in.

Oh, hell, he *was* falling for her. He'd always wondered how it would feel if that ever happened—he was thirty-two now and it hadn't yet—but he knew this *was* happening.

He'd once told Slater that when the woman of his dreams walked into his line of vision, he'd know it.

That might be true, but he wasn't sure he wanted it to be Lucinda Hale. They lived in different states, an obstacle in itself, and he sensed that her interest in him was based on her intellectual pursuits—but it might have evolved into something more. He couldn't pick up the ranch and move it somewhere else, so unless she was willing to completely change *her* life, it wasn't going to work.

How had he gotten himself into this situation?

Wait, *he* hadn't done it. She had.

Was he really that serious? He'd met her only a short time ago.

Maybe he was…

"That's so beautiful," she whispered. "Drag me out of a bar and carry me across a river anytime."

"Count on me."

The hell of it was he wanted to reach over, haul her into his arms and prove he meant it, but he wasn't comfortable with this kind of emotional impulse. He led a simple life and liked it that way. He got up early, saddled his horse, went to work and came home. Yup, simple.

Luce was throwing a hitch in his stride. She was a complication, and that was the truth.

It didn't help matters when she turned and smiled almost tremulously. "I could very easily fall in love." She amended quickly, "With Wyoming, I mean."

Damn, he was going to kiss her, and the worst part was that she knew it, too. There was an expectant look on her face, and when he leaned in and slid his arm around her waist to pull her close, she accepted it willingly, one hand coming up to rest on his chest.

It was quite the kiss, starting tentatively, but then it deepened with alarming speed. Still, he didn't care to analyze it. Luce was warm and pliant against him, her hair smelled like flowers and was tangled around his fingers. His heart was pounding and—

A familiar sound broke them apart, and to his complete shock, he saw the stallion, probably less than a hundred feet away. He'd come up here to drink from the stream and snorted again in displeasure at their presence. Then he lowered his head and drank, anyway, always vigilant but apparently thirsty.

If he could've had a conversation with that mare-thieving bastard, Drake would have pointed out that *he* was the one who should be ticked off.

To make it worse, Luce seemed to forget the kiss entirely. "I can't believe it," she said in a hushed voice. "Look how close he is!"

"Yeah, he sure is." Drake spoke in his normal tone, because while he had affection for all creatures on the planet, he was greatly irritated by this one at the moment.

"Shh. You'll scare him away."

"That would be fine with me. I don't have a tranquilizer gun, and if I did, there's no way I could transport him from this spot, anyway. So I guess if I spook him, it doesn't bother me too much."

"We agreed you weren't going to do that. Use a tranquilizer gun, I mean."

Oh, good. Great kiss followed by an argument. "We didn't *agree* on anything. *You* made the declaration that you'd become his new best friend, and I told you flat out that you were delusional."

"I do remember you being extremely closed-minded

now that you mention it." She stood up and Drake gave an inner sigh.

Smoke, the coward, turned and melted into the shadows. Smart horse.

"*Practical.* That's a better word." He stood, too. He might as well ride fences tonight, even though Red had it handled. Never hurt to check twice.

"Whatever," she muttered and started to walk toward the stream, stopping to yank off her shoes, holding them in one hand. "No need to carry me, by the way. I can take care of myself."

"Look, the herd's growing. If I wait too long, it'll be impossible. So I'm not going to wait. I can't afford to."

"The government will auction them off!"

"But not to a slaughterhouse or the glue factory, if that's what you're worried about. I wouldn't condone that, either. The real problem is that you're getting unreasonably attached."

Those gorgeous eyes sent him a death glare to rival Thelma's. "*I'm* unreasonable?"

Really?

In just one evening, Drake Carson had ordered her to leave a restaurant with him, picked her up without warning, kissed her senseless and then infuriated her. It was becoming pretty clear that he did things his way, and if she didn't like his approach, he wouldn't lose sleep over it.

Oh, the moon rising up over the mountains was gorgeous, no question about that. Not to mention romantic, which might've been why she was so drawn into that passionate kiss. She could tell that her research project meant little or nothing to him, and *his* agenda was what mattered.

It was his ranch, true, but he hadn't done anything about the horses yet. Maybe they could figure something out...

Maybe *she'd* figure out what that something could be.

She splashed through the cold stream, finding the bottom rockier than she'd expected. She gritted her teeth and went on, the current swirling around her thighs. She understood he was running a business; that part was fine. But the fact that he seemed to think she was pursuing a frivolous degree set her teeth on edge. No, he'd never *said* that. He really didn't need to.

Drake Carson was bullheaded, and that was all there was to it.

To make matters worse, he knew she was mad and didn't try to talk about it. He just walked behind her and didn't stop her when she rushed forward to open her own door. He closed it, climbed in the driver's side—both of them wet—and started the truck.

Clearly, if it was up to him, they weren't going to have a conversation.

Well, she had a news bulletin—it *wasn't* up to him, not entirely.

Luce began by asking, "Why did you kiss me?"

"I wanted to." He put the truck in gear and drove down the rutted track.

"I could swear you don't even like me. I told Mace that earlier."

"Mace is nothing but a pain in the ass."

"*And* he's your brother, and a really nice man."

"Nice? When did *that* happen?"

"You're joking and you know it."

"Luce, what do you want from me?" He kept his tone even. "I assume you realize I'm attracted to you. Not sure

I want to be, but there it is. I don't do casual, so that means it has to be serious, and in the end, you're going back to California. It might be better if we stayed away from each other, but you're there every time I turn around. This is a hard rock or a deep pool situation for me."

He had a point. She murmured, "I don't think that's quite the right saying. Devil or the deep blue sea? Between a rock and a hard place?"

"Close enough. That's Red talking. He always says that you could be stuck on a hard rock or drowning in a deep pool."

She laughed. "I can imagine him saying that. So what now?"

"If you want to fall in love, Wyoming is your only choice."

That was honest. A play on her words, but honest.

Still, this was moving far too fast. "I don't know if I want to fall in love—with you *or* Wyoming—at all. Anyway, I can't fall in love—in just a couple of weeks."

"It does seem to defy logic, but my impression is that logic doesn't enter into falling in love."

Time to give him some perspective. "I was kissed by a sexy cowboy near a waterfall during a full moon while a wild stallion intruded on the moment. Let's not confuse romantic with deeper feelings."

Drake only grinned. "I'm sexy?"

"Oh, yes." She wished he wasn't.

"Nice to know you're inclined to think of me that way." His smile flashed again.

"Like you didn't already know that."

"I'm not sure I did."

"Just do me a favor and don't play that card, okay? You're

totally aware of what's going on between us. And by the way, I don't do casual, either."

"So—what, are we making a pact not to get involved?" He did that thing with his hat, tipping it and then adjusting it back down. "I'm not positive it works that way. That choice isn't yours—it's made *for* you."

"Voice of experience?" She looked at him curiously, hanging on to the car door, since they were bumping along on something that only resembled a road. "Have you ever been in love?"

"No details available. This isn't a sorority gossip session."

Fine. Whatever Drake's opinion of her, she actually did respect his privacy. So, no questions.

No reason *she* couldn't be honest. "I thought I was in love once, but the man I fell for slept with my roommate. She blamed him, and he blamed her. I blamed them both. End of story. I lost a friend and a fiancé in one fell swoop. I did thank her, though, for saving me from making a big mistake. I got the flat-screen TV when I moved out. That gave me some satisfaction. She could watch the empty space on the wall."

"Ouch, but she did do you a favor. Faithful is not negotiable in my book."

"*The Cowboy Guide to a Successful Relationship*? I assume that's the title." She didn't conceal her amusement. "Let me guess. Chapter One is 'Never Discuss Previous Relationships.' What's Chapter Two?"

"Chapter Two is 'Avoid Beautiful Graduate Students Because They're a Passel of Trouble.'"

"What trouble have I caused you?"

He didn't budge an inch, but his mouth twitched with laughter. "I sense it coming."

"Do you now?" She was laughing, too. "So you think I'm beautiful, or were you just trying to be polite, since I said you were sexy?"

"You'll discover that I don't say anything I don't mean. Then again, I didn't mention you by name, did I?" He spoke in that low deliberate drawl she found so charming. "But yes, I think beautiful applies."

Maybe changing the subject would be a good idea. He was right; she was going to gather all the information for her thesis this summer and then return to California. Involvement with Drake was the last thing she needed. Her whole life was in California, including every member of her family. "So tell me, why did you give a seven-hundred-dollar tip to a waitress who was so grumpy I hesitated to ask her for a glass of water?"

"Someone hit Frankie."

Luce wrinkled her brow. "Frankie is…who? Husband? Dog? Cat?"

"Car. She doesn't really have the money to fix it. We all pitched in. This is Mustang Creek. She lives frugally, takes care of her elderly mother, and everyone knows she loves Frankie." He shrugged in a nonchalant way. "We all brought money for the poker game, so we pooled it together and gave it to her."

"That's generous of you."

"I've known her my whole life."

Softly, Luce said, "I'm guessing Chapter Three is titled 'Loyalty,' right?"

"If it isn't," he responded as they reached the paved road, "it should be."

CHAPTER SEVEN

SOMETHING WAS UP.

When he came in for lunch the next day, after that moonlit kiss he and Luce had shared, Drake saw Harry's knowing smile, and before he could ask any questions, she presented him with one of his all-time favorites—a corned beef sandwich. He devoured it and would've counted himself a lucky man, but Mace came into the kitchen before he was finished. The smug grin on his brother's face would have made it hard for a saint to resist punching him out on the spot.

Drake was no saint.

"What?" He set aside his plate and forgot all about having seconds of the potato salad. Harold and Violet, waiting patiently at his feet, were obviously hoping for leftovers.

Mace tried to look innocent but didn't quite pull it off as he plucked a sandwich from the board and spooned up enough potato salad to satisfy a bull moose. "What? You and Slater cross paths today?"

"Not yet."

Come to think of it, when he'd passed Grace in the hall, she'd also had an amused expression on her face.

What now?

For starters, he wasn't going to pass up the extra potato salad, and he never gave the dogs any table scraps, so he ignored them. He took his own sweet time eating, even rinsed his plate. Only then did he take the bait. "You going to elaborate? Just tell me. You're obviously dying to."

Mace had his mouth full, so he finished chewing and swallowed before he answered. "He's in his office. Maybe before you head out again, you should see him."

The fact that Mace found this funny was not a good sign, whatever was going on. Drake maneuvered the hallways to the back of the house, the dogs following. Slater was at his desk, talking on his cell phone, but he waved him into a seat. Drake chose to stand and gaze out the window, because that was one damn fine view. His father had known what he was doing when he'd selected this room for his office. Plus, he wasn't going to stay long, anyway.

Slater ended the call. "Sorry about that."

He turned. "No problem. We're even if you'll tell me why everyone's acting like there's something I don't know that they all find hilarious."

Oh, great, another big grin. His older brother said, "Can't thank you enough."

"What the hell does that mean? Thank me for what?" Drake was getting exasperated and he didn't care who knew it.

Slater touched a key on his computer. "I've been struggling with how to start the new documentary. We've begun some of the filming, but I needed an opening. It's all about Wyoming, specifically this area—and you handed my opening scene to me on a platter. Sterling-silver platter, in fact. Look at this."

The minute the image came up, Drake understood the snickers. It was certainly a familiar one. Moon rising, mountains, waterfall glistening, a wild stallion in the background…

Man and woman kissing.

"You had cameras there last night? At that very spot?" Drake took off his hat and wanted to throw it across the room, but he ran his fingers through his hair instead. "Damn, Slate, that was kind of a private moment!"

His brother leaned back in his chair. "Now, think about it. How in the hell would I know you'd conveniently show up—cowboy hat, boots and all—and kiss the girl? I just wanted to catch the waterfall and the moon rising, so we set up remote cameras. We handle things that way all the time. The stallion's an extra perk. I can't *not* use this shot. The chances of getting something like this are out of the ballpark. This *is* Wyoming. I'm opening with it."

Oh, *that* was good news.

His brother went on, going all Showbiz. "It's great footage. I showed it to my assistant, and he about flipped out. Sent it to the director, and he couldn't believe it, either. Done, and on the first take, too. No actors involved, and the staging and lighting are perfect."

This *was* his brother. He would've told anybody else what they could do with their perfect staging. Slater was Slater, though, and he was telling the truth—he hadn't planned on filming that kiss. It had just happened. No one's fault, but Drake's level of enthusiasm for sharing his love life—if that term applied—with the world was hovering around minus twenty.

So he looked for a way out. "Don't you need our permission?"

"Yeah, I do. I'm counting on you to sign, and to persuade Luce to do the same. You ought to be able to convince her—the two of you seem to like each other well enough, if that kiss is any indication."

This was a headache he didn't need. At least he and Luce weren't really recognizable, he thought as he studied the screen. They were practically silhouettes. "Well, I'm guessing since those were remote cameras, they kept on rolling, so you also caught us having an argument and her stomping off. I wouldn't count on me influencing her."

Slater didn't look fazed at all. "And yet I *am* counting on it. Grace said it might be the most romantic moment she's ever seen—which made me question whether or not I've been handling things right."

"She's pregnant with your child, so you've obviously done things just fine." Drake rubbed his forehead. "Did you *have* to show it to other people?"

"Mom walked in when I was reviewing the film to ask me a question. Most people wouldn't recognize you from your profile, but she would. Of course, she told Harry and Grace. They both asked to see it. Grace is kind of dangerous right now that she's in her last trimester, so I couldn't refuse. And I learned a long time ago that if Harry asks me to do something, I should simply do it. You can't disagree with me on that."

"Someone told Mace."

"Drake, if the way you dragged Luce out of Bad Billy's didn't start everyone talking, then I don't know what would. I heard about it from Raine, and she'd heard it from someone else because she and Daisy were out to dinner with us during that little scene." He paused, looking closely at Drake. "Oh, and I'll need Luce's permission in writing. My lawyers will be in touch."

"Lawyers?" This was getting worse by the minute.

"They handle situations like this. Don't act as if you don't know that."

He did, but still…

"I don't want to be part of your movie."

"You didn't intend to be part of it, but it's going to be perfect. You didn't have to act or anything. You just behaved naturally, and it was exactly what I needed. So you and I both won. Look at the picture again. Classic."

Hell, double hell and triple hell.

"It's that damn horse." Slater could easily get another couple to kiss in the moonlight by the waterfall, but that horse was so beautiful—when he wasn't kicking down fences and creating other chaos. "Fine with me, but *you* get to ask Luce about the footage. I've got a full afternoon and she's being fairly testy with me right now. You stand a better chance."

He stalked out the door and ran into her in the hallway. Figured. She was in full-on outdoor gear, ponytail and all. "Slater needs to talk to you," he said, trying to sound as normal as possible. "He's in his office, and just so you know, this isn't my fault."

"What does that mean?" Luce wasn't letting him off the hook. She caught his arm as he tried to leave. "What isn't your fault?"

"This." He grabbed her, kissed her the way he had the night before, then let her go. At least she didn't smack him, but he did see her bewildered look when he spun on his heel and walked away.

Chapter Four of his book should be titled "Romantic Moonlit Kisses Are a Bad Idea."

BLYTHE WAS ON the porch, watering her flowers. Luce went out there and sat down, sighing deeply. "Your sons are giving me fits."

"Welcome to my world." Blythe glanced over with a smile hovering on her lips. "Specifically?"

"I know you saw that picture of me and Drake." She felt a flush hit her cheeks.

"I could lie," Blythe told her, "but I'm not good at lying, and besides, why should I? I saw it. Slater is elated and I don't blame him one bit. That shot couldn't be orchestrated in a thousand years. Drake would never do that in front of a camera on purpose and that horse is definitely an…interesting addition."

Luce gave a small hiccup of a laugh. "Drake's going to view him as more of a nuisance than ever."

"I assume you mean the horse. Well, Drake viewed *you* as a nuisance when you first got here, but he seems to have decided otherwise in a very short period of time. I was going to have a cup of tea. Care to join me?"

"I'd love to."

"I'll be right back. We'll sit at the table in the corner."

It was a pleasant afternoon, pots of pansies vibrant in the slanting sunlight on the veranda-style porch. When Blythe returned with a tray holding an old-fashioned teapot and two delicate floral china cups with saucers, Luce hurried to take it from her, letting her hostess choose a chair first.

"Of course, Harry insisted on the oatmeal chocolate chip

cookies, since she was just taking them out of the oven." Blythe sat down and reached for the teapot, pouring them each a cup. "She makes those for Drake, lemon bars for Slater, and Mace's favorite is her blue-ribbon-winning pie. If asked, I'm fairly sure the boys would describe her as the most thoughtful tyrant in Bliss County. Now, then, what are you going to do about Drake?"

That was certainly direct.

But so was the picture, and he'd just kissed her *again*. Drat the man. Not that she'd pushed him away or anything...

The raspberry-lemon tea was wonderful. "I have no idea," she said with a rueful smile. "I don't know if I *can* do anything about him. He lives here and I live in California."

"His father lived here and I lived in California." Blythe took a dainty sip. "I really fell for that hardworking, honest-as-the-day-is-long cowboy. Slater looks like my late husband, but Drake *reminds* me of him more. Stubborn as all get-out. He's also a very good, kind man. Intelligent and yet compassionate enough that children and animals are instinctively drawn to him."

Luce nibbled at a cookie. She could level with Blythe, and she did. "You don't have to sell me on Drake. You saw that film."

Blythe's smile deepened. "I did indeed. A lot of people will see it. You're fine with that?"

"No one will know who I am. I told Slater I was okay with it."

"There are worse things than a woman being kissed by a handsome young man."

She couldn't agree more. "Everything in life is about timing. Did you catch that bus on schedule? Or if you missed it, did you also miss being in an accident? Did you walk across the street at the wrong time? Did your parents divorce when you were in high school? Did you catch your fiancé with your best friend? All kinds of scenarios like that. I just don't know if this is the right timing for us."

Blythe laughed, the sound light and musical. "Honey, you can't wait for 'right.' There's no such thing when it comes to love. I'd never tell you what to do, but to me, effort is the key to any relationship and I'm living proof that you have to do your share and maybe a little more if you want a man like Drake."

Luce shrugged. "I'm not convinced it's an option."

"Sure it is! Keep in mind that Drake's never going to be forthcoming, especially regarding anything emotional. That's just who he is. Mace expresses himself effectively, Drake not enough and Slater's in the middle."

That didn't bother her too much. He was a loner and she understood that, but he was also an intelligent, articulate man who *could* talk about his feelings; he wasn't inclined to do it.

Talk about being between a hard rock and a deep pool… Red needed to write his own book of quaint sayings and shelve it right next to *The Cowboy Guide to a Successful Relationship.*

"So I chose the difficult one, didn't I?"

"Maybe." Blythe didn't evade her question. "In a lot of ways he's the easiest. He does what he's going to do and that's it. He's never going to pull you in fifteen different directions, and he won't lie to you. If you want it straight from the hip, that's exactly what you're going to get, like it or not."

Chose was a dangerous word. It implied that she'd made a decision. Perhaps she even had…

Blythe took difficult and made it simple. "He's worth it."

It would be different if Luce disagreed. But Mace had said the same thing.

"I wasn't looking for this."

Blythe took that in stride. "Sometimes it just finds you."

"Now you sound like Drake."

"Or maybe he sounds like me?" She smiled. "We *have* spent some time together in our lives."

That did bring a laugh. "Okay, I concede that he might sound like you. Pragmatic and down-to-earth."

Grace pulled up just then, got out of her car and slammed the door. Hard. She stalked up the steps—as much as a very pregnant woman could stalk—and dropped her purse on the wooden floor of the veranda. "If I could drink, I would, but I can't. Is it wrong to say I had a bad day at the resort? That doesn't seem right. Who could have a bad day at a beautiful resort? Me, that's who. Some of those cookies have my name on them. Don't risk both your lives by eating them all while I go to the bathroom for about the four hundredth time today."

Blythe was unfazed. "Harry made an extra batch."

"She has a good sense of how the universe works. I'll be right back."

Blythe was laughing out loud, but she had a sympathetic look on her face as her daughter-in-law disappeared into the house. She settled comfortably back in her chair. "Near the end it gets rough. Childbirth right in front of you and either you don't know what to expect or you *do* know what to expect. Between a—"

"Hard rock and a deep pool?" Luce supplied helpfully. "According to Drake, it's one of Red's favorite sayings. It's become my new favorite, too."

"Red is quite the character, no doubt about that." Blythe poured another cup of tea. "Speaking of babies, this is a personal question, but I do hope you want children."

Wow, talk about moving too fast.

Luce didn't have a facile response to that one. She was rescued by Grace, who returned to the porch and lowered herself into a chair with a sigh of relief. She'd discarded her shoes in the meantime and come out barefoot, her red hair loose, and accepted a cup of tea and a cookie. "I've been waiting for this all day."

Through a mouthful, she added directly to Luce, "Slate loves the footage of you and Drake. Thank you. He's been struggling with how to open the film. No pun intended, but that's picture-perfect."

He might be happy about the picture, but Drake wasn't. Faintly, Luce said, "My pleasure."

CHAPTER EIGHT

It had been a long week.

Drake had come to the conclusion that those shots of him and Luce might be the death of him.

Mostly because everyone knew about their unwitting role in the film, and the ranch hands had plenty to say. His current infamy—because he'd kissed a young woman under a moonlit sky—was drawing laughs from everyone, and not just on the ranch.

"Hey there, Romeo, what can I do for you?" Jack Dunlap, who ran the hardware store, grinned unapologetically. He was a tall, lean man with iron-gray hair who always wore suspenders and, if there weren't any customers, wasn't averse to stepping outside to smoke a cigar. The place was a labyrinth of packed aisles, but he knew where to find every nut, bolt and screw, and tell a customer exactly how to use every item he sold.

Romeo. Drake was pretty sure he could thank Mace for the new nickname, although he couldn't prove it. In a very short time, it seemed that everyone in Mustang Creek had heard the story. It didn't help that the entire population of Bliss County was fascinated by the idea that Slater was filming a documentary right there. His out-of-town crew was staying at the resort, eating at the local restaurants, shopping at the stores, so it could've been one of those blabbermouths. He'd decided to ignore it all.

When he could, anyway.

"I have a list." He handed it over to Jack. "Most of it's for Mace. He's planning to build a newfangled contraption for fermenting a certain kind of wine, I guess. I just need the usual to do repairs in the stables."

Jack slipped on a pair of spectacles and surveyed the list. "Can do. Take me about fifteen minutes. Heard what you did for Thelma. She's hopping mad at you."

That was Thelma, but it probably meant she was hopping mad because he'd found out she'd cried over the gesture in front of people. They were in real trouble now.

"Did it for Frankie," Drake said blandly. "And it was all of us. Point me in the right direction and I'll help you with this list."

"Back of the store, last aisle, for those hinges. I'll get the rest."

As Drake headed toward the right section, he rounded a corner and came face-to-face with one of the few people he truly detested. Reed Keller straightened, a box of roofing nails in his hand. "Carson. Or I guess I should call you Romeo?"

He tolerated it from Jack, but he had his limits.

"Keller." Drake nodded curtly, trying to ignore the man's smirk. He walked past as swiftly as possible. They'd clashed since grade school when he'd caught Keller pushing Mace around, and their relationship hadn't improved in high school, when Keller deliberately went after Drake's girl-friend.

The ploy had worked for him, too. She and Drake broke up, Keller had gotten her pregnant—there went Danielle's dreams of college—and married her. They had a couple of kids now, but he'd heard they'd recently separated.

Not his business.

Still, seeing the guy at all added a sour note to his day.

Exactly fifteen minutes later, just as Jack had promised, Drake was in his truck, on the way home. He thought the day was improving—until he saw Red outside the barn with Luce, leaning on a shovel and definitely chatting her up. He had the distinct feeling there was another Romeo reference in his future.

He parked the truck, texted Mace that he'd bought his supplies so his brother could come and unload them.

Unfortunately for him, Luce looked *very* cute in a pair of jeans and a T-shirt, with her hair whipped back into a no-nonsense ponytail as usual. She was wearing her hiking boots and held a lightweight backpack slung over her arm.

"Hey, Romeo." Yup, just as he'd predicted. Red obviously thought he was being funny.

Luce blushed. Drake took it in stride. "First time I've heard that today? Uh, not really. Word of warning, I'm starting to lose my sense of humor over this."

Red adjusted his position. He might be older, and was certainly wiser, but he understood boundaries. He raised his hands. "Just joshing, son. Usually, you let it roll off your back. What has you as grouchy as a grizzly crawling out of his cave on a spring day?"

"Yeah, well, word about that film is all over town." He

took out the bag with the new latches for two of the stalls and slammed the door of his truck.

Red winked at Luce. "Who cares if the world knows you kissed a pretty girl?"

Exasperated, he avoided looking directly at the woman in question. "I don't particularly care, but surely people have something more important to talk about. Slater kisses Grace about fifty times a day—I'm always walking in on them by accident. No one hangs around talking about it. I'm going to replace those two latches and then ride out to the north pasture. Mind helping Mace with his stuff?"

"Don't mind at all." Red ambled toward the truck.

"I feel I should apologize for something, but I don't know what." Luce smiled tightly.

Drake wasn't taciturn by nature, or didn't think he was, anyway, and he relented, meeting her eyes. "It isn't you. I ran into someone who called me that, and while I don't mind being razzed a little, I didn't appreciate it from this person. We have some history. You have absolutely nothing to apologize for."

He was the one who'd kissed *her*, after all, not just once but twice, and he really wouldn't mind doing it again, but next time he'd check for hidden cameras.

"I'm hiking up to the ridge to see if the horses are there again this afternoon," she said.

"If you want to wait a few minutes, I can take you most of the way." That was the least he could do. He hadn't been very cordial since he'd run into Keller, but he shouldn't take it out on anyone else, particularly not Luce.

She didn't look too enthusiastic. "On your horse?"

"Yeah, on my horse. If I tried to walk everywhere on a ranch this size, I wouldn't get anything done. I do use the

ATV sometimes, but it spooks the cattle. Horses work best. Always have and still do. Luce, you're the one who thinks you can tame a wild stallion! Maybe you need to get used to horses. I'm talking about real horses. Not just horses as an abstract idea or an academic interest."

Defensively, she shot back, "All I want is for Smoke to trust me so I can get close enough to observe them better. I never said I'd tame him, nor did I say I want to ride."

"Riding him would be a neat trick."

"You know full well I didn't mean him."

He was just teasing her, but also serious. "Your choice. It's quite a distance on foot as *you* know full well. Starburst and I can take you about halfway. I just have to change out these latches on a couple of stalls. Won't take me long."

She was still thinking it over when he walked away, but he did have things to do, and as much as she might promise she wasn't going to interfere with his daily life, she already had. He found it entertaining that she was so eager to be around the wild horses, and yet Starburst, who was perfectly well behaved, intimidated her.

He used his handheld drill to remove the old latches on the stalls, attached the new ones quickly and then put his tools away.

As it turned out, Luce had decided to wait.

Judging by the tilt of her chin, she'd done it because he'd practically dared her, but he knew one thing.

He was looking forward to that ride.

DRAKE FELT WARM and solid as Luce sat behind him on the saddle. She was determined to put on a brave front, so when he urged the big horse into a gallop, she did her best not to panic.

As promised, he took her about five miles in easily half the time it would've taken her to walk, reined in near a field of grazing cows and dismounted to lift her off.

She appreciated the courtesy and was getting used to the fact that Drake Carson was a man of old-fashioned manners. A man who took care of other living creatures and was used to physical work, he thought nothing of picking up another person—literally!—and transferring her from point A to point B.

"It isn't smart to hike out here alone, especially if you're not used to rugged country. I hope that's come to your attention," he told her in his low drawl. "Don't be fooled by all the scenic wonders—the place came to be called the Wild West for a reason. Lots of bad-tempered critters around, besides wild horses. We have venomous snakes, bears, big cats. And of course people can be the most dangerous predators of all. I can't stop you, but I can tell you I don't like it."

Fair enough. He was giving her practical advice without being dictatorial, and she appreciated it. "I carry pepper spray."

"Not a bad precaution. But all I'm saying is be alert. An animal, human or otherwise, can catch you unawares."

Smiling, she said, "So you want me to survive to annoy you another day? I'm surprised."

"No, you aren't."

Okay, she wasn't. Not really. He wasn't just another good-looking cowboy; he was a kind man, a decent one. Whether he liked her or not, he wouldn't want any harm to befall her. "Drake, I—"

He raised a hand. "Look, be careful, okay? There's no

cell service as you go higher up. I sure hope you put on sunblock if you won't wear a hat."

"You aren't my big brother. Stop with the lecture."

"Lecture's over." He swung onto his horse in a single smooth movement and touched the brim of his hat. "And just so we're clear, I'm happy I'm not your brother. Have a nice walk. Wave hi to Smoke for me."

With that, he rode off and left her standing there, watching him go. She squared her shoulders. The ridge where she knew the horses frequently grazed was still some distance away. She headed off in that direction, and thanks to his advice, she was more aware of her surroundings rather than simply preoccupied with her destination. It was a lovely sunny day so, yes, she'd put on a combination of insect repellent and sunscreen. The wildflowers were entrancing, and since she wasn't a botanical expert, she didn't know specifically what kind they were. But every variety was beautiful. Yellow, blue, red, violet...

She heard the familiar snort and immediately halted. The horses were much closer than she'd realized, having moved down toward the ranch. She was starting to grasp the dynamic of how the horses interacted with the ranch, which was exactly what she wanted.

They did intrude periodically, but then they made themselves scarce.

Smoke was there, on the fringes of his herd, watching her. He had an elegant head, reminiscent of Spanish horses in historical pictures she'd seen, and although he was cautious, she got the impression that maybe, just maybe, he knew she wasn't a threat. Such as when he'd drunk from the stream even though she was there.

He turned away and went back to grazing, cropping the long grass.

To her mind, that was progress.

Some of the mares in the herd were used to people, so she didn't worry too much about them. She eased closer very cautiously so they didn't all run. Unfortunately, Drake was right; she didn't know enough about horses. Still, she was learning more every day.

The mares with foals watched her, as did Smoke. When he lifted his head, she stood her ground and waited. Evidently, he'd confirmed that she wasn't a threat, because he didn't come any closer, but let her stay perched behind some sort of conifer, probably a Douglas fir. She got some good snapshots and started on her notes, sitting cross-legged behind the tree. The mustangs tolerated her presence. Smoke was paying attention, but he obviously wasn't worried, and that was her goal.

Trust.

It couldn't be bought, and it couldn't be sold, and in her view, it was the most important commodity in the world. Smoke trusted that she wasn't there to threaten anyone, so he wasn't worried about her.

Step one.

She did observe some of the horses taking an interest in her, but the stallion quickly shut that down. She assumed they were some of the mares Drake had griped about losing. Smoke shooed them back into the group, and he got no argument.

She wrote: *It's interesting. He's a dictator and yet protects them all. From what I understand, when the younger males start to challenge him, they'll either win or be driven out. Not a democracy. His private fiefdom is under guard at all times.*

When she looked up again, she suddenly noticed that one of the foals was missing.

She checked her notebook twice. The little black one with the white star on his forehead was gone. She'd carefully noted them all over the past few weeks, describing them, and she was horrified. She even tried to call Drake, but he was right; her cell didn't work up this far.

Darn it, there were tears in her eyes.

As if Drake could fix it. As if he could rush in and save the day, find the colt or filly and solve the problem.

Luce sat down on a fallen log. Okay, she told herself, maybe she didn't know how to ride horses, but she did love them. Where did that little one go?

The sound of a horse nickering made her look up. Smoke stood about twenty feet away. She felt that an unspoken understanding had passed between them and that he recognized her concern.

"I hate to lose any of them," she said quietly, at the risk of sending the horse flying away because she'd spoken. "I can't even imagine how you feel."

The stallion took a tentative step toward her, then another one, until he stood less than a yard away. She couldn't believe it.

Under other circumstances, she might've taken his picture, but this wasn't that kind of moment.

This was...private.

Not that she was an expert, but she estimated that he got close enough to take in her scent. His breath ruffled her hair. She stayed perfectly still. Then he whirled around in a graceful movement and galloped off.

CHAPTER NINE

DRAKE WASN'T SITTING on the porch because he was waiting for a certain hiker to show up, safe and sound.

Nope. Absolutely not.

A man had every right to sit on his own porch and enjoy a cold beer.

No reason to worry about Luce because she happened to be a tenderfoot.

No reason at all.

He wasn't fooling his older brother. Next to him—in one of those rocking chairs their mother insisted on that were actually quite comfortable—Slater said, "Relax. She isn't an idiot. Far from it. Grace tells me Luce is a very experienced hiker."

Was he that transparent? He sure as hell hoped not. Drake summoned up his most indifferent expression. "I'm just sitting here having a beer. How'd the filming go today?"

"Nice try, Ace. Sometimes deflection works, but not tonight. Don't worry, I'm not going to initiate a deep, soulful discussion about your tender feelings. I'm saying the woman intended to camp up near that ridge during this whole study deal, so just because she's staying with us doesn't mean you get to monitor when she comes home—like she's a teenager out on a date or something. She knows better than to miss dinner. If she isn't smart enough to keep on Harry's good side, then I've severely misjudged the woman."

Drake nodded. Being late for dinner…no way you'd want to do that.

He could deny his concern, but he doubted that would work. "I should have ridden up there."

His brother mimicked their mother's skeptical expression. "You have time for that?"

"I'm sitting here having a beer with you, aren't I?"

"A rare occasion."

It was true. He didn't knock off this early very often.

"I was basically done for the day."

His brother wasn't buying it. "No, you're sitting on this porch worrying about her."

Maybe. He couldn't disagree. "Big mountains out there."

"Yes, big mountains. Drake, it isn't a bad thing to admit you're concerned about Luce."

He thought it over, boot heels on the railing. This was going to be a beautiful sunset. "I don't think that the words *concern* or *worry* really apply. I just wish she'd show up so I could forget about her and not have to wonder if she's been eaten by a bear—or attacked by a wild horse. That would sure make my life easier."

Slater choked on his beer, laughing and wiping at his shirt. "A woman shows up and makes your life easier? Oh, yeah, happens all the time." Then he sobered. "She might make your life better, but not *easier*."

"So speaks a married man."

"So speaks a happily married man. Grace is the love of my life, but is it easier? Nope."

"Wait until that baby arrives." Drake chortled as he imagined his older brother changing diapers. That mental image made the beer taste even better.

"Well, laugh it up all you want, but I think you've caught the same disease I have, and there isn't a cure."

"You're talking about love. Lust isn't the same thing."

"I agree. Completely."

That shook him more than a little. "She's smart and she's pretty. With the full moon and all, it was...just a kiss."

"I kinda thought the same thing with Grace. Just a kiss. Wrong. But at least you can relax. Here she comes."

Drake knew his relief was telling. He had to force himself not to get to his feet; he managed to stay camped in his chair until Luce reached the porch. Then he *had* to stand or his mother would have his head. Slater got up, too. His faint smile was irritating, but Drake could live with it better than with Keller's.

Luce sent him a direct look. Her shirt had wet spots on it from perspiration and she seemed distressed and out of breath. Yet she still managed to look damn beautiful, even after hiking about a million miles. "We've got a missing foal."

Her expression asked what he was going to do about it. That signal came through loud and clear.

"Okay," he said tentatively, waiting for her to explain.

"It isn't okay at all! I mean *missing*. I was there all afternoon. He's gone."

There could be any number of explanations. Horses got sick, just like any other creature. The foal could have wandered off and gotten lost. Mares were vigilant, but mistakes did happen in the natural order of things. Or there could be a predator stalking the horses, like the one taking his calves now and then. He said in what he thought was a patient tone, "I get it, Luce, but you can't expect me to ride herd—so to speak—on a bunch of wild horses. I've lost calves, too."

He and Slater exchanged a glance. "You thinking what I'm thinking?"

"Sure am." This wasn't news, more like an unwelcome update. "It's a big cat." Drake threw it out there as he grew more certain. "I thought it was wolves, but no, a mountain lion's staked out territory around here. He's got to be big, too. Remember that mauled deer I found last year?"

His brother nodded. "Could be a she. And if she's got little ones, she'd be more dangerous than a male."

That was a valid point. He turned toward Luce. "You're not going up there alone, not anymore."

She obviously resented his authoritative tone. Leaning against the porch railing, she snapped, "Excuse me? *What* did you just say?"

Perhaps he should've put it differently, but he stuck to his guns. "How much clearer do I need to be?"

"There's this part where you get yourself declared my legal guardian. Otherwise, you don't have jurisdiction over what I do and don't do. I believe you mentioned earlier today that you can't stop me."

"I've changed my mind. Carson ranch, Carson rules."

"How am I supposed to study the horses, then?"

"Figure it out, but you aren't going up there alone."

She pulled the high card, taunting him. "I bet Harry

would back me up. I know your mother and my mother would."

"Maybe." But in this case, maybe not. Harry was no stranger to how things operated in these parts, and if there was danger, he didn't think either of their mothers would be on board. "I doubt it, though. You aren't a regular part of a mountain lion's diet, but on the other hand, they aren't picky. They've attacked people before. You don't weigh more than the last calf I lost."

"Oh, that's comforting. Are you comparing me to a cow?"

Drake groaned. He'd stepped into that one. He'd said *calf*, but maybe he should just abandon this particular tack. Instead, he turned to his brother. "What do you think?" he asked. "She shouldn't go up there on her own, right?"

"If I want to be part of an argument, I'll hang out with my very pregnant wife. I'd advise you to take Grace with you, Luce, but I doubt she's up for the long walk—and she insists on working until the day she goes into labor. However, I maintain that at this time she could kill a mountain lion with her bare hands." Slater rose, saying over his shoulder, "See you two at dinner. Have fun resolving this."

He beat it, and Drake envied him that option. He sighed. "Luce, I worried about you all afternoon."

Finally, he'd apparently said the right thing. She leaned back against the railing, arms tightly crossed. But she softened. "Oh," she said in a quiet voice.

"I had work to finish, but I was too distracted because I was anxious about you."

"That's sweet."

Probably the last thing he'd ever wanted to be called was *sweet*. It was better than her being mad at him, but sweet?

"I don't want you eaten by a rogue cougar. I hardly think that qualifies as sweet. Don't feel special, okay? I don't want *anyone* eaten by a big cat."

"I was referring to how you worried about me all day."

"Afternoon," he corrected.

She waved a hand loftily. "I'm going with *all day*."

The breeze stirred her ponytail; he wished he hadn't noticed that.

And the flirtatious smile she gave him did something interesting to his composure. He made an effort to lean casually against the railing, too. "Look, Luce, Slater can put up remote cameras near the ridge. Then you can skip going off by yourself and still watch the horses."

"That's like sitting on the couch watching television! No, thanks. I came all the way here for the full experience."

And his mother referred to *him* as stubborn? "You can't stay up there by yourself for weeks. Are we really going to continue this conversation?"

"Nope. I'm off to have a shower before dinner. Harry told me she's making French chicken. Not sure what that means, but I trust it'll be fantastic."

It was, and *he* trusted that this discussion wasn't over.

DINNER WAS DIVINE.

The chicken, simmered in white wine with garlic and then served with crispy potatoes, and a salad tossed with homemade green goddess dressing would have shamed the most elite foodie place in California.

"So, Moonshine, how's the still coming along?" Drake asked between helpings. Luce was fairly sure he was going for his third.

Mace responded, "It's not a still. I'm trying out what I

think will be a better fermentation process for a small line of liquors."

Drake looked at Luce and said in a loud whisper, "It's a still. No wonder he wanted me to buy the stuff for it, so *I'll* look like the guilty party if he gets caught making his illicit potions."

"What you know about making wine—or any kind of potable—could fit in the stomach of a tree frog." Mace plucked a roll from the basket on the table. That quaint expression had Red written all over it. She choked, laughing, on a sip of wine.

"How big is the frog?" Slater asked helpfully with a grin.

Mace grinned, too. "Real small. One of those little green ones about the size of your fingertip."

"It isn't useful knowledge in my chosen profession." Drake said it in a superior tone. "By the way, that last lemon bar has my name on it."

"Like hell it does," Grace piped up. "You all sit there swilling your wine and I can't have any, so that last lemon bar is for me and Junior."

"I'd listen to her, guys. She's in as good a mood as a rattlesnake branded with a red-hot poker." That was Ryder, Grace's teenage stepson, and his grin echoed Slater's. He was fifteen, Blythe had confided. His father was in the military, and even though he and Grace were divorced, she'd taken on her ex-husband's child, because his birth mother had no interest due to a second marriage and other children. Luce was under the impression that his father was gone most of the time, so when Slater and Grace got married, Ryder had been part of the deal.

The Carsons were an interesting family, to say the least.

Drake immediately passed the plate to his sister-in-law. "You win hands-down, Grace."

"You've always been my favorite. Thank you." She grabbed the last cookie.

"Hey!" Both Mace and Slater said it.

After dinner, the ritual seemed to be that the men cleared the table while the women, including Harry, sat and had a cup of tea or decaf coffee. The dining room suited the overall grand style of the house, and the table was obviously an heirloom that could comfortably seat the whole crowd. There was a stunning quilt hanging above an old sideboard, and Luce couldn't help commenting on it. "I love that as a wall decoration."

"It's by Hadleigh Galloway," Blythe told her. "She owns the quilt shop in town. She does beautiful work. You can commission one if she doesn't have what you want. I promise you won't be disappointed."

The image of wild horses immediately danced through her head. "Really? I might stop by there."

"She's super nice, too." Grace yawned. "Is it too early for bed? Maybe I ate too much."

"Or maybe there isn't a lot of room in there for food. He's growing like a weed," Harry suggested with a kindly twinkle in her eye, although her expression was stern. "I just ordered a book online about making homemade baby food. No jarred stuff for the new addition."

They'd learned that it was a boy, but Grace and Slater had refused to reveal the name they'd chosen, to the amusement of the whole family, Luce gathered.

Grace certainly didn't argue. "If you make it, I bet he'll eat it when the time comes for solid food. Anyway, I'm off to bed. I have a romance novel waiting for me and hopefully about ten hours of sleep."

Blythe was laughing as her daughter-in-law departed. "I enjoy this experience a lot more when someone else is going through it. But I can't wait to hold this one in my arms, even though the last thing we need around here is another male."

Harry got up, too. "Ain't that the truth. I have to go to the kitchen to see what's happening. Those boys could be doing anything. I hear a lot of banging of dishes and pans."

"Who knows?" Blythe shrugged, still smiling. "They need to be managed. I'll go with you."

That left Luce to wander out onto the veranda by herself, tea in hand, until Drake suddenly joined her. "I was banished," he informed her. "I wash, they're supposed to dry and put away. But Harry took over my job, probably because of you. My mother not so subtly suggested we go for an evening stroll. That's how she put it—stroll."

He sounded disgruntled enough that Luce sent him a mischievous smile. "I take it there's a country song out there called 'Real Cowboys Don't Stroll'?"

"I couldn't tell you. Now, I'm going to *stroll* to the stables to check on the horses like I do every night, so if you'd care to join me, feel free. It's another pretty night, but Red says tomorrow's going to be as blustery as an old hag on a rant."

"Oh, come on, he didn't say that. You're making it up. I think you're all teasing me by inventing Red-speak."

Drake looked boyishly unrepentant. "Okay, yeah, I did make that up. But doesn't it sound like something he'd say? What he did say is that the weather's going to turn. That man should've been a meteorologist. He's right. You can count on it." He gestured toward the porch steps. "I know you've walked your share today, but shall we?"

It really was another lovely evening, and for once the incessant wind wasn't blowing. Maybe it was the calm before the storm. "Thank you. I need to walk off dinner, anyway. If you think Red should've been a meteorologist, I think Harry should be a chef somewhere in Paris, basking in her four-star rating. The chicken was superb."

"Not gonna argue with that one." He followed her down the steps and walked beside her, slowing his pace to match hers. "How's the research paper coming?"

Nice of him to ask, especially since he hadn't wanted anything to do with it in the first place. "I'm still making notes," she told him. "I have pictures and videos of the horses, and I know this is a sore subject, but thanks to your descriptions, I've identified the mares that were yours and belong to the herd now. So to sum up, it's coming along nicely."

"Glad to be of help," he said sarcastically.

"I'm not trying to rub salt in a wound, I swear it."

"I believe you." He had his hands in his pockets and his expression was reflective. "I also believe that life involves weighing decisions, and figuring out if they're good or bad. I realize some people don't bother with that—they see only one approach, which is usually whatever they've already decided. I have to consider every situation from as many angles as possible." He shrugged. "All I can do is my best. The reality is that these wild horses are a problem for someone in my position."

"I know. I owe you an apology, or perhaps a couple of them. I'm too focused at times. I admit that."

"Darlin', if you think I haven't noticed that you're too

focused at *all* times, you're mistaken. In my defense, this is my life and this is who I am. I can't change that."

Truer words were never spoken. He was *him*. Drake Carson.

"Why would you want to?" She meant it. "We don't understand each other all that well, but I wouldn't want you to change. And I wouldn't try to change you."

His response was unexpected—a low groan. "Don't do that."

"Don't do what? Give you a compliment?"

"No. But my mother always told me never to get involved with a woman who wanted to change me. It's a life lecture she gives all her sons. She likes you already, so I'll keep that information to myself."

She liked Blythe, as well. "*Are* we involved?"

Maybe she'd just said the wrong thing.

"You tell me."

She winged it. "Yeah, it might be leaning that way. Like a knotty pine on a windy slope."

"Not bad, but my try at Red-speak was better."

This time she really did give him a playful punch in the gut. It was flat and well muscled, which didn't surprise her because she'd seen him stripped to the waist. "Quit that, or I'll beat you up," she said.

"Think you can take me?"

Maybe she was falling in love with him because of his smile. He didn't show it often, but when he did, it was memorable.

"Oh, come on. My saying was a good effort, right?"

"It was too poetic. It should be more like 'Does manure fall in a horse stall?'"

"Well, I'll take that advice."

Then he kissed her for the third time. Best one yet. They were in each other's arms, and Luce knew this was exactly what Blythe had intended, and yet it was hard to resent when it turned out so well. There was a lowering dusk and privacy, and Drake's body against hers…

He lifted his head. "I forgot to check."

Luce had to admit she was dazed from that kiss. "Check?"

"For cameras." He scouted theatrically around. "I don't see any, but that means nothing. I'm not Showbiz with his diabolical staff, planting surveillance equipment everywhere, so I don't get how they think. Who knows where they might've put one? Under a bale of hay? Strapped to the belly of a horse? It's possible."

One of the things she liked most about him—aside from that smile—was that he had a dry sense of humor. Grace had told her he was one of the funniest people she'd ever met, and Luce could see why. "You're being paranoid," she told him, hiding her own smile.

"Damn straight I am. After what happened last time, shouldn't I be?"

"No one will know who we are."

"Really? Is that why everyone around here is calling me Romeo? But that's not even my point. It was supposed to be just you and me. First kiss. Alone."

He certainly didn't have to take Romance 101. He got an A—due to his natural talent, she supposed. "A kiss is more than just a kiss?"

"Wasn't it? To you?"

"It was." Luce took a breath. "Do you even have to ask me that?"

"No." He let her go and walked about five feet away. "I didn't see this particular storm on the horizon, that's all."

"I'm a storm? Isn't *that* too poetic?"

"Kind of." He swung around. "I'm afraid if I kiss you again, we're going to end up on some horizontal surface, comfortable or not."

"And since neither of us do casual—"

"And you live in California," he interrupted, but he reached for her again and pulled her against him, their mouths no more than an inch apart.

Who knew what might have happened next if Ryder hadn't come down the path to the stables just then, carrying a small sack of apples. He stopped dead in his tracks when he saw them in an embrace. "Oh, uh, s-sorry," he stammered, looking embarrassed. "I was going to give these to the horses…"

Drake didn't miss a beat. As he released her, he said in an easy tone, "I was about to check on them, so that works. Let's go do it. Luce?"

"I'll wait here and admire the view." Luce chose to not join them, but she stood on the path, gazing up at the starlit sky.

"Sure. I'll see you in a few minutes."

After they'd walked away, she whispered out loud, "Well, *now* what do I do?"

The stars didn't answer but twinkled cheerfully back. Even Venus, hanging low on the horizon, just smiled serenely.

CHAPTER TEN

THE STARS WERE not on his side.

Not that he was a big believer in the zodiac or in horoscopes, but he could tell he wasn't going to win anytime soon. Unless you counted one very intent graduate student and a slew of horses he'd never wanted in the first place, he was on his own. So Drake was resigned to navigating this love business without any other guidance.

Oh, his mother and Harry would be glad to chime in, but he had a feeling he knew what their advice would be.

Get together with the pretty girl and settle down. Have babies.

Ryder wasn't helpful. "She's really cool."

"Luce?" He fed Trader—an aging gray gelding who was extremely picky about letting anyone come close to him—an apple. "I think so," he said slowly.

"Kinda noticed that." The kid was too grown-up for his age, but at the same time, refreshingly honest. His expression was sheepish. "Sorry I showed up right then."

"Don't worry about it." That had probably been for the best, anyway. Although privacy seemed to be in short supply these days… Still, despite that, he wouldn't have traded where he lived for anywhere else in the world.

"What she's doing is pretty interesting." Ryder handed an apple to one of the mares. He was a natural with the horses, which had surprised everyone, since he was a city kid who'd been transplanted from Seattle to Mustang Creek.

"*She's* interesting, for sure."

"What's going to happen with the wild horses?"

Oh, great. All he needed was another bleeding heart on Luce's side. "I have to run a ranch. They can't stay here."

"You aren't going to shoot them!"

"Jeez, Ryder, you know me better than that. Do I seem like someone who'd shoot them?"

"Okay, no. Sorry. But we already have horses. Can't we keep those other ones, too? The wild horses?"

He checked the water in one of the stalls. "The size of that herd has doubled since they decided to take up residence. A few of them isn't a problem, but a lot of them really is. Where would you suggest we keep them? We need the grazing land for the cattle. Our horses are useful. The wild ones aren't, and they impact the ecological balance. And let's not even talk about our missing mares. I've lost stock and I've spent time and money repairing fences. They're an expensive nuisance—especially that damned stallion."

Ryder frowned. "Guess I hadn't looked at it that way."

"I have." Luce was standing in the stable doorway of the stable, her arms crossed. He couldn't help noticing that the light caught her hair.

He handed over the last apple, patted the neck of the horse munching away and turned to face her. "But your whole purpose is to study them—and protect them, right? Not to interfere with the herd."

"At the beginning. Now I see the whole situation with... more complexity." Her voice was soft and her eyes looked like shimmering gold.

Had he really just thought "shimmering gold"? He was an idiot.

He weighed every response he could make that might reverse the idiot progression, but he couldn't find one.

Fortunately, Ryder spoke up. "This place kind of grows on you. I didn't want to come here at all when Grace told me where we were going, but now I like it." *Way to go. Good sell.*

The only question was how she'd respond. "I like it, too."

Nothing definitive there, but he'd take it. Drake muttered, "Then stick around."

Why'd he say that? He had no idea. When she'd arrived, he'd wanted nothing more than for her to leave pronto.

She quickly caught on. "Is that an open invitation?"

Ryder started to get the gist of their conversation. He hurried toward the stable door. "Uh, I've got some homework to do."

They both watched him scoot outside.

"He just ditched us for homework. That's a powerful rejection of our company right there." Drake put the bucket away and washed his hands in the big metal utility sink.

"He's a nice young man."

"Thanks to Grace. And Slate, too. I sometimes forget he isn't actually their kid. Ryder might've gotten into real trouble if both of them hadn't stepped in. When Showbiz first asked me if the kid could work here, I was skeptical. However, I will say, if you work with Red, you *work*. He doesn't tolerate anything but the best you can give. Ryder stepped up."

"Good for him. And good for you."

"I didn't do anything."

"Drake, yes, you did. Grace told me you helped out so much with Ryder she can't thank you enough."

Sure, he had empathy for kids trying to find their way. Who didn't? "It isn't easy being a teenage boy," he said. "Your body changes, more and more people expect you to take care of yourself, to act responsible. You start to look at girls in a whole new light. I believe I was looking at you like that when he walked in on us." He needed to clarify something. "Feel free to weigh in, but I don't think our agreement to stay detached is working out."

"Not so much," Luce agreed. Then she added in an off-hand tone, "Oh, I'm camping up on the ridge tomorrow night."

Like hell.

He stared at her. "Didn't we recently have this conversation? No, you aren't."

"I'm not doing this project on a sort-of basis. I have to observe the horses at night."

"You do know you're trying my patience."

"No, I'm objecting to your assumption that you have the right to tell me what to do. Not the same thing."

"Luce."

"I have it on excellent authority that I'm not the mainstay of a mountain lion's diet. Wait, that would be yours. The authority, I mean."

"I'll join you."

"On the ridge? Oh, *that's* a good idea."

"You aren't staying up there alone." He paused, then said recklessly, "We can share a tent, tell campfire stories, roast marshmallows, stuff like that."

At least he'd made her smile. "Yeah, I'm sure that's precisely what we'd be doing."

"Remember, the weather's supposed to get nasty. We might have to stay in the tent."

She tilted her head, all that fabulous hair brushing her shoulders. "That's what you're going for, isn't it, cowboy? Same tent?"

"Same sleeping bag, something like that."

"I'm not going to be able to stop you, am I?"

She had that right. He offered her another option. "You could abandon the whole idea and sleep alone in a nice, safe, dry house. Or you can share a tent with me."

"I've camped alone before, and a little rain won't hurt me, and—"

Drake cut her off. "I think we have a date. Now, let me walk you back to the house, and then I need to close the front gate. After that, I'm going straight to bed. It's been a long day."

Luce set aside her almost-empty cup of hot chocolate, hoping that the splash of peppermint liqueur Harry had dashed in with a sly wink would help her sleep. Her secret recipe, the older woman had confided, guaranteed to cure whatever ailed you.

Somehow, Luce thought a cup of heavenly chocolate might not do the trick for her particular affliction.

What she needed was good old-fashioned therapy in the form of girl talk.

There was only one thing to do—call Beth Madison, her older sister and best friend.

After only one ring, she got an answer. "*Mi chica!* What, you psychic? I was just thinking about you. How's life out there in the Wild West? Please tell me they have indoor plumbing."

Considering that she was sitting at a polished mahogany desk in a guest room that could vie with a suite in the most elegant hotel... She glanced around at the silk bedspread and pillows, reading lamp and chair, wall-mounted television with about a million channels, plus a private bathroom. "Yes," she said drily. "They do, believe it or not."

"That's good news. I'm relieved. Men can pee in the woods and all, but for us it's a dicier proposition."

Luce was already laughing, which wasn't unusual after about two seconds on the phone with her older sister. "I often spend all day outside. You get used to the lack of facilities. What are you doing? It's not too late to call, is it?"

"I'm doing yoga. I need some form of relaxation after the diaper I just changed. Who knew a six-month-old could wipe out a whole outfit and his crib sheet in one fell swoop? Or do I mean poop? I won't go into the dreadful details, but a bath was involved. Is it too early for potty training?"

"Six months is probably pushing it, but I'm not an expert. My impression is that they have to be able to walk and maybe even talk." Luce laughed again, knowing that Beth adored her son, born after years of trying. "Have you decided whether you're going back to work?"

"Greg and I talked it over, and after several different versions of what added up to basically the same conversation, I'm going to work part-time from home. I'm on the computer all day, anyway. Who cares if I'm sitting in my sweatpants—I still need to lose about ten pounds—at home, or in an office. I think it'll work for all of us if I cut back a little, since it means I can stay home with Ian."

"Makes sense to me. Day care is good, but Mom is better, right?"

"That's our take on it. Baby sister, why'd you call? There's a reason. I can hear it in your voice."

Beth knew her. Luce fiddled with the handle on her cup for a second and then sighed. "I need some advice. You love Greg."

"I must. I live with him, endure his sometimes annoying habits, and we just had a baby together. And let's not forget I married him. You stood beside me at the wedding, remember? Oh, no way! Who'd you meet out there in the wilderness?"

That was her sister. Quirky at times, but always smart as a whip.

"Picture a tall, blond cowboy. Pure Wyoming, from his Stetson down to his dusty boots. He keeps his conversation sparse but really knows how to kiss."

"Woo-hoo! You found *your* cowboy."

"*My* cowboy?"

"Those sound like your requirements. Tall, good-looking and knows how to kiss. You were about fifteen when you spelled that out."

"I'd read a few too many Western romance novels."

"That you pilfered from Mom. I did the same thing. I still read them, by the way. For that matter, so does she. Tell me more about him."

"He doesn't discuss his feelings. He's close to his family, cares about animals and works long hours, but that's not enough of a description. I think, with him, any kind of relationship is an all-or-nothing deal."

"Oh, decision time, is it?"

It felt that way… "Beth, you're jumping to conclusions. I have the job of my dreams lined up in California. Plus, you and Mom and Dad are there."

"You can come and visit us."

"It isn't that simple. I don't even know what I'd do if I stayed here, and worrying about that is presumptuous, anyway. There's no guarantee he'd even *want* me to stay. He told me he isn't interested in casual relationships. I believe that, because if you look like him and *are* like him, you'd certainly have plenty of opportunities…"

"Did you listen at all to what you just said?"

She had. Part of the reason she'd called was to work it out in her own mind. Beth was always a good sounding board. "I'm in trouble, right? I've known the man for less than a month."

"I want to meet this slow-talking, fast-moving dreamboat. Invite him to California."

Only Beth would use the word *dreamboat*. "We aren't serious. We hardly have a relationship! I'm not sure if he'd go, anyway."

"Aren't you? Sounds to me like he would."

Luce tapped her fingers on the desk. "How do you *know*?"

"Good question. I wish I had a better answer, but I guess it's a sense I'm getting. An intuition, if you prefer. Despite what you say, you're responding to this guy and he's responding to you. So…invite him."

"That's not helpful."

"You hate it when I give you advice."

"I listen, but I don't always follow your advice. I just needed to talk to someone about Drake."

Oops. She hadn't intended to mention his name.

Beth pounced. "As in Drake Carson? *That's* who we're having this deep sisterly discussion about? Does Mom know? She'd be thrilled."

"Don't tell her."

"All right." Beth meant it, but her answer was accompanied by a disappointed sigh. She was a person who could keep her mouth shut if she had to. She had flaws—who didn't?—but that wasn't one of them. "If you don't want me to, I won't say a word, but I'm positive she'd be thrilled."

"Thrilled about what? I can't promise anything. He might know how *he* feels, but I'm...uncertain about myself. Am I in love with him? I'm starting to think so. But all the changes to my life plans have to weigh in, too, right? I've been told more than once that he's worth it."

Beth sighed. "You've worked this all out. I'm so glad, because I need to get to sleep soon. My son still wakes up about six times a night. I hate people who tell me their newborns slept through the night on the second day they took them home. Congratulations on figuring everything out and making me do nothing. I knew I adored you."

When they ended the call, Luce stared at her phone and laughed softly. Okay, perhaps she *had* figured it out—to a certain extent. Did she want Drake? She did. He represented an ideal she'd held close her whole life.

However... Kind, compassionate and all those other qualities were important, but there was also the fact that he couldn't and wouldn't change his life. She'd have to do everything on that end. What was more, he was going to relocate those horses. She saw his point, but damn, she hated it. If it was up to her, the entire Carson ranch would be wild-horse heaven.

Her dissertation was getting more and more difficult to write. She powered up her computer and went back to work, anyway. Tomorrow was another day, as Scarlett O'Hara had declared, and she'd analyze it then.

CHAPTER ELEVEN

WHAT DRAKE WAS doing felt like taking out a billboard ad on Times Square, but he didn't have much choice, did he?

He needed shaving cream and toothpaste, but that wasn't the main reason he'd made this trip to town. He eyed the display on the drugstore shelf and reminded himself that he wasn't sixteen, so he shouldn't be embarrassed. But this *was* Mustang Creek, and all the Romeo jokes were about to get worse. If he'd had the time, he would've driven out of Bliss County and shopped someplace else, where everyone didn't know him. But he didn't have the time; he was already going to use part of his morning to ride up with Luce, help her find a decent campsite. He had one in mind, since he and his brothers used to camp out in that area as kids.

He picked up a box of condoms and resigned himself to the fact that the cashier had greeted him by name when he entered the drugstore. He tried to look impassive as he walked to the counter to check out. Maxine was a sweet lady, but she played bridge with his mother in some women's church club, and there was something about buying condoms from a grandmother of six that made him feel like an adolescent.

With luck he'd need them. Maybe he should look at it that way. Maybe Maxine would just scan it and not notice.

She noticed, of course, with raised eyebrows. At least she didn't address it. Well, not directly, anyway. "How's Grace doing?"

He swiped his credit card. "Good. As far as I know. Slate jokes about her being touchy right now, but she's fine. I think she looks beautiful. He does, too."

Maxine handed him the bag. "You are a very diplomatic young man."

"I'm a cautious man," he said and then winced at the unintended reference to his purchase. "Grace really *is* beautiful. I'm not just saying that."

"I've seen her." Maxine was now laughing at him as he tried to scramble around what he'd said. "That she is. Tell your mother and Harry I said hello."

"Sure will." He hotfooted it out of there. With Maxine's tendency to share information, it was a lost hope that everyone would think all he wanted was a clean shave. They'd almost certainly guess he wanted something else— and they'd know what that something else was.

Worrying about it gained him nothing, though, and he preferred not to waste his energy, so he drove home. He hadn't caught the weather report that morning, but he usually didn't bother with it anymore. Red was invariably correct. And this morning, as he'd predicted, there was a hint of rain in the air—a higher proportion of humidity, which signaled a change from sunshine and blue skies.

Unlike Red, Drake wasn't a human barometer, but he'd lived outdoors pretty much his whole life. He could feel a front coming in.

Maybe he could talk Luce out of plans to camp up on the ridge.

Maybe he couldn't.

He already knew he'd lose the argument.

Maybe he didn't want to talk her out of it.

THE MORNING WAS GORGEOUS, but there'd been a reddish glow on the horizon at daybreak, and Red had warned her as he saddled Starburst that the weather might turn ugly at any time. He eyed her backpack and shook his head.

She assured him she'd be fine.

Drake had suggested they ride up together so he'd know where her campsite was, if she was hell-bent on doing this—his term, not hers. She was more than capable of pitching a tent on her own, but what he'd said made sense; if he really was going to join her later, he should know where to find her.

As she thought about spending the night with him, her stomach did an unfamiliar flip-flop.

"Wait for Drake," Red advised, slapping the side of the horse. "This fella does whatever that boy says, but he doesn't listen to anyone else."

Oh, yeah. Like she'd jump on and ride off. "No worries. Starburst and I are on good terms."

"He does seem to like you. Here you go." He handed her the reins and left her there, holding the horse. Her entire life, she'd heard that if you were nervous around horses or dogs or any other critter with four legs, they knew it and they reacted. So she stood very still and let Starburst take a gander. He was…huge. He sniffed her hair and nuzzled her shirt and apparently decided she wasn't all that interesting. To her relief, Drake walked in just as she was starting to feel she'd fallen short of the horse's expectations.

Drake looked startled, coming in wearing the usual ensemble of faded jeans, boots and, since the air was cool this morning, a red flannel shirt over his white T-shirt. Naturally, his two sidekicks trotted in right on his heels. "*You* saddled him?"

"No. Of course not! I couldn't saddle a turtle."

"That's what I thought. Ryder did it?"

She could swear the dogs had that same inquiring expression.

"No, Red."

Drake did laugh about the turtle comment, although that wasn't flattering.

She needed to learn the art of saddling a horse before she left Wyoming. A whole summer on a ranch and no saddling skills? Yup, she needed to learn.

"Red wouldn't leave you here alone with this big guy. No way."

She took exception to that. "He says Starburst likes me."

Drake nodded. "Starburst's kind of picky about people. I think he knows *I* like you, so he behaved himself. He's a decent guy." Drake affectionately patted the animal's neck.

Luce was relieved to hand over the reins. "I assume that's what Red thought, too, or he's just so used to horses he figures everyone is as comfortable with them."

"Hard to tell with Red. He seems like a down-to-earth soul, but he's a sight more complicated than that. He might've thought that you needed a nudge and counted on Starburst to realize it, too."

"Do I need to apologize for not growing up on a ranch?"

He shook his head. "Now, don't try to make me feel sorry for you."

"Sorry for me?"

"Everyone should grow up on a ranch."

It wasn't as if she didn't realize she was being teased. "My parents have a beach house in Malibu, besides the place in Napa."

"Little rich girl, huh?" He regarded her in that singular way he had. "You very carefully avoid the subject of your family. You want to study wild horses, but you're obviously not used to being around the domestic variety. Your camping equipment is top-of-the-line, and even though you dress down, I think you seem like a Napa girl. I'm guessing you got the invitation from my mother because she knows your family."

It didn't surprise her that Blythe hadn't completely explained the situation to her son, considering the shameless matchmaking going on.

Okay, maybe it was time to come clean. Luce looked into those very blue eyes. "My mother and yours were best friends all through school in California. They took vacations together and were bridesmaids in each other's weddings—real best friends. *I* wrote to your mother, but I suspect there was a private conversation between the two of them. Trust me, I would never have agreed to stay at the house if I didn't know something about the person who invited me."

"I wondered."

"Yes." She put her hands on her hips. "Why didn't you ask before?"

"That information should be offered, not gained by prying into your life."

A valid argument—and perhaps an example of why animals liked him so much. He was laid-back and considerate and didn't invade a person's space. Usually...

He shrugged. "I just *did*."

"Right," she conceded. "And I answered. Now I'm headed up there." She pointed in the direction of the mountains. "If we're going together, let's get moving."

He checked the cinch, probably out of habit. "We can. Let me saddle your horse first."

Her *what*?

"Drake, listen, I—"

"You'll take Grace's mare, Molly, since she's gentle. It'll be faster for both of us."

He was already opening a stall and leading out a very beautiful horse and slipping a halter on her. "Wait while I get the tack. Give her a carrot. Hold your hand out flat like this." He demonstrated. "That way she won't accidentally bite you, because she does love her carrots. I'll be back in a minute."

Luce tentatively held out the carrot he'd given her, following his instructions. It worked out—hand intact, horse docile and happy as she crunched away.

Drake returned with the tack and made short work of it, expertly handling the straps and stirrups, then turned to help her into the saddle. "Ready? I'll take your pack."

As she handed it over, he looked at her skeptically. "There's a tent in here?"

"Seven pounds or so. All-weather, plus a thermal blanket. I've camped before. Oh, and a lunch, courtesy of Harry."

"Then you're ready."

No, she really wasn't. "I didn't count on this when I got up."

"On what? Riding a horse? Things aren't always what we expect them to be. Happens to all of us. I'll give you a leg up. Just relax, and she'll do the rest." He caught her around the waist and balanced her as she tentatively put one foot in the stirrup. "It'll be fine," he reassured her.

Easy for him to say. However, she did manage to land in the saddle. As he adjusted the stirrup length, he said, "Hold the reins loosely and only use them to communicate with the horse, let her know what you want her to do. This little lady is well trained or Slate would never let Grace ride her. She'll probably just do whatever my horse does. The worst thing that can happen is you fall off, and even the most experienced rider takes a tumble now and then. You get up, dust yourself off and climb back on—just like that old cliché says."

Two seconds later, he was in the saddle, too, and Molly was docilely following Starburst out of the stable.

Once she'd begun to relax, and the horses were walking at a sedate pace, the experience wasn't as intimidating as she'd feared. In fact, with Drake right next to her, the ride was a surprisingly soothing and pleasant experience. Beautiful mountains, handsome man, cool breeze… What more could a girl want?

He pointed to a huge animal grazing by itself in an enclosed pasture. "That's Sherman. Jim Galloway's lined up some good leads on new bulls for me. Sherman's done his time. My father picked him out and I'm pretty fond of that cranky critter. I'm hoping to get one a lot like him. He's dangerous—all bulls can be dangerous—but he's cooperative unless he's riled up. He hates change, so if we keep his routine the same, he's fine. By the way, did you know Slate wasn't always Mr. Showbiz? He competed on the rodeo circuit for a couple of years during college. He was decent at it, too. Those trophies in his office aren't just for his documentaries."

"I noticed them when I was in there." She stopped, not wanting to mention the image of a moonlit kiss. "Come to think of it, I haven't seen *your* office.

His smile was wry. "Don't have one. I keep a ledger and receipts on an old table in the tack room and I bring them to the accountant once a month. Can you picture me sitting in an office? No, thanks. My mother handles everything to do with the house and, of course, Mace takes care of the winery."

"I see what you mean. But I can't picture you in tennis whites, either, although I know you played in college."

"I needed something physical to do if I couldn't have all this for four years." He gestured at the vista around them. "Sending that ball over the net at a hundred miles an hour releases the frustration."

"I heard you could've gone pro." She was pushing it, getting so personal, but that wasn't any more personal than what he'd done—yanking her into his arms and kissing the heck out of her.

"I hate crowds."

That was the Drake Carson she was coming to know. Explanation over in three words. *A possible Grand Slam title and cheers from the stands? No, thank you. I'd rather saddle up, ride out at dawn and get back after dusk, dirty and tired.*

The man wasn't interested in glamour, but she wasn't,

either. All those fancy wine-tasting parties with appetizers and swirly dresses were fine once in a while, but they weren't anything special. Not to her—no doubt because she'd grown up with people who talked about the stock market at dinner and drove cars that cost more than some people's houses. Drake was right; she was a rich kid, and her parents would've been happier if she'd decided to become a doctor or a lawyer. Ecology was just more interesting. She loved nature and that was why she enjoyed hiking so much. Looking at film and photographs of the great outdoors was fine, but experiencing it was very different. When her father had suggested a trip to Europe, he'd meant Rome and Paris and London; she'd accepted his offer and hiked the Alps instead.

"I prefer being outside myself." Luce drew a deep breath. "This is a breathtaking place, but so is Napa."

"Are we making comparisons here? Or choices?"

What a question! She floundered for an answer. "Should I be? The only choice I made this morning was to let you force me up on this horse."

"You chose to *let* me *force* you? Hmm. Sounds like a bit of a contradiction."

"Give me a break," she said tartly. "I'm concentrating on not falling off."

"Or into my arms?"

Now she truly had no idea what to say. Drake Carson was teasing her. Again. She came up with a retort, although it took her a moment. "At least you don't seem to have any lack of confidence, despite your flaws." A little weak, perhaps, but it was the best she could do under the circumstances.

They were in a meadow of wildflowers that smelled

heavenly. He swept off his hat and scratched his head, pretending to consider that, but his mouth was twitching with laughter. "Flaws, huh? Care to be more specific? I'm always up for self-improvement."

"No, you aren't. You do what you think you should do, and that's that."

"I hate to be the one to tell you this, but that's not a flaw. You'd better pick another one."

"You...you argue with your younger brother a lot."

"Nope, that doesn't work, either. *He* argues with *me*. Go on." He replaced his hat and adjusted it. "If you continue at this rate, I'll start to feel damn near perfect."

"You're...too tall," she said with a laugh.

"Too tall for what?"

She didn't respond but rushed into her next bogus complaint. "You talk to your dogs more than you talk to people."

"Hey, Harold and Violet are smarter than most people. So if I want intelligent conversation, I usually do pick them. They're also very good listeners. Besides, aren't I talking to you now? That was a compliment, by the way. I said *most* people."

"So, you're saying I'm smarter than your dogs?"

"Oh, heck, no. I was talking about people, remember."

If she could throw something at him, she would, but then she'd probably fall off and there was nothing available to chuck in his direction, anyway. She agreed with Grace; he was very funny.

And far too attractive.

He pointed at a spot she recognized. "I'm thinking we should pitch the tent there, by that spring. I'd leave Molly with you, but I can't, not with the other horses nearby."

He studied the location, a small, protected valley. "Good cover for when it starts to blow."

She looked at the cloudless blue sky. "Are you sure—"

"I'm sure."

CHAPTER TWELVE

THE CLOUDS WERE THICKENING.

"You aren't going to leave that pretty little girl up on that mountain by herself."

Drake glanced up. Red wasn't asking, he was *telling*. Right behind him stood Ryder, and the kid looked as bent out of shape as the old man.

Well, they could back off, both of them. He'd been busting his ass to get everything done so he could take off and he didn't need them crowding him. "Uh, no, I'm not. I'm waiting for Jax Locke to get here so I can talk to him about those two sick cows."

"Wind's picking up."

"You told me it would." Drake straightened. "I checked my phone and the Doppler confirms you have it right, as usual."

"Get going. I'll talk to the doc." For the second time that day, Red had Starburst saddled and ready to go. He handed over a large insulated bag. "This here's a present from Harry. Supper. Don't know what's in there, but I bet it's good."

He'd bet on that, too. He accepted the cooler. "Any instructions?"

"Didn't think you needed any. Just do what *comes* naturally, son." Red guffawed at that remark. Luckily, Ryder had gone back to mucking out stalls.

Oh, news about the condoms had gotten around for sure, but by now Drake was resigned to that. "I meant for the food, Red."

"Sorry, couldn't resist that one." He was still chuckling. "Nah, Harry knows a campfire meal might be kind of difficult tonight, so she kept it simple. No instructions. All she said was *enjoy*."

Drake sensed another bad joke on the way and staved it off by mounting his horse with lightning speed. "I trust you to deal with the situation if those cows need to be quarantined. I don't want the entire herd getting sick."

"I was handling cattle before you were born. Good call to bring in the vet, but I'm guessing he'll agree with me that those two just ate some plant they shouldn't have. I've seen it before." Red waved him off. Drake pointed at the dogs. "Stay."

Both obediently sat down. At least *someone* listened to him.

It was one thing to spend a stormy night in a tent with a beautiful woman, and another to share the experience with two wet dogs.

He went before Red could repeat *enjoy*. He wouldn't have put it past the old coot.

The air smelled like rain, and that rising breeze sounded faintly like a wail. Part of him said he shouldn't have left

Luce alone for most of the day, but another part reminded him that she was an intelligent and determined woman, smart enough to take care of herself. Besides, he'd had plenty to do. The first time they met, he'd explained that he wouldn't babysit her, hadn't he?

And yet... If he could, he'd keep an eye on her all day—and night.

He was looking forward to the nighttime shift, in particular.

The darkening sky told him the storm was bound to roll in before sunset. He squinted up at the slate-gray clouds roiling overhead and gave Starburst a gentle nudge to pick up the pace. The horse didn't like the distant sound of thunder, his ears going back.

"You'll have shelter soon," he said reassuringly, patting the horse's neck. "I chose a good spot."

He had. It was a place where he and Slate and Mace had fashioned a lean-to for their horses, back when they were teenagers and still camped out fairly often. It was hardly master construction, but he'd left it because it reminded him of those outings, and no one saw the place, anyway. Truth be told, he'd replaced part of the roof last fall, just in case he ever had the urge to spend a night.

Good decision. The trees sighed as he got closer to the ridge, and flashes of lightning illuminated the silhouette of the mountains.

When he pulled up and slid off the horse, the drizzle had already started, and his boots made a soggy noise as he hit the ground.

Although the tent had been pitched, it was empty.

Oh, hell.

He stood there, holding the reins, trying to make a decision. He figured that was the moment he first knew he was in love with Luce Hale, because he was ready to jump back on his horse and go looking for her.

Good luck with that. There was a lot of country out there, and she could walk places he couldn't get to on horseback. He wasn't even sure what direction she'd gone.

She'd done some camping; she wasn't inexperienced.

She'd know enough to come back to the site—wouldn't she?

Drake hated waiting around, but right now, it was the most sensible thing to do.

Another hour passed before Luce finally turned up, and by then, the weather was really going to hell. The wind was practically tearing the tent off its pegs.

He was inside, fretting, thinking he couldn't recall the last time he'd been so on edge.

When someone unzipped the flap of the tent, he actually ran a shaking hand over his face.

She was back. Thank God.

He was instantly furious. "It's about time! Where've you been?"

Luce stumbled through the opening, lost her balance and landed squarely on top of him. There was no room to stand—and he had no objections at all. It took him two seconds flat to realize she was soaking wet and shivering. Her teeth were chattering. "I jumped in the stream. Not like I had a lot of choice. Oh, thank heaven, you're warm. Take off your shirt."

She certainly wasn't warm. Wet, cold and delightfully female. But she was shaking so much he could hardly understand her.

He stripped off his T-shirt and dropped it. "Jumped in? Why?"

She wrapped her arms around his neck. "I'll get to that. For now, just help me off with my clothes. I'm so cold my fingers don't work."

Well, he wasn't about to refuse that request. He did have questions about her fall in the river, but…

"Hold still." He unfastened the buttons on her blouse. Underneath she wore a camisole thing with a built-in bra; he helped strip that off, too, and she settled against him, bare breasts to his bare chest.

It felt as wonderful as he'd predicted. This had been coming all along and he'd known it, but he hadn't expected it to happen quite this way. Outside, the wind was shrieking.

He asked," You aren't hurt?"

She buried her face in his neck. "No…no. Frozen, but not hurt. What do you do up here, pour ice into your rivers?"

"Mountain runoff." He kissed her underneath her ear. They were very close to altogether naked. He'd had fantasies about this. Her hair was damp and he smoothed it back, combing it with his fingers. "Any warmer?"

"Yes, thanks."

"Get as close as you want."

"I want closer. Take off my jeans."

That would be his pleasure, as long as she was okay with it. His voice was huskier than he'd intended. "Luce, if I do…"

"Take them off. While you're at it, take yours off, too."

"You sure?"

"I am. But I'm so seriously cold I know I couldn't work the zipper."

It was really going to happen. He helped her out of her wet jeans and some very sexy panties he hoped she'd selected just for him. He'd probably set a world record at getting out of his own clothes.

He held her until she stopped shivering. In their intimate position, there was no doubt that she could feel he was interested in a lot more. Her arms were tight around his neck, but they relaxed bit by bit until she sighed against his chest. "Much better."

"Is it okay for me to let go of you for a minute to get something from my pack?"

She artlessly kissed his jaw and ran a hand over his bare chest. "Hmm. What would you need at this particular moment?"

"I assume you'd prefer that we use protection. I'm old-fashioned enough to like things done in the right order."

"Oh! Yes. Glad you're thinking straight. Maybe my brain is still frozen." She shifted onto her side so he could reach over. He'd brought a battery-powered lantern, and the light revealed every supple curve and hollow of her perfect—in his opinion, anyway—body. Nicely rounded breasts, feminine hips that emphasized her long athletic toned legs…

His hands weren't quite steady as he found what he needed and rolled it on.

"Red was right about the storm."

"He always is," Drake agreed as the tent shuddered under another blast from Mother Nature.

"Harry said you need the rain."

"We do."

"I started back here when the sky was getting so dark, but—"

"Luce, stop talking about the weather." He brushed his thumb across her lower lip in a slow caress, pulling her close again.

"Um, sounds like a good idea. Kiss me?"

"That's an offer I won't turn down."

He thought he did a thorough job of it and then moved lower to her breasts. He took a taut nipple in his mouth. There wasn't a single mention of the rain now pelting the tent. There might've been a gasp of enjoyment he missed because of the storm's noise, but he certainly got the message from the arching of her body and the way her fingers ran through his hair.

His own message to Luce was loud and clear. He wanted her. He'd always believed that meant for his entire lifetime, and that desire and passion were naturally linked to commitment. But now, with the wild storm rushing through, he wasn't going to do anything except make love to her.

The big questions were left for later. The growing love affair, the proposal, the response…

He wasn't ready to propose. Not because he didn't want to head in that direction, but they hadn't really talked about her return to California. Right now, they didn't need to have that conversation.

He slid his hand over the smooth curve of her hip, down her thigh and upward to touch her intimately. She quivered against him, not at all shy about how much she enjoyed it, her thighs parting in unspoken invitation, her hands tightening urgently on his shoulders.

He'd been trying to go slow, take his time, make sure she was ready, and that he wasn't rushing things because his body was sending him signals like the sudden flashes of lightning outside. But apparently she was impatient, too.

"I'm in love with you," he whispered.

He stopped whatever response might have been with a searing kiss. He'd just needed to say it.

HERE SHE WAS, making love with a very sexy cowboy. As usual he didn't want to talk; all he wanted was to get to the business at hand.

She might ask later how he'd learned what he was doing so well, but she doubted he'd answer. Every touch had been reverent and gentle, and he certainly knew his way around a woman's body. And that brief declaration—good timing. But she wasn't interested in talking. Not yet. Maybe one day they'd have that discussion, but not now. She didn't own his past and he didn't own hers, either.

But…he was in *love* with her?

If anyone other than Drake had said that, she might've thought it was nothing more than an opportunistic line. Drake wasn't like that.

He truly did mean everything he said. Down to the last word.

She wasn't prepared for any life-changing discussion, but she decided she had to say *something*, meet him halfway. "I think about you from when I wake up in the morning until I go to sleep," she admitted. "Is that love? Help me out."

The way he responded was so Drake. "Can't right now. I'm kinda busy."

Busy translated into driving her crazy with his mouth and hands. When he finally did slide deep inside her, she was already on the edge, so that didn't take long at all.

They moved together naturally and were so lacking in

awkwardness that she might've marveled at it, but at the moment she couldn't think anything remotely profound.

Sexy cowboy, score one. She wasn't sure she was still breathing after her first orgasm. After the second, she didn't recall her own name. Then, with a fine sheen of sweat on his skin and his face buried in her still-damp hair, he went rigid and groaned in pleasure. They lay there in the breathless aftermath, intertwined, sated, silent. He finally lifted his head. "The storm's passing. Tent stood firm."

Luce traced the arch of his brow with a fingertip. "So far, so good. It could've blown away and I probably wouldn't have noticed."

"Could be a rocky night. Who knows what might happen next." His grin held pure male satisfaction.

He didn't seem inclined to let her go, which was okay with her. Despite the events of the afternoon and the volatile weather, she felt safe nestled there against him. "Could we just live right here?"

It must have been the afterglow talking. He'd never once mentioned marriage and she'd avoided the subject, as well. She was instantly appalled that she'd spoken out loud.

Luckily, he didn't seem fazed. "Too far from the day-to-day on the ranch. Getaway for the weekend, maybe? A nice little log cabin. I bet Slate and Mace would pitch in to build it because they'll want to use it, too. That's a great idea."

"I wasn't suggesting—"

"Suggest away. You could convince me of anything right now." He raked back her hair, feathering the strands with his fingers. "Unfair advantage."

The lantern light and the fading sound of thunder did lend a romantic ambience, and the rain had let up, too.

She looked into his eyes. "I think the advantage is all yours."

"Hope that's true, but we can debate it later. In the meantime, Harry sent us a present. If you aren't starved, I am. Let's see, I spent all afternoon worrying about you and working like a fiend so I could get up here, you fell into an ice-cold river and I still don't know why, and we finally acknowledged something I think we both figured out a long time ago. Oh, I have a dry shirt in my pack. Why don't you wear it so we can have dinner?"

She was hungry, too, she realized now that everything was ramping down.

Or...ramping up.

"I'll borrow the shirt, thanks. And anything Harry sends me is welcome."

"We'll eat first, but after that maybe you could tell me why you fell in the river."

"Deal."

A few minutes later, she was sitting across from him, eating a fabulous Greek sandwich that involved feta, olives and marinated meat she assumed was lamb. The cucumber salad was tangy, and Drake had brought a bottle of Mountain Vineyards wine she'd never tasted before; it was a mellow red she really liked.

Life was good, even sitting in a tent in stormy Wyoming.

It could be good all the time. He'd made the first move. Luce weighed her words carefully. "I have to finish my degree. I can't fall in love right now."

"I have to finish my sandwich. Keep going. Why?"

He looked incredibly sexy in jeans and nothing else, and yes, he did seem hungry. He kept eating.

She gave up. Why fight it. "Okay, fine. I'm in the same

untenable position. But there's a difference. You have ties here and I have ties somewhere else."

"*Untenable?* How many people use that in a sentence?"

She would've tossed the rest of her sandwich at him, but it was too good to waste. "You do realize that the reason you aren't married is because you may be the most exasperating person on earth?"

"I'm not married because I hadn't met you yet."

She had to fall for the most forthright, no-nonsense man on earth—and that was exasperating in its own way. She hadn't wanted to discuss it yet, but he'd brought it up.

Love. And marriage?

She chose to deflect the topic. "I can confirm that you do have a mountain lion problem."

The tactic worked. He choked on his last bite. "Excuse me. You can confirm this *how*?"

"I was hiking back here when I noticed something following me. He wasn't shy, either. I turned around and he was standing right behind me."

"Are you okay?"

The single most ridiculous question ever asked. She had to smile. "I think you inspected every inch of me, so you should know I'm fine." Then she shrugged. "He—the lion—was beautiful. He just watched me, but since I thought running would be a bad idea, I chose the stream. I guess he doesn't like that cold water any more than I do. I stayed in until I was positive he'd gone."

Drake helped himself to another sandwich. "This is where I get to remind you that I didn't want you up here alone in the first place."

Luce ate a large bite of salad and washed it down with wine. "Excuse *me* for making the argument that I'd probably be in more danger getting into my car and having some idiot on his cell phone run a red light. The mountain lion was there stalking the horses, not me. Remember the missing foal?"

"I remember. Those big cats have large territories." Drake rubbed his forehead.

"In any case, Smoke scared him away. I'm not going to get all melodramatic and say he saved my life, but maybe he did."

"The stallion scared him away?"

"Yes." She took more salad, spooning it out of the plastic bowl. "That's exactly what happened. I was watching the horses all day, and when they bolted, I thought it was because of the storm. I decided I should come back, and that was when I realized I was being followed. I turned around and saw the cat, but Smoke came out of nowhere at full speed, and I jumped in the stream."

"The horse saved you?" He still seemed incredulous.

She nodded.

Drake seemed to be striving for patience. "Give me a minute to put this together. So you're out all afternoon watching the horses, taking pictures and making notes. A wicked storm blows up, so you decide to head back to the tent. Then a mountain lion follows you and a rogue stallion chases him away. Do I have this right? Quite the eventful afternoon, Ms. Hale."

"Oh, and don't forget when you and I made love."

"Not likely I'll ever forget that." His voice dropped in timbre and he held her gaze. "I did just say 'ever,' didn't I?"

She hadn't planned to say this yet, but... "My sister thinks I should invite you to California for a brief visit." She hesitated. "I know you're really busy, but if you could

find the time, maybe we could go for a couple of days? My
parents have a house very close to your grandfather's vineyard. That's how my mother met yours, remember? They
both grew up there. You could see him, too."

He didn't respond to that, but his brows rose. "Your
family has a country house?"

"Look, the Carson ranch isn't exactly a slum, so I don't
want any rich-girl comments. My parents don't support me.
They haven't for quite some time. I want to inform you,
though, that I'll have student loans to pay off."

He seemed amused at her defiant statement. "Good information. You do realize it doesn't reflect badly on you
that your parents are successful people."

She was probably too sensitive about the subject. "It always makes me feel as though my accomplishments are due
to them, not me."

Drake just shook his head. "You do very well all on
your own. Mind if I eat the rest of that salad, or do you
want more?"

Therapy, Drake Carson—style. *You're okay and pass the
salad.*

She passed it. "I *can't* be in love with you," she said again.

"But you are?"

The least she could do was be as honest as he was. "Yes."

He handled it with his usual composure. "I'll take a
weekend and we'll go to California. Red can manage the
ranch for a few days."

CHAPTER THIRTEEN

LUCE WAS ASLEEP next to Drake, one arm curved over her head. He could see one enticing bare shoulder, and her lips were slightly parted.

He'd kiss her awake, but he had a feeling she could use the sleep. He, on the other hand, rarely slept past dawn. Drake eased out of the sleeping bag, doing his best not to disturb Luce and succeeding except for a small sleepy murmur. Yanking on his jeans, he pulled a clean shirt from his pack. Then, dressed and barefoot, he made his way over to check on Starburst, giving him a handful of the oats he'd brought along. Then he sat on a fallen pine, stretched out his legs and watched the sunrise, inhaling the crisp air that still smelled of rain in the wake of the storm.

He didn't have enough moments like this. Oh, lots of solitude, but he was usually on a ranch mission of some sort. Rarely did he just sit and breathe and indulge in the luxury of reflection.

So Luce wanted him to meet her parents. That was as

good as a *yes* to a question he hadn't yet asked. The stumbling block was that they were facing a long-distance relationship, at least for a while. He was torn over whether or not that kind of marriage could work, but the decision seemed to have been made for him.

And now, in addition to relocating the wild horses *and* trying to recover some of his mares, he'd have to do something about the mountain lion. It had been poaching on Carson property since last fall. Ironically, *without* the horses here, the problem was likely to get worse. The foal Luce had noticed was missing probably wasn't the first. Animals, like people, fell into certain behavioral patterns, and not only that, the young ones were an easy food source for a large predator. A friend who was a park ranger had told him once that he never failed to advise families hiking in the mountains not to let their children or dogs run ahead on the trails. Kids should walk between the adults, he'd said.

Wyoming was a wonderful place to live but, like anywhere else, it had its dangers. No hurricanes or tidal waves, but there were plenty of other things to be cautious about—blizzards, forest fires and tornadoes among them.

"You seem deep in thought."

He glanced up to see Luce emerging from the tent, dressed in a set of clean clothes, her hair in a ponytail. She could pull off a face free of makeup unlike any other woman he'd ever met. She was naturally beautiful, fresh-faced and vital.

"Just mulling over the dynamics of the universe," he said, summoning a smile. "Sleep well?"

"You know exactly how I slept because you were beside me."

"Uh, that's right, I sure was. Wouldn't mind doing that again."

Drily, she said, "How come I think you aren't referring to sleep?"

"You have a suspicious mind?" The smile came more easily this time.

"I hate to be the one to tell you, but you don't do innocent very well. Now, if you'll excuse me—"

"I'm going with you." He'd stood when he heard her voice and he reached out to touch her cheek. "No argument. I'll turn my back to give you privacy, how's that?"

Of course, she argued, anyway. "I was out here by myself all of yesterday. I've been up here alone plenty of times before. I don't need a bodyguard."

"I'm really fond of your body. I'm guarding it for me. Purely selfish reasons." He picked up his rifle, which he'd brought out with him and hoped he wouldn't have to use. But he knew the cat was close, so better safe than sorry. No way was she hiking anywhere alone.

Luce didn't look very happy, but obviously understood that he wasn't going to budge. He thought it was possible that she muttered the words *stubborn ass* as she walked into a copse of small pines.

When she emerged safely and bent to wash her hands in the small spring, he admired the graceful curve of her spine and said, "I could use a good cup of coffee. What about you? Should we pack up and ride back to the house?"

She shook the drops off her fingers and he could swear he saw a tinge of color in her cheeks. "Everyone there is going to know we spent the night together."

"Yeah, that's true." He almost made a comment about his trip to the drugstore but stopped himself in time. All of

Mustang Creek knew by now, but she didn't have to realize that. "Last I heard, you and I are both adults and unattached. If we want to sleep together, that's our business."

"I don't care so much about everyone else, but I do care about your mother, mine and Harry."

"The three most conniving matchmakers in history?" He didn't put the brakes on fast enough to stop that one. "You have to be kidding, Luce. Two of them lured you here to Wyoming, and one of them made dinner for us last night. What about those heart-shaped cookies… Oh, *that* wasn't a hint? Do you think Mace included the wine and the glasses? Don't overrate him. He isn't that sensitive. No, it was Harry. She and my mother are probably doing fist bumps over their morning tea."

"That would be flattering," Luce said with a laugh.

"They both like you."

"They both love *you*. That's different."

"I know. I'm not saying they aren't both great. I'm saying you don't have to worry that they'll be anything but happy about it. The two of us getting together, I mean." He was the one likely to endure a talk on how he should go about choosing a ring. Yeah, he was looking forward to that. No doubt someone of the female persuasion would want to go along so he didn't mess it up. He could rope a bull, but there were clearly misgivings in some quarters about his ability to select a suitable ring.

"Any chance Slater caught it on camera? I'm talking about the fist bump."

"Hell, no. He'd never risk his life. Between the two of them, they could certainly take him. Grace would help. He'd be toast."

"You do realize you have an eclectic family, right?"

She'd lightened up, if her laugh was any indication.

"They're an interesting bunch. Let me help you with the tent, and then I'll saddle Starburst."

He thought she'd put up a fight, insist she wanted to camp out again, but maybe despite her comfort with the outdoors, her experience the night before had made an impression. Sure, he and his brothers had camped out many, many times, but they'd brought their rifles, knew how to store food to avoid attracting unwanted guests, and they'd grown up knowing you had to keep your eyes open. Practice and familiarity counted for a lot.

She said without equivocation, "I can handle the tent. Go get your horse."

If he forced the tent issue, he had a feeling he'd be in trouble.

IT WAS NICE to slip into the house unnoticed and bolt straight to her bathroom for a shower. As she stripped off her clothes, she registered soreness, partly from horseback riding and partly from...well, uninhibited sex. On the positive side, the shampoo and conditioner might make her hair manageable again. And she needed a chance to think about the night before.

She already had an offer from a private college for a teaching position once she completed her graduate degree, assistant professor, not associate or full, but she was still in her twenties; there was plenty of time to advance in the academic ranks. She'd gotten a teaching certificate as part of her undergrad program.

As she'd pointed out to Beth, what would she *do* in Mustang Creek?

She'd put a lot of time into figuring out her future. Drake was totally mucking that up.

She did hope this wasn't a problem with trust on her part. Previous men in her life, notably her erstwhile fiancé, had proven to be jerks, but Drake wasn't, and intellectually she understood that. In her heart...she just wanted to make sure she was independent, confident, solid on her own.

It was her problem to solve.

The hair was indeed a challenge, but she won the battle, wielding conditioner and a hairbrush. Because she was self-conscious, she decided mascara was in order. It was closer to lunch than to breakfast, and she found the entire family in the dining room, chatting and having Sunday brunch.

She walked in, and all conversation paused but slowly resumed as she took her seat That was followed by cheerful hellos from everyone present.

"I'm a little late," she said apologetically.

"Yep, you are." Drake, the king of the three-word sentence, rose with his empty plate in hand. "Listen, I'm running behind. Gotta go."

But he didn't leave the dining room right away. Instead, he leaned over and kissed her in front of his entire family, just a light brush of his lips on hers. "See you later."

Luce was speechless. Everyone else was grinning. He used his elbow to open the door and disappeared into the kitchen. Grace jabbed Slater in the ribs. "Admit I called that one."

Blythe interjected, "I think *I* called it."

"Saw it coming from the start," Harry said serenely. "Luce, can I pass you some biscuits and gravy?"

CHAPTER FOURTEEN

"WANT TO FLY-FISH the Bliss?" Slater propped himself against the doorway. "Where's Ryder, anyway? Isn't this his job?"

Drake wiped his forehead. "Believe it or not, he went to the movies with Red. Some sort of John Wayne marathon at the theater downtown. Red's been talking them up to the kid. They were both so excited I told them just to go. Ryder called Grace to ask if it was okay, and then they lit out of here."

"So you're voluntarily mucking out stalls?"

"I am, but fishing sounds better. Feel free to pitch in and, after that, yes to the Bliss. You're done filming for this afternoon?"

Slater picked up a shovel from the wall rack. "I'm not a slave driver. It's Sunday, after all. I'm going to bet half my crew is watching John Wayne, along with Ryder and Red, and the other half is at Bad Billy's. I gave everyone the day off."

It was true that there wasn't a lot to do in Mustang Creek, and that had always been okay with Drake. Plenty to do on the ranch and there were mountains practically in his backyard. He did go skiing now and then, but fly-fishing was more his kind of thing. They'd all gone with their father as boys and those afternoons were among his fondest memories. Being with his dad. The quiet, the sunshine, the gleaming water. The thrill of getting a hit on your line…

"We going or what?"

He turned to see Mace carrying their fly rods and a tackle box, hip waders draped over his arm.

Drake gestured around him. "Get busy mucking. Two more stalls and we can go. Showbiz is on board with helping, as you can see. How about you?"

His younger brother muttered a word he'd never say in front of his mother or Harry, but he obligingly set everything down. "I'll do the straw and feed. I'm not touching Heck, though. Slater can brush his own damn horse."

They'd worked together so many times the work was done in minutes, and then they all piled into Slater's truck. Mace was in the back, and he patted a cooler on the seat next to him. "I told Harry we'd be bringing back trout. Don't make me do all the work because you both suck at fishing."

"Yeah, right," Slater said sarcastically.

"After the storm last night, a successful haul might be a neat trick," Drake observed. "River's going to be high and muddy. I thought I'd end up somewhere around the south pole the wind was blowing so hard."

He shouldn't have said it, because—predictably—Mace jumped on it. "I'm sure you clung to Luce for comfort, Romeo."

There were two ways to react to that sort of comment, and he chose the high road. "I did, as a matter of fact."

Both of his brothers laughed. As they turned onto the county highway, Slater asked, "So, is it pretty serious or just a fling?"

"I agreed to go to California with her." He really hadn't meant to let the proverbial cat out of the bag. Luckily, his brothers wouldn't tell if he asked them not to, and he did. "That happens to be top secret information, by the way. Mom and Harry are running the show too much as it is. If they get wind of this, I'll know it was one of you two."

Slater shook his head. "Not necessarily. You'd better hope Luce doesn't tell Grace. They seem to like each other and they aren't too far apart in age. I get the impression they talk."

Mace was his usual cheery self. "They probably complain about the two of you. I know I would."

"We could just drown him in the river," Drake suggested caustically.

"That's a plan," Slater agreed. "Think we'd get caught?"

"Hmm. Spence is a smart lawman. He might catch on."

"Yeah. We'd have to be clever about it."

"Thanks to Spence I'm saved? Good to know." Mace took it in stride. He might be a wiseass, but he did have a sense of humor. "I'll thank him later. Why do I get the feeling I'm going to be the last holdout Carson bachelor?"

"Because no one would ever want to marry you?" Drake muttered. Apparently, he viewed that as a logical observation.

"I'm choosing not to take offense at that."

"If you two start arguing again, I'm going to park the truck and walk the rest of the way, and you can follow,"

Slater said. "Then you guys get stuck with bringing the gear." He was probably only half-kidding. He'd been the peacemaker for a long time.

"Don't worry about it. I'm not going to waste an afternoon off. The river looks high, but there's not too much runoff." Drake, looking out the window, was happy to see the water running clear. The Bliss had to be one of the most beautiful rivers in the world. Crystal-bright and rippling gently, it had a variety of trout and also grayling. "We did need that rain. No significant runoff."

Slater parked in a flat grassy area they'd used before, then it was waders on and flies tied. As he waded into the water, Drake felt a twinge of nostalgia and sorrow that the fourth of their party was long absent and would never join them again.

Mace echoed his thoughts. "This always reminds me of Dad."

"I know." Drake flicked his pole. "For me, that's good *and* bad. I like to remember him, but missing him is still painful."

Slater, a few feet away, water swirling around his thighs, murmured, "Try having your wife expecting his grandchild. I grieve for him, and for the fact that my children won't know their grandfather."

At this stage of his life, Drake could only imagine that feeling. He was distracted from his melancholy mood a moment later, when he got a clean strike and the battle was on. Fly-fishing was truly a sport. It wasn't just hauling them in once they took the hook; it was wearing them out enough so you could net the fish.

He won in the end, a nice rainbow trout. He turned to his brothers. "The score is currently me one, you two zero.

I don't know what Harry's backup plan is, and I'm sure she has one, but I'm having trout for dinner."

"Whoa, don't get too smug, brother of mine." Mace's pole had suddenly bowed.

"Try landing that fish," Drake told him. "Let it run."

His brother *was* playing it expertly, giving line and taking it back. "The day I need fishing advice from you is the day hell freezes over."

"Seems to me I'm the only one who's actually caught a fish so far." Drake cast again, working the line with what he considered his lucky fly.

At the end of it all, everyone was having trout for dinner and Slater had caught the most fish. Go figure.

"I'm just lucky," he said when they got back in the truck. "Beautiful wife, wonderful daughter, and let's not forget I'm a better fisherman."

Mace rubbed his jaw. "If he's better at anything, it's at being conceited. I've always thought that. How about you, Drake?"

"Yeah, he's full of himself, all right." He stowed away the poles.

"You two are poor losers."

"You get to clean them, remember that."

"Yeah, Harry's Law." Slater rolled his eyes. "She'll bake a double-layer chocolate cake and make coconut frosting from scratch, but she won't clean a fish."

"So clean it and remember she cooked the fish."

"Thanks." Slater slanted him a derisive look. "It seems to me we'll *all* be cleaning fish, correct?"

Mace gestured expansively. "Hey, I'm starting to feel blessed 'cause I caught the least, so I won't—"

"No, no," Drake interjected. "You don't get a free pass for that."

Slater backed him up. "We'll make it a family affair. One for all and all for one. We're the Three Carsoneers, aren't we?"

Drake and Mace booed. "Jeez, that's feeble," Mace said.

"The fish are all in the same cooler," Slater added. "You can't tell which measly few are yours."

Mace grumbled, "Fine. But if you're going to brag the whole time, Slate, you might want to keep in mind that I know stories about you in college that I doubt Grace has heard. Like the one when your buddies bet—"

"Okay, no more bragging," Slater interrupted in mock terror.

"Thought you might feel that way." Mace grinned and so did Drake, listening to the lighthearted banter. All three of them worked so much they rarely had a chance to spend time together. As kids, they'd often gone riding, fishing and camping as a trio. There were a lot of arguments, but those usually blew over as fast as that storm the night before.

The storm.

Luce, soaking wet and clinging to him, and the very different kind of storm that followed. He hadn't asked and he wasn't going to, but he wondered if her betraying jerk of a former fiancé had been her only lover. She wasn't shy by any means; however, he had the feeling that she'd been shocked by the intensity of her sexual response.

He shouldn't have kissed her in front of everyone, but their evolving relationship was hardly a secret. Hell, their first kiss was going to be in a movie!

Time to broach an important subject. "I want to surprise Luce. I'm thinking we should build a cabin up on the ridge. Do you two agree? Nothing fancy. A bedroom or maybe two, small kitchen, but we'd have to bring in coolers for food. We'll need a camp shower, and we could set up a wood-burning stove for heat. If we wanted to, we could put in a generator for electricity. We could run that off a small propane tank. Glorified camping."

His brothers jumped in with both feet. Slater said with conviction, "River-stone fireplace that burns wood. Grace would love that. Two bedrooms—I have children, remember?—and a nice deck."

"An outdoor grill for cooking." Mace was part of the project. "A good one with a burner on the side. Put it on the covered deck, so if the weather's bad, you can still cook. We'll need to improve the horse enclosure, too."

Slater said, "I agree with that. Plus a fire pit for sitting around. When we're ready to build, we should get the logs from the property and have the mill strip them for us instead of buying lumber. For the floors, we could use some of the siding from the bunkhouse we remodeled for the winery."

"That old barn door would make a fantastic dining room table." Mace looked thoughtful. "I could refinish it."

"And we could use the chairs up in the attic," Slater suggested. "Those are antiques from our grandmother, and I've always felt bad that they've just gathered dust for years. Hadleigh Galloway could reupholster them."

This was quickly spiraling out of control. "I was thinking simple," Drake said in protest. "Did I even mention a dining area? What kind of home-improvement TV shows do you have time to watch? All I want is a small rustic cabin, not something that could be featured in a magazine."

"Be quiet." Slater frowned at him. "We need a place to

eat. So we're doing a dining room. It would be great to have a place to go for weekends. Yup, it's a brilliant idea. Can't believe *I* didn't come up with it."

Mace said, "He's full of himself again. I'm so telling Grace that story."

Drake shrugged. "Go for it, I say."

THE WILD HORSES had moved.

Luce had made a diagram of where they usually grazed, and they weren't there. Interesting. Smoke had decided on different territory.

They were closer to the ranch again, which she suspected would not make Drake happy. For her purposes, it was easier, since she wouldn't have to walk for hours.

There was a beautiful new foal.

Pure Smoke. He was gray, with that same black mane, and she was riveted. The mother was one of Drake's stolen mares, and Luce snapped pictures on her phone and took more with the high-tech camera her father had given her for Christmas.

Wonderstruck, she allowed herself to dream that by the time the colt had matured, she might be skilled enough to train and ride him.

Of course, the little one *could* be a filly, but she had a feeling she'd guessed correctly.

Would she even be here when the foal was grown?

Not wanting to pursue the prospect of either going *or* staying, she shifted her attention back to the magic of the moment.

She felt a sudden thrill. She'd come to Wyoming in the hope of having experiences like this. She was learning so much and her ambitious approach to this project made more and more sense—to her and, she thought, to Drake Carson, too. Whether he was ready to admit it or not.

Drake. Before her arrival here, before that first meeting, she'd never imagined what he might come to mean to her.

She texted him the picture. He might be annoyed—this was the stallion's handiwork, after all—but she suspected otherwise.

When she got back to the house, she went straight to her room, fired up her computer and downloaded the pictures. She emailed one to Beth and one to her mother. She was in the middle of putting her notes into a more logical order when Blythe knocked on her open door and stuck her head in. "I know you're working, but care to run into town with me? I want to order a special gift for your parents' anniversary and your opinion would be invaluable."

Her gift would be showing up for the surprise dinner party Beth was hosting for them. She hadn't told Drake about it, although he was her designated date—designated by her, anyway. He'd agreed to California for a weekend; might as well meet her whole family at once, like ripping off a bandage. If she knew Beth, the party would be casual and fun, cocktails by the pool, and her mother's favorite caterer would do the food. Lots of children everywhere, since most of Luce's cousins were older than she was and had growing families.

"I'd love to go." She saved the file. "Let me change. It'll only take a minute."

"Sweetie, you're fine in jeans. Where we're going, the business owner will be dressed the same as you are. You'll like her, too. I know you met her husband, Spence Hogan. Melody makes the most artistic pieces in this entire state. When she got married, she moved to Spence's ranch and turned her own house into a studio. No specific hours—you have to call ahead or drop in and hope she's there. You aren't allergic to cats, are you? Ralph, Waldo and Emerson are usually there, too. I have no idea how she wrangles them back and forth with a little one to boot, but she manages it."

"Her cats are named that?" Luce went to grab her purse. "That's clever!"

"She's an artist, what can I say?" Blythe laughed. "I love her free spirit. She's beautiful, too, but I don't think she realizes it, just like you. She's a jeans kind of girl. What you have on right now is perfectly okay."

That was a nice compliment—the one about being beautiful—but she didn't think Blythe was exactly unbiased.

If Drake loved her, the entire Carson family was going to love her, too. Hands down, no questions asked. They were that sort of family. Look at how they treated Raine, the mother of Slater's child, even though she and Slater were never married. Regardless, she was part of the family.

The drive into Mustang Creek wasn't too long. They pulled into the driveway of a small well-kept house with a neat yellow car. Blythe parked her sleek Mercedes next to it and twirled her hand. "We're here. Get in tune with your creative side. She has a display of her work, but mostly she does commissioned pieces. That's excluding what she sells to the shops in town."

Melody Hogan answered the door in jeans and an old T-shirt that announced she'd graduated from Mustang High School. As Blythe had said, she was strikingly beautiful, a vibrant, energetic blonde. A baby wailed somewhere in the background.

With a smile, Melody said, "Welcome to the land of

chaos. We're having green beans today and, as you've no doubt guessed, *somebody* around here hates anything green." The child's cries escalated, and Melody winced. "Sorry about the noise."

"If you think I haven't heard a baby cry before, think again," Blythe said, obviously right at home. "Melody, this is Lucinda Hale—aka Luce. Her mother's a dear friend of mine, and I need a special anniversary gift for her." She waved one hand. "Go handle the green bean crisis. We'll check out some of the pieces on display in your studio."

Melody Logan nodded gratefully. "Look around all you want. I'll be back." She sighed, heading for a nearby door. "Bananas?" she muttered to herself. "Or mashed carrots?"

Smiling, Blythe led the way to Melody's studio-gallery. The space was cozy and colorfully cluttered and, somehow, elegant, too. There were cases of jewelry, bracelets and earrings, and unique custom-made clocks on the walls, along with a few paintings, mostly landscapes.

A couch stood near the fireplace, currently occupied by three napping cats so similar that they might have been cloned. A worktable scattered with sketches and a baby monitor sat next to a computer.

Luce was immediately drawn to the charm bracelets, one of which would be a perfect gift for her sister's upcoming birthday. She was particularly interested in a charm that featured a mother's hand clasping a baby's.

"Do you suppose Melody would do a horse charm?" Suddenly inspired, she pulled up the picture on her phone. "Look at this little guy. He and I just met today."

"Melody would do it." Blythe's mouth held the hint of a smile and there was a twinkle in her eye. "You should give it to Drake."

That made her laugh as she pictured one of these delicate pieces on his brawny wrist. "I was thinking of me, but he won't approve of that, either. He and Smoke have a love/hate relationship."

"He told me you named the stallion. I hadn't seen him up close until that image Slater's film crew took. He really is a beauty. I like the name Smoke. It suits him." Blythe turned back to the display. "Look at these gorgeous rings. Get Melody to show you her engagement ring. My friend Lettie Arbuckle tricked her into making it, and Melody didn't know it was intended for her. It's truly a work of art."

As far as Luce could tell, everything was.

When Melody came back, there was a suspicious yellow stain on her shirt, and she was shaking her head and laughing. "Nap time. Even the bananas were rejected. But give him the right stuffed animal and he's out like a light. It's nice to have a nursery here where I work. Now, what did you have in mind?"

"Like I said, I need an anniversary gift, but it actually has to be for both of them." Blythe gestured at one of the pieces in a display case. "I remember you made Lettie a set of rings that would fit on the neck of a wine bottle. They each had a charm. My friends live in Napa, so a wine-related gift works well. They entertain a lot, so I'd need six of them. Would it be possible for you to do this in two weeks?"

Melody nodded. "Of course. The ring and the chain aren't the issue. I need an idea about the charms. Want them all the same or six different?"

"I was thinking the letter *H*, done in pewter." Blythe turned to Luce. "Sound good?"

It did; it sounded like a very tasteful gift and perfect for her parents. But Luce had already cottoned on to the fact that this wasn't why she'd been invited on Blythe's shopping expedition. She waited for it—and she didn't have to wait long. Very casually, Blythe said, "Oh, Melody, please show Luce your ring. I was telling her how lovely it is."

Drake was going to die laughing when he heard that one of the "conniving matchmakers" had invited her on an excursion to look at engagement rings. Melody extended her hand. The ring, a sapphire surrounded by small diamonds, was exquisite. "I wasn't aware I was making it for myself," Melody explained, "but maybe you've heard that story."

Might as well play along. "Gorgeous," she said with a smile, "and yes, I've heard it."

"Blythe is about to ask you if that would be the kind of ring you'd like and what center stone you'd choose. She'll do it wearing her most innocent face. I have informants in the Carson household."

"That Grace!" Blythe threw up her hands. "What a traitor. If I didn't adore her and she wasn't about to give me a grandchild, I'd be offended. I'm just trying to help my son, who's a wonderful person but who's likely to walk into a jewelry store somewhere, squint at the case for five seconds and then say, 'That one looks fine to me.' Now, if he was buying her a saddle, he'd really take his time and know what he was doing."

Luce was touched *and* amused. One of the cats rose and yawned and then stretched and the other two did the same thing. They settled back down, facing the opposite direction, once again in the same pose.

"We haven't even discussed marriage. He hasn't asked me yet."

"He will," Blythe said with conviction.

Melody echoed that. "From what I hear, he will."

Luce's phone beeped, signaling an incoming text—from Drake. Dinner out? Just us?

Was that timing or what?

She responded, Yes. Then she told Melody, "Should the subject ever come up, I've always loved rubies."

"Good choice."

CHAPTER FIFTEEN

DRAKE WAS ABSURDLY nervous and couldn't understand why.

The evening ahead was no big deal, just dinner at the resort his sister-in-law managed.

Calmly, Drake changed into a white button-down shirt and tan slacks, thought about wearing a tie, but he'd have to borrow it from Slater, since he didn't own one. Hated the things actually.

Finally, when he figured he was as presentable as he was going to get, he texted Luce.

Meet me downstairs in five minutes?

Hey, Cowboy, she texted back. I'm already down here, ready and waiting. If you're primping, stop it. I've seen you covered in dirt and you've seen me sopping wet.

He couldn't stop himself. Not to mention, naked. That was the best part. Be right there.

Taking Luce—or anybody else—out for a formal dinner was a little out of character for Drake, but he wanted more one-on-one time with her.

When he got downstairs and saw Luce, he had to catch his breath.

Hot damn, she looked good. She wore a skinny black dress, shoes with heels and some sort of long sweater in a silvery gray. All that luxurious hair was loose and she'd gone a little Hollywood with the makeup, compared to her usual outdoorsy style. It wasn't excessive or anything and he definitely approved.

Drake wasn't a hermit. He dated, but not very often, since he was always working. Occasionally, he'd meet someone through friends or at community events, and he'd even gotten semiserious a time or two, especially back in college. So far, though, he'd never met anyone like Luce.

Maybe because there *was* no one like her.

He gave her a deliberate once-over. "Damn."

That was eloquent. He wanted to groan at his own awkwardness, but she laughed, so maybe it wasn't too bad. "I was going to say that about you," she said.

He opened the front door and, for the second time in two nights, ordered Violet and Harold to stay. They both looked disappointed—those two had expressive canine faces—but they immediately sat down.

As they went down the steps toward his truck, Luce asked him, "How did you train them so well? My mother's Yorkies are the cutest dogs, but it took obedience school to get them to listen. I can't picture you doing that."

"I got them as puppies and I just talked to them. They caught on fast. Animals are so much smarter than most people give them credit for. It's just a question of whether they choose to go with what you tell them to do. They both learned right away that if they didn't do what I asked, I wouldn't take them with me the next time. So they do it. These two have to be some of the best herding dogs anywhere."

"I believe it." Somehow she managed, even in that skimpy dress, to get gracefully into the passenger seat of his truck. In retrospect, he should've borrowed his mother's expensive classy car. His truck was expensive, too, but probably not what a lady wanted to ride in to a nice dinner.

She didn't seem to mind.

"What a beautiful evening. Very different from last night." She gazed out the window as they went down the drive. "Wyoming has such beautiful sunsets. I love the mountains."

He did, too. "California doesn't do too poorly in that department, either. I've visited my grandparents fairly often, especially when I was younger."

Luce gave him a sidelong look. "I'm surprised we never met. My mother's always throwing some sort of party and your grandparents always come."

He shrugged. "For all I know, we did. Remember, I'm a lofty six years older than you. Until I turned twenty-four, you were beneath my notice." His grin held a tinge of humor. "Not to mention underage, and I don't do that any more than I do casual. By the time I graduated from college, the ranch was waiting for me. It's far easier for my grandparents to visit here than the reverse."

He didn't add that elaborate social events bored the hell out of him, and they had his entire life. Even as a kid he'd preferred taking a long afternoon ride or reading a good book in a secluded place, preferably outdoors.

"Speaking of which, I'm hoping a specific weekend will be convenient for us to fly out there."

Uh-oh. "Why?" he asked cautiously.

"An anniversary party for my parents."

He almost groaned at that announcement. He managed to stifle it, but only just.

She added lightly, "I believe your mother's also invited."

"My mother? That should be a relaxing, romantic trip."

"You were looking for romantic? That's reassuring."

"After last night, do you doubt it? But the idea of meeting your whole family, with my mother right there, sounds worse than a root canal."

"You'll like them. Anyway, I'm going to change the subject. I really want that new colt—Smoke's baby. I sent you his picture."

He stopped dead in the very act of pulling out of the drive onto the county highway, hitting the brakes and looking over at her incredulously. "What exactly would you do with it?"

"Eventually ride him." Her mouth was set in a firm line and she stared straight ahead.

"I see." He didn't discount the possibility that she could do anything she set her mind to because she'd succeeded quite often in his opinion. Her plan to study wild horses in unfamiliar territory didn't seem as illogical as he'd originally thought. She could handle herself well outdoors, and quite frankly, she'd managed to get a lot closer to the herd than he had. In his defense, he didn't have all day to sit around taking pictures and writing notes, but still… Luce had shown dedication and resolve.

He knew he'd have to tell her he was rounding up help

to move the horses. She'd asked for time, and the two weeks they'd agreed to were up.

"He'll need his mother for a while," he said calmly. "Red can train a horse like nobody else, but he's getting a little old to hit the ground that often. Slate, Mace or I can do that part."

"I can have him, then? The foal?"

"I sure as hell want that mare back, so yes, if we can work it out." *Here comes the hard part.* "If you want that horse, you'll have to move to Wyoming, Luce."

"Mind clarifying that?"

He gave an exasperated sigh. "You know what I'm saying."

"I'm not sure I do." She'd finally turned to look at him. "Drake, if there's a question dangling in there, just ask me."

So he did. "Marry me?"

"We've known each other less than a month and slept together once."

"The amount of time that's elapsed since you started annoying the hell out of me doesn't really matter, and thank you very much, but it was more than once last night, remember? I'll feel vaguely insulted if you don't."

Her laugh was encouraging. "Oh, yeah, I remember. You do know how to charm a girl, by the way. *Annoying the hell out of you?*"

"Maybe that wasn't well put. How about—annoying the ever-lovin' hell out of me. Better? I could elaborate and tell you that I think about you all day instead of concentrating on what I should be doing, I've had more sappy thoughts since I met you than in my whole life and I've even wondered if our children would have my eyes or yours. That's it. I'm done."

She was quiet, her face averted. Then she said, "That could be the best proposal in history. Yes."

"Yes?" He swerved a little, then straightened the truck. "Yes."

Well, that was settled. He muttered, "So, I think I should meet your parents. I mean, before we tell the world."

Now she was truly smiling. "That is so sweet—and so old-fashioned."

He smiled at her. "I like to do things right."

She let that one pass. There were plenty of things Drake Carson "did right"—in and out of bed. "We'll figure something out."

"Hungry?"

She nodded.

"Me, too," he answered. "Let's go to dinner, have a glass of Mountain Vineyards wine and see what Stefano has on the menu for tonight. I had the lobster ravioli last time I was there, and while Harry is a wizard, that's not in her repertoire."

"It sounds like I'm going to have a remarkable evening." She looked him right in the eyes and hers were luminous. "You have no idea how happy I am."

Wrong. He was just as happy. Maybe happier.

SHE TEXTED BETH, just two words, as Drake went to park the car after dropping her off at the entrance to the resort.

He asked.

The reply was immediate. I knew it!

You can't say a word to anyone. Drake wants Mom and Dad to know before we make any announcements.

I won't say a word. If I wasn't breast-feeding I'd drink a glass of champagne to celebrate. See you soon. Can't wait to meet him.

Well, she'd had to tell *someone* and her sister was a logical choice. She was tempted to tell Grace, too, since they were becoming friends. But Grace was married to Drake's brother and part of sharing a life was, after all, sharing everything. When Drake chose to tell his family they were engaged was up to him.

The resort was perfect for the area, rustic but classy. Luce could tell that while it catered to affluent clients, there was no sense of exclusivity. Western-style hospitality was the attitude, and the theme of the decor, too.

Drake steered her toward the restaurant entrance with a hand on her elbow. The place was high-end but low-key, she thought with admiration. The art was impressive—spectacular landscapes, exquisite horses, portraits of Native Americans in ceremonial dress. Several pieces were obviously Melody Hogan's work, such as the clever mobile fashioned from old spurs and stirrups.

Soft instrumental music played, and the tables were beautifully set, with white cloths, candles and gleaming china and silverware. A distinct change from Bad Billy's.

"Lovely," Luce said as they were shown to their table and Drake pulled out her chair. "But I would expect that with Grace in charge."

"She's a perfectionist. So is Slater. No wonder they get along so well." Drake sat down and smiled in a way that suddenly made her feel vulnerable. "I'd love it if you told me what makes *us* get along so well—despite our differences. Quite frankly, I can't quite put a finger on it."

"A love of adventure?" she suggested. "Or that I annoy the hell out of you."

"Could be," he agreed. "I—"

When he stopped in midspeech, Luce first thought it was because the waitress had arrived with their menus, but it took her about two seconds to realize that wasn't it.

The nervous waitress passed them the leather-bound menus with a tremulous smile. "Hi, Drake. It's good to see you. Can I get you all a drink?"

"Danielle. I didn't know you were working here." His voice was even, but the impassive look on his face spoke volumes. "How are you?"

"Getting a divorce. Which you've probably heard."

He nodded.

"Otherwise, I'm managing. I just got this job. Your sister-in-law really helped me out. Grace persuaded the restaurant manager to take a chance on someone who's been a stay-at-home mom for fourteen years. You know Reed. He's determined to make this as nasty as possible. The kids and I are living with my parents right now. But you don't need to hear my sad story. How's your mom?"

"She's fine. And I *asked* how you were. Which means I wanted to know."

"I guess. Well, thanks. Um, I'd better get to work. Drinks?" She flipped back the pad she was holding, pen poised, but her hand wasn't steady and her smile was forced.

Luce homed in on it. She just *knew*. He'd been in love before—he'd said so—and it was with the woman standing in front of her.

She couldn't blame him. The woman was one of those delicate blondes with a flawless complexion. She wasn't heavy, but not thin, with nice curves. She could still pass for a high school cheerleader.

Drake ordered a bottle of chardonnay, Mace's label, of course.

Luce knew she shouldn't ask, but she couldn't help it. "What's the story?"

He did his usual thing. "Long time ago."

"But you were serious."

"We were young."

"Quit with the three-word sentences and *tell* me. It seems to me that we're committed to a permanent relationship now. And I have to say, I don't understand why any woman would give you up."

His smile resurfaced. "I appreciate that, Ms. Hale."

She raised her eyebrows in question.

"High school romance. It might've gone further, but she got involved with someone else. Never liked the guy, but it was her life and her decision. Not a big deal."

Luce sensed that it *had* been a big deal for him. A healed wound still left a scar. He wasn't the kind of person to take betrayal lightly and she knew exactly what that felt like. A different waitress showed up then with their wine, which confirmed that the old romance—the broken romance—was significant for them both. Luce had the feeling that they weren't going to see Danielle for the rest of the evening.

After the tasting ritual, the new waitress poured them each a glass. Drake didn't comment on the change in waitress. This would be life with him; if he didn't want to talk about it, he wouldn't bring it up. On the other hand, if *she* brought it up, he wouldn't argue but would respond directly.

"Shall we toast?" She admired the golden liquid in her

glass. "This looks like that wine Mace served at dinner recently. I loved it."

"Could be. He's an alchemist. All I saw was a label I recognized. I usually drink beer."

"Like I haven't noticed." She noticed everything about him. He looked fantastic dressed up, but she still thought he was sexy as hell in jeans and dusty boots, wearing his favorite hat.

He raised his glass. "To us. To our future."

"Our *bright* future."

Their glasses touched and she knew she'd remember that light, delicate sound for the rest of her life.

The menu was an eclectic mixture of Italian, classic Spanish and, of course, things like elk steak and buffalo chili. She chose linguini with a delicate crab sauce; Drake opted for paella and, of course, ate every bite. Their plates had just been cleared when Danielle came rushing up to the table. She'd disappeared from the dining room at least half an hour before.

"I'm so sorry to interrupt, but I'm so glad you're still here." There were tears in her eyes and her mouth was trembling. "Can you help me? I've been waiting for my dad to pick me up because my car's in the shop. My mother just called. They think he had a heart attack and they're doing tests, but I need to go to the hospital right now. Can you give me a lift? I can't call Reed, and even if I could count on him, it would take him a while to get here. I know we've had our differences, but…please? My dad's in intensive care. My mother was hysterical. I could barely understand her on the phone."

Drake didn't hesitate. "Take a deep breath." He stood and pulled out his wallet to extract a credit card. "We haven't gotten the bill yet. Luce, can you take care of it with this, please? I'll run and get the truck."

"Thank you." There were tears running down Danielle's face and Drake handed over his napkin so she could wipe her face before leaving the table.

Was it possible to fall even more in love?

Luce wasn't sure, but he was convincing her otherwise. As he swiftly walked out the door, she put her arm around the shoulders of a complete stranger. "He'll get you there. Let me go take care of the bill."

"Catherine probably has it ready," she said through a small sob.

She did, and the young waitress processed it quickly, obviously aware something was wrong. "Is Danny okay?"

"She's pretty upset because of her dad. We're running her over to the hospital."

"Tell her if she needs me to pick up some of her shifts, I will."

That news brought on a fresh spate of tears when Luce got to the doorway where Danielle was waiting. "After all those years with Reed, I swear I'm not used to people being nice to me. I *knew* Drake would help."

Luce had the feeling there was something else she was saying. *Even after I treated him badly...* But this wasn't the time to worry about that. She stood in the doorway, and when the truck pulled up, she helped Danielle inside, settling her in the backseat of the extended cab.

As it turned out, the regional hospital was about twenty minutes away. Drake drove with his usual calm, but maybe a bit faster, while Danielle talked to her kids on her cell. Evidently, they were home alone, and worrying about their grandfather.

Luce felt double-sorry for those children. Their parents were in the middle of what sounded like a messy divorce, and now this.

It was a memorable way to spend the evening of her engagement, no doubt about that.

CHAPTER SIXTEEN

HE COULD'VE IMAGINED a better end to the evening, but maybe some things were simply meant to be.

Drake was happy that Luce seemed okay with doing this for someone she'd just met, and he was still flying high from her saying yes to his proposal.

A lifetime ago, he and Danielle had lost their virginity to each other, spent warm summer nights by the river talking about their future and been practically inseparable. Was he glad she regretted marrying Reed? No, definitely not. He'd like to think he wasn't that mean-spirited. Besides, then he wouldn't have been free to find the right woman, all these years later.

He parked as close as possible to the main entrance. "We'll go in with you."

Danielle had been sobbing quietly for most of the drive. With the combined stress of the pending divorce, having to move out of her own home, starting a new job and now this, Drake wondered if she could even locate the intensive care unit on her own. She looked almost dazed. He was uneasy about just dropping her off.

Luce met his eyes and nodded. From the ridiculously small stylish purse that matched her outfit, she'd extracted a packet of tissues for Danielle. She'd also turned to cast worried glances at their passenger more than once.

Luce murmured, "We'll come with you, make sure you and your mother don't need anything. What about the kids? Will they have had dinner? We can stop and pick up a pizza or something for them."

"Nathan is fourteen. He can heat up some leftovers, but it's kind of you to offer."

He wouldn't have thought of that, but he certainly wasn't opposed to doing it. "They could probably use a pizza. I know I would've preferred it at their age. We can also give them an update on their granddad once you've seen your mom."

"That would be wonderful." She looked miserable but sounded grateful.

He went to the desk to be directed to the intensive care unit. Coming here brought back memories of his father's death that he didn't want to revisit, but it wasn't as if he hadn't been back a couple of times since then. Once for a broken wrist when he'd been handling an unruly cow. On a later occasion it was because he'd had to admit his stomach pain was getting worse; they ended up removing his appendix.

All in all, though, he'd just as soon skip hospitals.

The friendly woman at the reception desk pointed him in the right direction and they hurried over to find Danielle's mother, Louise, in the waiting area, white-faced and exhausted. The community was small, so Drake saw her now and then at different events, and she looked as if she'd aged about ten years since they'd last run into each other. That was at the fall farmers' market, where he'd obligingly stopped to buy some pumpkins for the front porch. Picking out pumpkins wasn't really one of his skills, but his mother had asked him to do it. Louise had been there, and she'd helped him. She'd been his first-grade teacher, and at one time, he'd envisioned a future with her daughter. So they did have some history.

After she and Danielle had hugged, he asked gently, "How's Walter doing?"

"He's going through bypass surgery. He's in serious condition, but stable." Louise wiped her eyes. "He's always been so healthy. He's never even had a cold that I can recall."

"I know," Drake said. Danielle's father was a cattleman through and through. "He's tough. Remember that." He paused. "This is Luce Hale. We can stop by the house and check on the grandkids, if you want. We're glad to help in any way we can."

Louise smiled weakly and acknowledged Luce with a nod, then said, "I'd appreciate your looking in on the children. Please remind them to feed my cat. He's getting old. He needs medication for his joints and it has to be sprinkled on his food. So if you could—"

"Done."

He wanted to help, as he'd said, but he also wanted to get the heck out of this shell-shocked environment. Luce didn't say anything at all until they got back to the truck. When she'd clicked her seat belt in place, she finally spoke. "I hope you understand that I'm both confused and impressed by your sense of self. Or maybe more to the point, your sense of selflessness. Your kindness and generosity."

There was no real response to that in his estimation. He chose "Ah."

She reached over, gave his arm a squeeze. Her tone was light, but her expression was serious. "Listen to me, Carson. You can handle anything without blinking an eye. This has been one crazy evening and you just seem to take it in stride."

"What else are you supposed to do? Could you order that pizza? Let's say half sausage and half pepperoni. Leave the vegetables off, since some kids like 'em and others don't... Have I mentioned I hate lima beans? Don't ever serve them to me, please."

"Have I mentioned that I don't cook? You aren't in any danger of lima beans and I've never heard of them on pizza."

She *hadn't* mentioned that she didn't cook, but then, this could only be described as a whirlwind romance. They hadn't had time to talk about details—important ones—like that.

"I think lima bean pizza might be a big hit in certain circles," he said, realizing his life had dramatically changed this evening, "but I'm not destined to be a fan, and I can pretty much guarantee those kids won't be, either. So let's stick to the pepperoni and sausage variety. The number's in my phone."

"With Harry there, you still buy pizza?"

Legitimate question. "I sure do. Lunch for the hands once in a while. She deserves some time off."

"And when she fixes you lima beans?" Luce was laughing as she took his phone.

"I eat them," he admitted, "but not happily. She makes this thing called lima bean stew that both of my brothers love, so she serves it fairly often. Tomatoes, onions, whatever else is in there I like, but not the lima beans."

"The things we do not know about each other." She pressed a button and a moment later ordered a thick-crust pizza from the only decent place nearby.

When they'd picked it up, he drove to Louise and Walter's house. To his dismay, he saw a car parked outside—a car he recognized. He somehow doubted Reed was welcome at the house where Danielle had grown up, but at least he was paying attention to his children.

He told Luce, "I wish we hadn't offered to deliver the pizza because that's Reed's car. Danielle's soon-to-be ex. He and I don't like each other. Not exactly a state secret. I should warn you. Reed probably won't be very cordial."

"I'm getting the impression he's not what you'd call a prince."

"You have no idea."

"I have some idea. Danielle's very...what's the word? *Downtrodden* might work."

He hated that, too. The Danielle he remembered was bright and beautiful, with high hopes and a buoyant disposition. The woman he'd seen tonight bore almost no resemblance to that memory, and he disliked seeing the unhappiness in her eyes.

Reed, of course, met them at the door.

Luce was a good judge of people, or in any case, she thought she was, and the man staring them down didn't impress her. He was nice-looking with dark brown hair and regular features, wearing what she was starting to think of as the typical Mustang Creek uniform of jeans, boots and a button-up shirt. But he wasn't friendly, as Drake predicted. He leaned against the doorjamb with one shoulder and crossed his arms in a classic gesture of defiance. "Oh, look, it's Romeo. My wife called our son and said you were coming. May I ask why?"

Luce instantly understood why Drake resented hearing the Romeo nickname from certain people.

To his credit, Drake ignored the open animosity. "Just dropping this off. Ran into Danielle at the restaurant when she got the news about her dad. She wasn't sure what the kids would eat. I figured one less worry would be good."

"Knight in shining armor, huh? I always wondered if she'd leave me for you. When Danielle said she wanted a divorce, you were the first reason that came to mind. We split up and a few weeks later she runs straight to you. How long have you two been seeing each other?"

Luce was conscious of two things. One, that the man had been drinking, and two, that fists could easily come into this conversation. They were about the same height and weight. Reed Keller might be impaired, but he was also very angry. A risky combination.

"We haven't," Drake said flatly. "At all."

"I don't believe you. She's been seeing someone."

"I don't care if you believe me or not. Your marriage failed, but I had nothing to do with it." Calm as ever, Drake held out the cardboard box. "Before you get belligerent, have I mentioned this is my fiancée? Give your kids the pizza. Tell them their grandfather's in stable condition."

Danielle's husband seemed to notice Luce for the first time. He said sardonically, "You going to get married to him, Ms. Whoever-you-are? Save yourself and don't. That's my advice. I don't care who it is, Carson or not. Just… don't."

Drake didn't exactly drag Luce down the sidewalk, but almost. She was surprised he didn't pick her up and carry her; maybe he wanted to keep his hands free for a fight.

When they were back in the truck, he started the engine and muttered, "That actually went better than I expected."

"You've got to be kidding me! I was ready to call 911. That guy is a real jerk," Luce said. "How did she live with him for so long?"

They pulled away from the curb. Drake took a moment to answer, the streetlights outlining his profile. "He isn't always a jerk. I don't like him, but that's a problem between him and me. In case you couldn't tell, he doesn't like me, either. He got her pregnant, but he did marry her. Yes, he wanted her to stay home, not go back to school and not work. I guess he was pretty controlling. But…she made her own choice, too. She's smart, so she knew—to some extent, anyway—what she was buying into when she married Reed. As far as I know, her family didn't pressure her to do it, even though she was pregnant. And I don't think he's ever lifted a hand to her or his kids, because around here I would've heard about it. I'm not a fan, but what you saw tonight was a guy whose wife is determined to divorce him and he's apparently hurting because of it."

Luce still felt rattled by the acrimonious exchange. After a moment, she asked, "You always so fair-minded?"

"I was just assessing the situation. Being rational. Looking at both sides."

He meant it, she knew he did. "She made a poor decision. Choosing between you and him? I should've said a *very* poor decision."

"I hope so. Since *you* agreed to marry me."

She had. It still felt surreal.

He went on. "Yet I think you were just advised *that* might be a poor decision. Let's not talk about how I dragged you off to take an ex-girlfriend to the hospital. The night is young. Who knows what might happen next?"

It'd been an eventful evening. He'd had only one glass of wine, while she'd had two, and she was feeling uninhibited. "My bedroom or yours?"

"I like that plan. The evening's looking up again. Either one. You pick."

"Whichever isn't going to draw attention to the fact that we're spending the night together."

"It doesn't matter. We've discussed this before. We're both consenting adults." His sidelong glance was brief but held a world of meaning.

"Your mother talks to my mother and I want them both to approve of me." She confessed what was hardly a secret. "I know, I'm a grown woman and all, but I'm not promiscuous and I'd rather not be viewed that way."

Drake broke out laughing. "No one, sweetheart, would *ever* view you that way. Luce, you're the quintessential nice girl. Why else would I fall so hard?"

It was probably his way of explaining that she'd betrayed the fact that she wasn't very experienced in bed. She couldn't decide if she was chagrined by his comment or not. "I suppose that's a compliment."

"I'm in love with you. I asked you to marry me. What do you think? I like everything about you."

That made it better. Sort of. Should she protest the "nice girl" label or live with it? "Talking about nice... You're just as guilty. You were even decent to Danielle's husband when he accused you of having an affair with her."

"I told him the truth. Married women are off-limits in my book."

"Cowboy code, huh?"

He shrugged. "My code, anyway. Straight from the chapter titled 'Things to Do and Not to Do So You Can Still Look at Yourself in the Mirror.' You don't steal a man's horse and you don't steal a man's wife."

Luce laughed. "I'm going to guess the horse is more important."

He grinned in response. "Damn straight. You can live without a wife, but you need a horse."

"Hmm, I'll keep that in mind. Starburst first, me second. I'm trying to come up with a name for the new man in *my* life."

He took his eyes off the road for a second to glance at her. "The foal? He's not yours quite yet, but I'll work on it. Why are you so convinced it's a colt and not a filly?"

"I just am. What do you think of Tinkerbell?"

He turned onto the county road toward the ranch. "That's cruel. Poor horse couldn't hold up his head. Try again."

"Precious?" She couldn't keep a straight face.

"Oh, yeah. Now we're headed in the right direction. Better than Tinkerbell, anyway. Try again."

"What about Moonflower?"

"I'll knit him a skirt to go with that one."

"*You* know how to knit?"

"Hey, I have a lot of hidden talents. Actually, no to the knitting. But if you name that horse Moonflower, I'll learn."

This was one of the reasons she'd fallen in love with him. Grace was right; he was so funny in a droll way. Luce got serious. "I was kind of thinking Fire."

"As in, where there's smoke there's fire? Not a bad choice. And if it's a filly, that should still work. I like it."

They drove into the lane. The front porch light glowed as the house came into view in the distance. Her pulse had already started to accelerate, and she sincerely hoped no one was sitting there, reading a book and sipping tea. It really wasn't all that late.

Luckily, the porch was deserted when Drake parked the truck. As always, he hurried to open her door, but when she got out, he kissed her with a passionate hunger—a preview of what was about to happen. "We never settled this. My room," he murmured against her mouth. "I get up early. It's at the opposite end of the house so I won't disturb anyone."

She didn't care where they went. "Fine with me. Just don't pick me up and carry me in, please. I can tell you're thinking about that, and if we passed anyone in the hall, I'd be mortified for the rest of my life."

He admitted with a wicked smile, "You know me. I *was* thinking that might be faster, but okay."

CHAPTER SEVENTEEN

LUCE DISCARDED HER SWEATER, an action he found sexy as hell. Anticipating the rest of the outfit's removal had him on edge—and he was more than willing to help her get naked.

"Let me unzip your dress." He didn't wait for an answer, taking her shoulders and turning her around, sliding down the zipper.

He pressed his mouth to the nape of her neck, lifting all that silky hair out of the way. Her back was beautiful, smooth and feminine, and as he traced her spine with his fingertips, she gave a sexy little shiver.

She didn't comment on the minimal decor in his room. Bed, dresser, lamp and one comfortable armchair—that was it for him. It wasn't as though he hung out there much. The quilt with its mountain theme he'd bought from Hadleigh, and there was a pegged rack for his hat and coat, as well as a handwoven brown rug, but otherwise he'd kept it pretty simple. She turned around to face him. "Kiss me."

No way could he resist *that* invitation, especially when

she was so irresistible in a slinky bra and barely there panties. He really kissed her. A "this is the night we got engaged" kiss. In about a minute they were on the bed and
she was busy unbuttoning his shirt. To his mind this was
how it was supposed to be. Both so attracted it was inevitable, like the sun coming up on the horizon.

They made love in a breathless rush of desire and new-
found emotion and ended up damp and twined together.
Pleasure had taken on a whole new dimension. He wasn't
possessive, but he sure as hell wanted to keep her in his life.

She touched him. "I could get used to this."

"Sex?" He relaxed with her in his arms. "Oh, count
me in."

"I meant just being with you."

He tried for lighthearted, but he couldn't quite manage
it. "That works." Then he cleared his throat. "Luce, after
we go to California, I want you to come back to Wyoming
with me. How can we figure this out?"

He shouldn't have pushed. She drew back, and her body
tensed. "I have to finish this degree. I'm doing it for myself and I don't know if you understand this, but I've spent
a lifetime trying to please my parents and friends. This is
for *me*. You love what you do. I want that. I'm happy about
being a wife, but I want to be more than that, too. I don't
want to wind up—I don't know—like Danielle, working
at some job because I need it, not because I love the work."
She paused, shook her head. "Not that there's anything
wrong with waiting tables—that isn't what I meant—and
I'm not implying that you'd ever..." Finally, in a despair-
ing gesture, she threw up her hands. "I want to teach students about ecology, inspire the kind of awareness that

might save a species, or even the planet… You of all people know how I feel."

He absorbed her words, let her settle down a little.

"I hear what you're saying," he said after several minutes. Then he raked a hand through his hair, his other arm tightening around her. "How long will it take to finish your degree?" he asked.

"Until December."

He winced. "Ouch," he said. "I'm not sure I can be away from you that long."

"Mr. Carson, that might be the best thing you've said to me since the day we met." She playfully ran a finger along his stomach. "Maybe the university will let me do most of the remaining course work online. But I need to do this, one way or another."

Luce's tenacity was one of the qualities he loved most about her. He moved back onto her warm body. "It can't be December," he said, only half teasing. "We'll have to figure out something else."

She gave him a twinkly smile. "Think about a Christmas wedding."

"I'm thinking about a Christmas wedding night."

"I can tell that you are." She stretched suggestively beneath him.

He kissed her throat. "Will your parents like me?"

She laughed. "My mother will, for sure. She's one of the scheme team, remember? And my father will be okay with my choice of husband, since you've never been in prison and you're gainfully employed. Dad's priorities are simple." She touched an index finger to his mouth when he raised his head. "And my sister will adore you—I think she already does. Beth is a free spirit, so be prepared."

He cupped her breast, stroking her nipple. "I'm adaptable. My father told me once that ranch life forces you to change the game plan in no time flat. One minute you've got sunny skies, the next pouring rain. A dust storm could follow. You just never know."

She gazed up at him. "You still miss him a lot, don't you?"

"Yeah." He exchanged his caressing thumb for a flick of his tongue, not sure this was the moment to talk about his dad—although he'd brought the subject up. Luckily, she sensed his feelings and left it alone.

"I like your room. It's very...serene."

If she was willing, he was in the mood for a repeat performance of what they'd just done. "Feel free to stop by anytime. This is a room with a beautiful view."

"It doesn't face the mountains."

"I was talking about right now and I'm not looking out the window but at you."

She did that cute thing and blushed. "Nicely done. And I'm looking back at you, by the way."

"I think I noticed that."

"I thought you might have." She arched into his caress. "Maybe we should stop staring at each other and get down to business. Again."

"Yes, ma'am. You're insatiable. I like that."

"Only when it comes to you."

Only you. This wasn't the time to talk about her romantic history. Or his. They'd had enough of the past tonight with Danielle. It was an interesting experience to fall in love again, older and wiser. As a teenager, his psyche had processed information very differently. Lust colliding with immature emotion wasn't a good combination. This time, at least, he was aware of what he wanted and needed—as a man and not a boy.

"I love you." He wasn't really telling her; he was telling himself with a sense of wonder. "I can't believe it."

"Thanks." She urged him closer. "If I didn't know what you meant, I might've taken offense."

He kissed her again. "I just never thought I'd feel this way."

"This *is* going awfully fast," she whispered.

"I hope you aren't insulting my stamina."

She laughed. "So far, no complaints in that department."

"And I'll do my best to keep it that way." He shoved back the tangled sheets so he could see her better. "Can we have our wedding soon? Location doesn't matter to me."

"Um, just keep doing that and you won't hear any argument from me."

He did as he was told. She wasn't voluptuous, but those graceful curves were so feminine, so perfect... He stroked her intimately. "This?"

"Exactly. Don't stop what you're doing."

As if he would. "You have my word."

"I THINK I NEED to write a chapter in *The Cowboy Guide to a Successful Relationship*." Luce was limp in his arms after another earth-shattering climax, resting against Drake's chest. "Can I coauthor it with you?"

"Oh, I'm dying to know what your chapter would be titled."

"'Cowboys Are Not as Simple as They Seem.'"

"Oh, thanks. I'm not happy we seem simple in the first place."

"What I mean is that you're so straightforward, but

you're also sensitive. For that matter, Red is, too, along with Slater and Mace. You love animals, you'd do anything for your family, you rescue damsels in distress—"

He interrupted her. "I think you've been reading too many fairy tales."

"Okay, I loved them when I was a kid, but that's beside the point."

Although the moon was no longer full, light spilled in through the window, which had no drapes. He might not have a view of the mountains, but stars were visible in a vast sky and it was utterly quiet except for the far-off lowing of cattle.

Whatever she might have said next was interrupted by someone knocking on the door with alarming urgency.

"Drake." Male voice and it didn't sound happy.

Quickly Drake jumped up to grab his jeans. "Be right there!" he called.

Luce dived under the sheets. It was one thing if people knew she and Drake had been sleeping together, but quite another to be caught bare-ass naked in his bed.

Red opened the door. "Let's go. Right now. We've got trouble."

Drake didn't hesitate but picked up his shirt and thrust his arms into the sleeves. "Bad?"

"I'm hardly going to roust you out of bed otherwise, son." Red sounded grim. "Sorry to bust in like this, Luce."

Luce nodded. "Anything I can do to help?" she asked tentatively.

"Maybe. An extra pair of hands never hurts. Don't wear your favorite dress or anything. We'll be out front. Grab a towel and his cell phone, will you?"

Actually, one of her favorite dresses was the only thing

available. She waited until the door shut behind Drake and then slipped into it. She didn't bother with her perfect matching shoes because something in Red's voice told her this was not a perfect situation at all.

She found Drake's cell on the nightstand, ran into the bathroom for a towel and dashed out the door. She wondered if she needed a jacket, since it had started to cool off, and then didn't care when she opened the front door and saw the blood.

All over the front porch.

Harold was on his side. He was licking Drake's hand, but he wasn't moving in any other way. The big German shepherd's fur was matted with blood. Drake said tersely, "Luce, call Jax Locke. It's in my contacts. Tell him to get here right away. I mean *right* away. Throw the towel over to Red, please. This dog's been mauled pretty bad."

Luce's hands were shaking, although Drake appeared calm.

She found the number, got referred to a service and left a message, but about thirty seconds later, the phone rang back. Dr. Locke said, "Drake? What's going on?"

"I—I'm... Luce Hale...his fiancée." She was stammering. "Something...it must've been big, maybe a mountain lion, got hold of Drake's dog. There's a lot of blood."

"Harold? On my way. You guys tell the dog to hang in there. I mean it. Animals understand."

Drake was already doing that, talking softly to the dog, crooning words of encouragement. She was almost more worried about him than Harold—not to mention Red. Both of them were on their knees next to the dog, who was wrapped in the towel. Blythe came out, tying her robe. "I was still up reading and heard voices." Then she caught sight of Harold and gasped. "What's going on... Oh, no! Have you called—"

"He's on his way." Drake's voice cracked. "Let's hope he can do something. I just asked Red and there's no trace of Violet. I'm thinking that big cat got a little too close to the house. Dogs spook them. But mountain lions don't usually act this way. Something is off here."

Red shook his head. "I was asleep. I heard a commotion that woke me out of a sound sleep, like when a Canadian clipper starts wailing through the trees. I ran out of the stable and found Harold like this about five feet from the porch. Brave guy."

"No Violet?" Blythe looked as if she might cry but was struggling against it. Luce was having the same problem.

"Perhaps she's hiding," Luce suggested.

Blythe hugged her. "Yes, let's hope so."

There was an unspoken message between them. *Or else Drake will be devastated and neither of us can take it, and...*

"No Violet." Red looked tired but confirmed it. "I've called and called that dog. She's feisty and maybe the fight stirred her up. She's smaller than Harold, but she might've chased that lion right up the mountain."

"It's possible." Drake glanced over at them. Luce recognized that remote expression. There was blood on his forearms and his T-shirt, even smeared on his face. He was doing his best to hide his response and act calm, but he wasn't. Luce could tell he was shaken. She was, too.

It seemed to take forever as they waited, but she suspected maybe a new record was being set for traveling the distance between Mustang Creek and the ranch.

Headlights shone up the drive, and within a minute of skidding to a halt, a young man was out of the car and dashing up the porch steps. He stopped for a second, looking at the dog and all the blood. "Oh…damn it. You weren't exaggerating."

Drake was petting Harold's head, soothing him. "I know. Just do your best, Jax. Thanks for coming out right away. We didn't want to move him too much."

Locke snapped on disposable gloves and went to kneel by Harold. The dog whined as he was examined, but it was a weak sound at best. "Good call on not moving him more than necessary. I have to stitch him up and give him a couple shots, but he's a big dog, and in my opinion, he'll survive this. We'll have to wait and see. Bad news is it'll take a little time. Where's his sidekick?"

"Violet is missing."

Locke paused, frowning at them. "That's bad."

Blythe offered a timorous suggestion, repeating what Luce had said earlier. "Maybe she's hiding?"

"Shepherds don't usually hide, Mrs. Carson. Anyway, I don't think she'd leave Harold."

It was true. Luce had never seen one of those dogs without the other.

Drake got up and walked away for a minute, his expression once again remote. Both Luce and Blythe let him go. Red said forcefully, "I'm going to grab my rifle and go look for her. I'm useless right now and I don't like the feeling. The doc's already here, so if she's hurt and we can find her, we can do something about it."

Luce said instantly and ridiculously, "I'll go with you."

"Like hell you will." Drake had apparently needed a minute to collect himself; he stalked back up onto the porch. "Luce, you're barefoot and wearing a dress, and even if you were wearing a suit of armor, I don't want to risk you getting hurt. Stay here and help Jax. Red and I will go out. Mom, can you get the big flashlights, please? I'm going to get my rifle as well and wake up Slate and Mace."

Blythe went inside with alacrity and Luce might have resented his commanding tone, but she didn't know what to do and Drake was probably right. She'd be more of a hindrance than anything. She did say, "I want to help."

"Then do it like I said, by staying put. I have enough problems at the moment. I'm worried about how this animal is acting. Harold and Violet wouldn't have tangled with it if they hadn't felt there was a threat. If Red found Harold a few feet from the porch, the animal came right up to the house. Not normal mountain lion behavior. And listen to me, if you think you're going anywhere out there alone after what happened tonight, you're dead wrong. My mother isn't setting foot outside, either, not by herself, until we get this situation taken care of."

Normally, she would've argued, but she was starting to think he was right. He disappeared inside and came back a couple of minutes later with his brothers. He'd thrown on a clean shirt and washed his face. All three of them had rifles.

Slater and Mace swore out loud when they saw Harold, their faces grim.

Luce was an animal lover through and through, and she didn't want them to kill the lion, but she also knew they needed to stay safe. She knew Drake well enough now to know he didn't want to kill it, either, but his mother was a slender woman who was also an avid gardener. She was often outside, alone, tending to the flowers and the herbs she planted every spring for Harry, and Luce was truly getting an education about the realities of ranch life.

Jax Locke was still working on the dog and, without

looking up, said, "Priority one is finding Violet, but be careful. That cat did not get off uninjured. Not all this blood is Harold's. I'd usually trust this dog not to bite me, but I sedated him, anyway. I don't have to tell you that injured animals are hard to handle. And that also means your already dangerous friend out there isn't going to be happy."

"I'm pretty unhappy myself." Drake jerked his head toward the stables. "Let's go."

At that moment Luce jumped up and caught his arm, just before his foot hit the top step. "Hold on. Did you hear that? Listen! I swear I heard a dog bark."

They all went still, and just when she thought she'd delayed them for nothing, it came again, faint in the distance. Not a coyote or a wolf, but a dog. Even after her short time in Wyoming, she knew the difference.

"That's her bark. I'd know it anywhere. Thanks." Drake gave Luce's hand a grateful squeeze before all three Carson brothers ran down the steps, hell-bent for leather, as Red would say.

CHAPTER EIGHTEEN

"North."

Drake agreed with Slater and had already turned Starburst in that direction. "Yep."

He wished there was still that romantic full moon, but it was waning and the night was pretty damned dark. At least they could follow the sound, which meant they didn't need to search every inch of terrain. If she could bark, Violet was alive. He was damned fond of that dog, so he wanted to keep her that way. Harold was bigger, so he probably went after the cat first, but Violet was as quick as lightning.

He felt for her. If the mountain lion had hurt Harold, she'd go after it. That was the only reason she'd ever leave him.

They rode by the west pasture, then slowed to see if they could hear her She wasn't much of a barker unless it was necessary, so when it came again, he figured it *was* necessary.

"She's got it cornered somewhere," Red said with conviction. "There's nothing like hunting a big cat in the dark to let a man know if he's got fire or just smoke in his britches."

Drake might have laughed if he wasn't so worried. He'd have to use that one on Luce someday. She'd probably accuse him of freestyling again.

"I know that dog," Drake muttered. "She's fighting mad. Tomorrow I'm calling Ed Gunnerson. He's handled relocating lions before. Man, between this critter and the wild horses, you'd think we'd issued some sort of open invitation to ruin my peace of mind."

"But those horses also brought you a gift, son," Red said in a dry tone. "Unless I'm mistaken, you weren't exactly alone when I knocked on your bedroom door."

Slater murmured, "Why does that not surprise me?"

"We're getting married." Drake was spared having to say anything else, since Violet barked again and this time it was close enough that Mace unsheathed his rifle.

His younger brother said pragmatically, "I'm the best shot. You all manage the situation and I'll be ready if it goes south. Not anxious to do it, but I will."

He was right. Mace was the most accurate marksman Drake had ever seen. It just came naturally, like brewing up those concoctions of his. He had a very focused mind.

"Deal," Drake said. Violet always obeyed him, but on the other hand, this was a different scenario. Normally, he'd just whistle for her. But he was worried that if she turned around to come to him, the injured lion might attack her. At least Mace was likely to hit the target effectively—if it had to happen, which none of them wanted. At one time Mace had contemplated the military to become a sniper or law enforcement for a SWAT team position. He was really that good.

When they finally found the dog, she had, as they'd predicted, treed the big cat. Listening to Violet's ominous growling, Drake wasn't surprised that the mountain lion stayed put on a large branch about twenty feet up, although it was snarling right back.

"Violet, come." He could tell she didn't want to, but she trotted toward him with no apparent injuries except a long bloody scratch on the top of her head. His heart twisted at the sight of her, and at the same time, relief washed over him like a flood tide.

"What do you want me to do?" Mace asked. All three of Drake's companions looked at him expectantly. His ranch to run, so his problem to solve. Just like the wild horses. His brother added, "I don't have a clear shot."

"I'm reluctant to kill it," Drake replied.

Even with the powerful flashlights, the animal was difficult to see because of the foliage, but they knew where it was.

"He's going to continue to be a pain in your backside," Red pointed out, sitting his horse with the ease of an old cowboy. "I understand your position—that critter up there is just doing what comes naturally—but now's your chance."

He was right. However, it *felt* wrong. The animal needed to go, but relocation seemed a much better option.

"Let me talk to Ed," he said finally. "He's handled this kind of thing before. After what this cat did to Harold, you'd think I'd be inclined to tell Mace to give it a try. But if we can handle it another way, I'd prefer that."

"Your call." Slater sounded as calm as usual. "I don't

want to have to kill it, either. Although I'm going to walk my pregnant wife out to her car every morning until we fix this. After that run-in with the dogs, I doubt the cat will come near the house again, but who knows. I wouldn't have expected it to in the first place."

"Yeah, who knows what it'll do." Red thoughtfully rubbed his chin. "Had a friend with a cabin on Big Pine Lake and he said he woke one morning and there was the biggest bear he'd ever seen looking in the window, eyeing him up. About gave that die-hard ole cowboy a heart attack, and I can tell you, he doesn't scare easy."

Red had a story for every occasion, including, of course, this one. Drake said wryly, "I hope he's still alive and well." When Red grinned, giving him a thumbs-up, Drake added, "Good to know. I plan to emerge from all of this in the same condition. Let's just take Violet home. I'm not sure if Jax needs to stitch that wound on her head or not."

Red nodded. "Looks like she could maybe heal on her own, but if we aren't going to end the battle right now, we might as well go home, boss. Hey, girl, let's go see Harold."

Violet followed, wagging her tail, and the rest of them fell into line.

Red always called him *boss*, but Drake had to acknowledge that they had a careful balance of wisdom and authority between them, and he rarely ignored what Red had to say. Part of it was that he knew Red was as worried about both dogs as he was. Red was also a lot more sentimental than he let on.

When they got to the house, every single woman in residence was hovering over the injured dog. Harry wore an impossibly old bathrobe, while his mother, Grace and Luce were all fully dressed. Harold rested in a corner of the veranda, and Jax Locke immediately abandoned a cup of coffee, got to his feet and crossed the room to examine Violet. "Thank God you found her," he said. "Come here, girl—let's have a look at you."

The dog moved slowly as she approached Jax, but she seemed sound. In the end, all Violet needed was first aid, a shot of antibiotics and some loving attention.

Drake took Luce's elbow as everyone else went back into the house. As she looked at him questioningly, he pulled her close and said, "Get some rest. I'm going to grab a sleeping bag and stay out here on the porch with Harold and Violet. In his condition, Harold can't make it to my room and I don't want to move him. You can go back to my bed or use yours."

"I'm sleeping out here with you."

How did he know she'd say that? He had a feeling he was going to suffer from acute exasperation—and crazy, grateful love—for the rest of his life. "Why would you want to do that, Luce? Isn't a comfortable bed more appealing than a hard floor?"

She ran her fingers lightly through his hair. "I'd just lie awake and worry about you and the dogs, but if you were right next to me, I might be able to get some shut-eye, buckaroo."

For a moment, Drake hesitated, torn between wanting Luce beside him and wanting her to be safe inside the house. He didn't think the cat would be back tonight—or ever, for that matter—and if it did show up again, Violet would let him know. His rifle was within easy reach, too.

He could protect Luce—and the dogs—if he had to.

Anyway, it was a given that the determined Ms. Hale

would do as she damned well pleased, regardless of what he said.

He was sure of one thing—come hell or high water, he wasn't leaving Harold.

So he shrugged. "Suit yourself."

I'm camping out on the porch of a Western mansion with a handsome cowboy and a dog who was mauled by a mountain lion.

LUCE SENT THE TEXT to Beth's phone, then grabbed a pillow from her bed. That message would have her sister calling her back first thing in the morning, if not before. Beth was the queen of tantalizing texts such as: At mall and hoping I don't get arrested for murder.

The explanation for that one turned out to be about a purse she'd ordered, a hard-to-find item in a "positively delicious" color. When Beth went to pick up her bag, she discovered that a clerk at the expensive boutique had accidentally sold it to someone else. In the end, she bought the same purse—in black—at a discount store. Beth might have loved the original purse, but she was nothing if not practical.

Introducing Drake to her family was going to be interesting. His down-to-earth, sensible approach to life was not how she'd grown up, that was for sure. However... Blythe and her mother were lifelong friends, and Blythe had certainly married, by all accounts, a true Wyoming cowboy. She'd left California, where her wealthy family was as close to royalty as anybody could get, and settled into her new life. Luce had met Drake's sophisticated grandfather a couple of times. She highly doubted he could—or would—saddle up a horse and go after a mountain lion to save a dog.

Drake had laid out two sleeping bags on the porch floor. He was already half-asleep and she was tired, too, so she crawled into hers. The events of the evening piled up in her mind.

"Hmm," he said, draping one arm over her. "We aren't likely to forget *this* night."

Violet, lying next to Harold in his makeshift bed, lifted her head at the sound of Drake's voice. Luce replied, "I agree with that."

"We could have killed it." His face was shadowed and he looked weary. "I opted not to do it. I think we have a young rogue cougar that's just discovered a convenient food source. A lot of ranchers have had this problem."

"Some take the low road."

"Who could blame them? All of us considered bringing down the cat. One shot and it would be over, problem solved. Fact is, there are *some people* I wouldn't mind wiping off the face of the earth, but I'm more tolerant of animals. Most people know when they're committing a crime."

That pro-animal attitude of his was part of the reason she'd fallen for him. "I support that decision."

He spoke quietly enough not to disturb Harold, who was still sleeping off the sedative. "We're not going to be that couple with twelve dogs and fourteen cats, are we?"

"No." She shook her head. "It's too heartbreaking to lose one. How's he doing, anyway?"

"Harold? Violet will tell me if there's something wrong. He's a ranch dog. He's been hurt before. Not like this, of course, but he's had his share of injuries. Jax is a very good vet, and he wouldn't have left if he was worried. We got lucky when he moved to Mustang Creek. I trust him."

She did, too. Dr. Locke was obviously competent and empathetic, but forthright. It was heart-wrenching to see Violet standing guard over her injured sibling, but also heartwarming. Luce understood why Drake had decided to sleep outside, because Violet would be torn between her loyalty to him and her need to protect Harold. This way was much easier. It made sense for his dogs—and that was important to Drake.

Luce was surprisingly comfortable in her sleeping bag. The night sounds were soothing, the stars twinkled and the air smelled fresh and clean. While Drake might get a few hours of rest, she doubted he'd actually sleep.

On the other hand, she was exhausted. "Hmm, tell me a bedtime story."

His laugh was muffled. "What?"

He looked all cowboy, with his mussed-up blond hair and his arms now linked behind his head. Getting a pillow obviously hadn't even occurred to him.

"You know," she murmured, "the kind of story that helps kids doze off. I'm so tired I'm not sure I can sleep. I need a story."

"If you're looking for *The Princess and the Pea*, I'm afraid I don't really remember that one."

At least she'd coaxed a smile out of him. "Just make something up."

"You do realize you're pretty high maintenance."

"Not compared to my sister. Have a beer with my brother-in-law and see if he doesn't agree. Come on now, you can invent some yarn. You know Red, for heaven's sake. Has he taught you nothing?"

"I believe he told me when I was about fourteen to steer clear of women because they're a pain in the ass."

Luce jabbed his shoulder. "I didn't notice you feeling that way earlier this evening."

He clasped her hand and kissed each finger in turn. "I don't feel that way now, either. Nice of you to keep me company. Story? Okay, I'll give it a try. Let's see. Once upon a time—"

"You'll have to do better than that, Carson. Not very original." She liked being close to him, even though they were in separate sleeping bags. He grinned. "Hey, give me a chance. I've had an eventful evening. Okay, I'll start over, since you have such exacting standards. How about… Once, out on the range, there was this innocent, unsuspecting cowboy, minding his own damn business."

She couldn't help commenting, although she really was dozing off. "A good start," she mumbled, "but if you're referring to yourself, I don't think *innocent* applies."

"Do you want to hear the story or not?" His thumb stroked her wrist.

"I'm on the edge of my sleeping bag." And snuggled in with her comfy pillow and Drake right next to her. He wasn't the only one who'd had an eventful evening.

"I'm going to ignore that comment. Anyway, this extraordinarily good-looking and talented cowpoke ran afoul of a willful woman—and all hell broke loose."

Luce made a sound that could be described as a snort. "I think *extraordinarily* is a bit over the top. However, I might buy *noticeably*."

He went blithely on. "She seduced him with her hair. Sort of like that Rapunzel girl who lived in the tower. You know the one I'm talking about?"

He loved her hair? She really was drifting off. "Uh-huh."

"But a wise old bowlegged wizard warned him she might put a hitch in his normally peaceful existence and the darned fool didn't listen to what was plain common sense. He got involved with her, anyway."

"Maybe the cowpoke was stubborn and hardheaded."

"Hey, who's telling this story?" Drake ran his finger over the curve of her right brow.

"You are."

"That's what I thought. So, anyway, he wants to ignore her, but he can't. He *wants* to, mind you, but he just...can't."

"Noble of him."

"I think so. He was trying not to take advantage of her."

"What made him think he could?"

"She looked at him a certain way."

"Oh, I see, a love at first sight story."

"Ha-ha. Could be, I guess. Want me to keep going? You seem to be down for the count."

"No, no, I'm still awake."

Drake laughed softly. "Yeah, I can tell."

It was the last thing she remembered.

CHAPTER NINETEEN

HE HAD MYRIAD problems to solve.

Luce slept next to him with her face turned away and, between her and Harold, he doubted he'd close his eyes. So he'd resigned himself to a sleepless night.

Fine with him. He needed to figure things out.

He might've made a mistake by not telling Mace to end the issue with the big cat, but a man had to live with himself. Luce's entire thesis centered on how people and wild animals interacted and, in principle, anyway, he thought they could usually respect each other and achieve a balance.

But...not always. Animals were as individual as human beings. They had their routines and habits, and the lion had to go. He'd decided that last night. It wasn't about vengeance; he knew the critter was operating on instinct, but he couldn't risk letting it roam free. He had to think about the livestock.

Hell, he had to think about *people*.

Harold stirred and Violet was immediately on alert, as

was Drake. Part of the reason he was sleeping outside was to make sure the dog didn't hurt himself by getting up too soon. Harold truly was a ranch dog, used to working. The possibility that he'd struggle to his feet once the sedative wore off was very real.

Drake said quietly, "I'm here."

The dog settled back down. Maybe it was sentimental, but he wanted to be there when Harold woke up in the morning.

He wasn't the only one, as it happened.

Slater wandered out with a blanket and feigned a yawn. There was a reason he was a producer and not an actor—he couldn't fake a damn thing. "Can't sleep, and I didn't want to keep Grace awake, tossing and turning. Thought I might camp out here for a while."

Luce stirred but didn't wake. Drake stifled a laugh. "You were checking on Harold, weren't you? Make yourself comfortable, if that's possible. How long do you think before Mace shows up?"

"Two minutes, tops. I met him in the hall." Slater slapped down his blanket and sank on top of it. "He was trying to pretend he wasn't coming this way. Hmph."

"Slate," Drake said, "if you're going for casual, it isn't working."

"We're brothers. Therefore, I'm worried about you *and* the dog. Hell, Drake, all of us love Harold—even if his name is a mite on the stupid side."

Drake ignored the name comment. He had his reasons for calling his dogs what he did. "He just came to. Tried to get up, then changed his mind."

His older brother relaxed. "You know," he said, "it's kind of nice out here. I haven't done this in a while." He sighed companionably. "I remember sleeping out here a lot when we were kids. I'll never forget the night you and Mace got into it over a candy bar we'd snitched from Harry's stash in the pantry. While the two of you were brawling, I ate it myself—for the sake of peace and goodwill."

"Mace was just as annoying back then as he is now," Drake said. "We probably would've duked it out over something else, if not that chocolate bar."

"Who's annoying?" Sure enough, it was Mace, dropping his bedroll to the floor of the veranda.

"You are."

He shook his head in mock disgust. "Talking about me behind my back," he muttered. "I thought better of you." He executed a yawn only slightly more convincing than Slater's had been. "How's Harold? I came to keep him company."

"He's holding on," Drake said.

A moment later, their mother came out, too, toting a blanket and a pillow. She surveyed the now-crowded porch with a resigned look on her face. "Nobody mentioned a family campout," she said. "I'd think *one* of you might have invited me."

"This seems to be a drop-in kind of deal," Mace told her. "Come as you are, and all that."

Everyone was keeping it down, but Luce was so exhausted, even the extra voices didn't wake her. At least, Drake thought, they hadn't all wandered out here and found him and Luce sharing a sleeping bag.

Blythe wasn't naive, but she *was* his mother, and Drake would have been embarrassed as hell.

"Remember when we used to do this with Dad?" Mace asked. "I was considered one of the coolest kids at school when I told them we had a 'sleeping porch.'" He leaned forward a little, peering at the dog. "I see Harold's awake. That's good. Means he'll be okay."

"Quiet," Drake cautioned, watching Luce sleep through all the arrivals, wondering if she was going to be chagrined in the morning at waking up to a crowd scene. He shifted closer to her. "She's really tired."

"Of you?" Mace said. "Sure, who wouldn't be?"

"Don't be a wiseass."

Slater intervened, as usual. "I agree with Drake. If the two of you start to bicker and somehow wake up my pregnant wife, I can't answer for what might happen next. I might just end the argument myself, or I might let her loose on you two. Watch it. She's a force to be reckoned with at all times. That red hair does not lie."

Drake loved Grace. A former police officer, she knew how to put her foot down.

So did his mother. "They aren't going to argue. Go to sleep. You especially, Drake. There are more than enough of us to look out for Harold and Violet, not that Violet can't take care of herself."

The Blythe Carson method. Clear and succinct. It had worked when they were kids, and that tone was still mighty effective. Drake closed his eyes. He'd doubted that he'd catch even a wink, but it did help to know that there were other eyes and ears tuned in.

Five seconds later, he'd zonked out.

LUCE WOKE TO the smell of coffee, the scent of fresh bread and voices. She didn't even know where she was until Violet trotted over and licked her hand. She sat up on the hard floor of the porch and pushed her hair away from her face.

Daylight. She'd rarely slept that long. Or that deeply.

It seemed that breakfast alfresco was taking place on the veranda.

The round table at one end held a makeshift buffet, with muffins, a carafe of coffee and a pitcher of juice. There were also plates of sausages, along with a big glass bowl full of mixed fruit. People were sitting in various chairs or on the steps, talking and eating.

As she blinked in confusion at the blankets everywhere around her, Harry breezed through the door carrying a platter. "Scrambled eggs. And if anyone asks for ketchup or hot sauce, I'll have their hide."

Blythe, wearing some sort of lacy robe over silk pajamas, gave Luce a sunny smile. "Good morning, honey. If you're hungry, there's plenty."

Drake was, of course, nowhere in sight. Just her luck. Luce had on pajama pants patterned with tiny cows—a pair her sister had given her and christened "the moo pants"— and a faded old T-shirt. Crawling out of her sleeping bag was embarrassing; on the other hand, she'd apparently been snoozing away in front of Drake's entire family for who knows how long.

"I, er, might run inside for a few minutes." She made a beeline for the door, since a swift exit seemed prudent. When she got to the bathroom, she saw that her Rapunzel hair was out of control. She rarely wore makeup, so she'd done nothing to remove it, and there were definite dark smudges under her eyes. She scrubbed those away, tamed the hair and put on a pair of jeans, a better shirt and a pair of slip-on shoes. She was late for breakfast yet again.

The Carson household was generally unpredictable. It wasn't every day a girl woke up to discover that she'd slept on a porch, watched by half a dozen people. What *was* predictable was their softhearted attachment to the dogs.

She still found it hard to believe that she was going to become one of these people, a member of their family. She hadn't known Drake very long, but the doubts she'd experienced during her first engagement just weren't there.

How odd to realize it.

This was perfect for her. Okay, sort of perfect. She had the handsome cowboy, and the ranch life she was settling into so easily. But…her family was still in California and she'd have to give up her teaching dream…

Nothing worth having came without sacrifice, she reminded herself. Once she had her master's, maybe she could look for something with the park service. She wasn't cut out to bake cookies and pack school lunches—at least not as a full-time vocation. Centering your life on family appealed to her, but she wanted a professional life, too. In a word, she wanted it *all*.

She hoped to teach at the college or university level. The closest college in this area was quite a drive, even if she managed to land a position there. And completing her PhD, which was another lifetime goal, seemed unlikely if she lived on a remote ranch.

She also guessed babies would be involved at some point. After all, Blythe had already brought up the subject.

There were certainly some things she and Drake needed to discuss—sooner rather than later. Maybe when he was her captive on the plane to California, strapped into the next seat, she could bring up subjects like the actual wedding. She had the distinct feeling that the kind of elaborate wedding her mother was going to want would not be welcome news; Drake was bound to prefer something simple. Beth's wedding had involved a string quartet, hot-house orchids and waiters in tuxedos. Their mother was adamant when it came to entertaining. Beth had confided that she'd just thrown up her hands and bowed out of the decision-making process, except for choosing the dress.

"Have a seat." Blythe offered her a plate. They were alone on the porch now. "Drake is off moving cattle, Mace left for the vineyard a few minutes ago and Slater has a meeting with some of his investors, so he's flying to Chey-enne. Grace went to the resort. She's cutting back her hours but isn't quite ready to stay home and wait it out. I'm going to relax here with the dogs, keep an eye on them. I spend most of my time out here, anyway. I have this new book I'm itching to read, and poor Harold gives me an excuse to indulge myself. What are your plans?"

That was a transparent question. Luce was sure every-one in the household knew Drake had forbidden her to go out on her own, and they were waiting to see how she'd handle it. "I'm going to work on my paper. Don't worry. After last night, I won't go out by myself. But truthfully, that mountain lion's been out there the whole time. Maybe it followed me, and maybe it didn't. Life is full of risks."

"I'm not going to disagree with that. Risk is everywhere. Falling in love is a risk." Blythe sent her a matronly, know-ing look. "Have some fruit salad. Bex Calder's recipe. I had to practically bribe it out of her. It's so good."

Not sure what to say, Luce helped herself to a bowl of fruit salad and a muffin. She felt her future was spinning out of control. Unexpected things, positive things, were happening, but *she* wasn't controlling them any longer. She said faintly, "Thank you."

"Your mother's looking forward to meeting Drake. Well,

she *has* met him before, when he was much younger. And my father's thrilled we're all coming."

Luce couldn't picture the austere man being thrilled about anything, so she took a bite of her muffin instead of commenting. It was delicious, made with bananas and white chocolate, among the more notable ingredients. Finally, she said, "I mentioned the dates to Drake. I got the impression that when we go doesn't really matter. I assume he'll want to spend some time with his grandfather."

"He and his grandfather don't get along all that well." Blythe looked resigned. "You've met my father."

Luce nodded. She certainly didn't know him well but had a clear memory of the distinguished elderly man, owner of a renowned winery.

"Well..." Bythe sighed. "My father and my husband didn't see eye to eye, either. To Dad, ranching is something people should pay to have someone else do for them. It's fine to own the property and stock, but choosing to be a true rancher baffles him. He couldn't rope a calf or break a horse to save his life. He was raised in wine country and, to his mind, being a vintner is a cultured thing to do. Getting dust on your boots is not. I won't use the word *snob*, and he loves Drake, but they don't understand each other. My father can taste a glass of wine while wearing a thousand-dollar suit and tell you exactly what grapes were used. My son can move a thousand cattle to a different pasture. Both of them are capable and stubborn as all get-out, and just different enough to strike sparks off each other. Yet I love them both. Have you set a date for the wedding?"

The...what?

"He *told* you he proposed?" She was going to strangle the man. They'd agreed to break the news together.

"Drake?" Blythe smiled and poured her a cup of coffee. "Of course not. Sons don't tell their mothers anything that personal, but he didn't have to tell me. Remember when you and I went ring shopping? Cream in your coffee and no sugar, right?"

"I remember the ring shopping," she said, slightly startled by the abrupt shift from jewelry to coffee. "And yes, right. Cream and no sugar, please."

"And here I thought I was being subtle about the wedding."

Yeah, as subtle as a sledgehammer. Luce had to ask, "Um, how often do you talk with my mother?"

"Now and then."

The coffee was wonderful and she needed some caffeine. She took a long sip. "Why do I suspect that means almost daily?"

"Now that you're here, we chat a little more often than before."

"Drake wanted to talk to my father before we announced our plans."

"That doesn't surprise me. I won't say a word, but your mother's already emailed me several pictures of wedding gowns she thinks would suit you. I'm afraid I did mention the film footage Slater's crew caught of my son kissing her daughter. Forgive me, but having been friends all these years, how could I *not* tell her about that?"

That dratted picture. Still, Luce couldn't really blame *his* mother for telling *her* mother. After all, she herself had blabbed the news to Beth right away. As a matter of fact, she'd now told *two* people that she and Drake were engaged. At this point, the entire town probably knew, anyway—thanks to the film and to her visit with Melody.

Luce held her coffee mug between her palms. "Drake's going to hate visiting California, isn't he?"

Blythe leaned back, the slanting sunlight catching the silver in her auburn hair. "He dislikes leaving Wyoming, but for you he'll do it. In my opinion, that's better than an emphatic 'I love you.' The old cliché about actions speaking more loudly than words, you know? He wants you to be happy and you should let him make you happy. And that, in turn, will make him happy. Pretty simple actually. People tend to complicate relationships."

Luce didn't discount that. She'd watched a few of her friends try to change their various boyfriends without success or, perhaps worse, change for them. Compromise was necessary, of course, as her father had once told her, but being true to yourself was the best thing you could do for your marriage. It kept you from resenting your husband or wife. That was why he let her mother give her parties without complaint and she let him play golf as often as he wanted. He couldn't understand her endless need to entertain, and she thought golf was boring, but their marriage worked because they each understood what was important to the other.

The ranch and his family were part of Drake's soul. But he'd have to understand that all the compromise wasn't going to be on Luce's side.

A car coming up the driveway interrupted her reflection.

"It's Lettie." Blythe sounded pleased. "I'll bet she's already heard about Harold somehow. She has a network that's second to none. Mine doesn't even compare, and I've lived here for years. I warn you, she has a tendency to say whatever's on her mind, but she also has the softest heart of anyone I know."

The woman was wearing a tailored suit at— Luce wasn't quite sure of the time, but it couldn't be more than eight. She marched up the steps and walked straight over to where Harold still lay on his blanket, looked him over and nodded. "Jax Locke obviously did his job. Good man."

Harold wagged his tail weakly.

Blythe murmured, "Morning, Lettie. Have you met Luce Hale?"

"The girl Drake's going to marry. Prominent California family. She's here to study wild horses." Lettie Arbuckle-Calder moved to the table, settled into a chair, then crossed her elegant legs and accepted a cup of coffee. She leveled a stare at Luce, who now felt distinctly grubby even after cleaning up, and asked, "What's your young man going to do about the mountain lion?"

She didn't know what Mrs. Arbuckle-Calder was hoping to hear. "He could've killed it last night, but that isn't Drake. He has a friend who's relocated lions before. He's going to call him and review his options."

Mrs. Arbuckle-Calder relaxed visibly. "I approve of that."

Whew. Right answer.

"What about the wild horses?"

Now, there was a tricky one…

Luce took a gulp of coffee. She hadn't expected an interrogation this morning. "He says they can't stay."

"I have a solution to his problem."

The lady sounded very sure. Luce liked her more by the minute. "I can't wait to hear it."

CHAPTER TWENTY

IF HE KEPT a diary—which he didn't—Drake might've written, *Best day of my life, but not without problems.* First day as an engaged man. That was the happy part. He could also note that Red, although he'd never admit it, seemed to be coming down with something—maybe the flu. Which could be dangerous at Red's age.

Slater was out of town, so he couldn't help, and Mace had gotten in a huge order for Mountain Vineyards wine that had him dancing in the streets but working like a dog.

And speaking of dogs... Harold was doing very well—considering. It still hurt to think they might've lost him. Working with animals his entire life, he tried to not get too attached, but...

Ed Gunnerson answered on the third ring. "Drake. We haven't talked in a while. What's up?"

Drake was multitasking, stacking hay bales and talking on his cell. "I need your help. I've got a problem with a mountain lion, and he needs to go. One way or the other, but I prefer the other. He and my dog got into it, and the dog essentially lost the fight. Seems like he's going to make it, though. This cat's been raiding my calves since last summer, but he's getting bolder. Thoughts?"

There was a pause. Ed always took his time. "Big cats have big territories."

That wasn't news. "Could you track him?"

"Oh, yeah, if he has a pattern, and they all do. Done it before. Track him and move him."

Maybe he could cross that off his to-worry-about list. "You are officially invited to the Carson ranch."

"I know where he could be content to live to a ripe old age and help keep the deer population under control. I'll try to get the arrangements in place."

"I'd appreciate it."

"I prefer a humane solution myself. That's why we're here."

"Thanks." He ended the call and contemplated what he should do next. There were always chores, needless to say, but he should check on Harold and Violet.

And Luce. When he'd gotten up, she'd still been asleep. Everyone had been asleep.

He rode back to the house and saw a recognizable car in the drive. He liked Lettie Arbuckle-Calder, but the woman was difficult to dissuade when she made a decision. He'd once tried—and failed—to deflect her from purchasing a nearby piece of property. She'd later sold it, and he figured that proved he'd been right, but he was never going to hear that from her. *I was wrong* was not part of her vocabulary.

Why did he have a sinking feeling that this had something to do with him? If Mrs. A-C felt the need to meddle, leave him out of it.

No such luck.

When he walked onto the porch, he saw Harold had gotten up and was eating. An encouraging sign. Violet was keeping him company, munching kibble from her bowl, too. She deserved a double helping.

"Hi," he said lamely to the three women sitting there. "I'm checking on the dogs, but I see they're in good hands. Red isn't feeling well, so I'm feeding the horses." A pause. "Beautiful day, isn't it? See you later."

Just as he spun around, Lettie said in a steely tone, "Not so fast, young man."

At thirty-two, he wouldn't describe himself as young anymore, but with his mother sitting right there, he wasn't going to argue. However, he wasn't going to apologize for his reluctance, either. The fact that he could tell Luce was laughing to herself didn't make the situation any more comfortable. "Yes?"

"I want to talk to you about the horses."

"Which ones?"

What man *wouldn't* be wary with three women looking at him expectantly? He certainly was.

It was Luce, as bewitching in her faded jeans and plain shirt as she was in her stylish dress, who finally said, "The wild ones."

His mother added, "I think it's a brilliant plan."

Oh, a supposedly brilliant plan involving wild horses and women? Just what every man needed. Both unpredictable. It would be rude to point that out, so he hedged. "I'm listening. I guess."

"The old Winston homestead. The one where you believe the herd winters, correct? I've looked into it. The state owns the property now because it was abandoned and no

taxes were being paid. You know how slowly the government works." Mrs. A–C sniffed in disapproval at the slow-
moving wheels of bureaucracy. "But I have some influence
here and there."

She probably had more influence than the governor, although he refrained from mentioning that. "I'm following
you, but only so far. What's your suggestion?"

"I'd like to propose that the state of Wyoming make the
property part of their park system on the basis of its being
a historical landmark. If you can relocate the horses there,
your problem's solved and they won't have to be shipped
off anywhere." She seemed very…self-satisfied. Yep, that
was the word for it.

He propped one foot on the top step, wishing it was that
simple and not knowing how to delicately explain that it
wasn't. "Uh, well, it sounds great in theory, but—"

"In *theory*?" Luce interrupted. She plonked down her
coffee mug. "It sounds *great*, Drake. In reality. Not just in
theory."

He gave her a quelling look. "You've been studying
them, right? Doing research? Then you're aware of how
fast the herds grow. By the time this arrangement was set
up, my problem would be a lot worse than it is now. Not
to mention that I don't know if the federal government
would even agree to let a state park keep wild horses when
it's allocated land to manage them. And don't forget that
stallion's kicked through almost every fence *I've* ever put
up. Plus, there's no guarantee the horses would stay put,
because he moves them all the time. My bull is easier to
contain. Sounds simple, but I promise you, it won't be."

That reminded him he had to meet Jim Galloway in a

couple of hours to go see a young bull owned by a friend of his.

Full day. At least Harold seemed to be doing as well as anyone could hope. Jax had said he'd stop by later.

Mrs. A-C tapped the table and said thoughtfully, "Probably valid points. I will ask all the right questions, then. Nothing is insurmountable."

He hoped that was true, but he'd stumbled across a few situations that were pretty daunting. Yet he had to admire her confidence. He didn't envy whatever official in the state government got her call. They'd be scrambling to accommodate her, no doubt about it.

"I'd better get back to work." He touched his hat. "Ladies."

Then he beat a hasty retreat—although not as hasty as he would've liked. Self-preservation was rarely unwise. He could stand his ground if he had to, but his philosophy was to be polite and get the heck out of there when it was three against one and he was the one. A minority position was always difficult. Besides, he had things to do, plenty of them, and he even took his truck so he wouldn't have to go back to the house.

Of course, when he got to the stable, Red was hard at work. Drake frowned. "I told you to knock off for the day. You really look like you could be running a fever."

"Nonsense." Red continued to brush down a horse. "I don't get sick."

"You don't *admit* you get sick. There's a difference." He plucked the brush from the older man's hand and went to work on the gelding. "I'll finish this. Go take a nap."

"Naps are for old ladies," he said gruffly.

Time to play the trump card. "I told my mother you

weren't feeling well. She'll tell Harry. Mrs. Arbuckle-Calder was there, too. Do you want the three of them catching you not resting? If I were you, I'd at least pretend to be asleep. Otherwise, in addition to whatever ails you, there's a lecture in your very near future. Maybe three." He fake-squinted at the door. "I think I see them coming now."

Red was no fool. He beat it. Drake shook his head and laughed sympathetically as he finished grooming the horse. He left a note for Ryder to clean the tack room when he got home from school; it was going to be good when the kid was out of school for the summer, because he did a great job with the smaller chores. Slater was teaching him how to ride, Drake was teaching him how to rope and Mace was teaching him how to shoot. For a city boy, he was catching on, too, and roping a calf when you hadn't been riding long wasn't all that easy. The first few times, the horse went one way and the kid went another and bit the dust, but he was getting the hang of it.

Drake glanced at his phone and saw that it was time to go over to Jim Galloway's. He probably smelled like horse with more than a hint of manure mixed in, but Jim wouldn't mind that one bit.

Jim and Pauline lived in a neat little house in town, perfect for two people, with tidy flower beds out front and a fenced backyard for their dogs. Jim looked younger since he'd married his second wife and won his battle with cancer, and he was grinning when he answered the door. "So you're getting married, eh? That's almost as fast as me when I met Pauline. What are you trying to do, beat my record? Pauline and I got hitched practically the moment we met. Hey, I have a request. Could you play the Texas two-step at the reception? My wife's one hell of a dancer."

How had Jim found out? Was that just a lucky guess?

He hadn't told anyone. That meant Luce had, which he doubted, or his mother had figured it out. Maybe Mrs. A–C had looked in her crystal ball. Oh, yeah, Red had known Luce was in his bed the night before…

Anyway, he wasn't going to lie to Jim. He admitted, "We've talked about it. I don't think I'll be part of the entertainment committee, but I'll be sure to mention your request. Now, let's go see this bull."

Jim climbed amiably into the truck. "I'm not going to say he's easy to handle. Sherman's moody, too, so you know how to deal with that. Impressive animal. I went and took a look at him before I called you."

"You didn't need to do that."

"I have time on my hands now, so it was a pleasure to pretend I was still running a ranch, even for an afternoon. He's a dandy."

"Bloodlines?" Drake shot off some rapid-fire questions about the bull as he started the truck again, got the answers to his questions, and thirty minutes later, they pulled into the yard.

Jim's friend Mike Gorman was old-school, with overalls and a bald head, and it was clear that he assessed Drake before he nodded and they walked over to the fenced pasture. He liked that. The man wasn't going to give this animal away to just anyone.

"He's a handful," Mike said, keeping it short and sweet. "He'll get the job done and he'll tone down some as he gets a few years on him. No one wants a lazy bull. I named him Tobias, but you can call him whatever you want."

The price was reasonable, and Drake couldn't argue. This was a beautiful creature. He wrote a check then and there, because both he and Red trusted Jim's judgment. They hashed out the details for getting Tobias to his new home, and when they got back into the truck to head for Mustang Creek, Drake was feeling decent about life. The mountain lion was going to be handled, he'd solved the bull problem and Luce had said yes. If Mrs. A-C's ridiculous idea actually worked out, things were looking up.

His phone beeped and he pressed the button that let him talk hands-free. "Yep?"

It was Tripp. "You buy that bull from old Gorman?"

"Sure did."

"My dad's a traitor. I kind of had my eye on it."

"Son, I can hear you." Jim was chortling. "I'm right here. You waited a shade too long, that's all."

Tripp muttered something they couldn't catch, but then he laughed. "So I'm talking to both of you? Since you're there, Dad, I'm supposed to tell you that whatever you're having for dinner tonight, Pauline isn't going to cook it. You choose the place, but you're taking her out. And via Melody to Hadleigh, I'm supposed to tell Drake the ring is ready and he can pick it up whenever. Why *I'm* expected to have time to relay all these messages is a mystery to me, because I'm watching the baby right now and that's no picnic. I'd rather be herding ornery cows."

"Ring? What ring?" The moment the words were out of his mouth, Drake felt he already knew the answer to that question.

"The one your mother ordered for you. Damn, I smell something suspicious. This diaper needs changing… Gotta go. Drake, see you on poker night. Dad, take Pauline someplace nice."

Jim looked as if he was going to burst out laughing as

the call ended. "Don't tell me. You didn't know about the ring?"

"No." Drake felt like laughing, too, but his laughter would've had an edge to it.

"You've been corralled. Blythe Carson's always been a woman who gets things done."

He'd be more annoyed, but truthfully, his mother had probably done him a favor. She'd have a much better sense of what Luce might want in a ring than he did.

He wanted a companion on evening rides. He wanted to see her smile, to hear the passion in her voice when she argued with him, to touch her, to taste her kiss, to imagine their children laughing and playing.

So all he said was "You're finding this way too funny. I guess after I drop you off, I need to go pick up a ring."

Jim agreed with a cheerful grin. "I guess you do, son."

LUCE BIT HER lower lip, thought about the sentence she'd just written, then went back and erased it.

She sat with her laptop on the front porch, since Blythe was out running errands. Violet was in the kitchen with Harry, but Harold had hobbled over and was keeping her company, sleeping at her feet. She found it touching that he was guarding her for Drake, even though he could barely get up.

She'd come to Wyoming to gather information, and now she had far more than she needed. The dissertation was getting harder to write as she went; there was a lot of ground to cover.

She was about to give it another try when her phone beeped. A text from Beth. I swear I didn't tell.

What did *that* mean?

She typed back, Clarify?

Operation Wedding has begun.

Luce blew out a breath of frustration. She believed Beth, and she knew Blythe would keep her word and hadn't said anything. So that meant her mother was evidently jumping to conclusions—the correct conclusions.

At that moment, Drake pulled in, parked his truck, and Harold barked in greeting, then settled back down. He rested his head on her foot.

"So *she's* your new best friend?" Drake came up the steps looking accusingly at his dog, but he smiled. "Well, Harold, here's a poorly kept secret. I like her, too."

"It isn't a secret at all," Luce informed him drily, although she felt the same way about Harold. "I have to tell you something. My mother seems to know about the engagement. She didn't hear it from me, or from my sister *or* your mother. Oh, and Blythe's already booked our flights for the anniversary party."

He was quiet, obviously thinking it through. "Okay," he said finally. "That's not ideal, but we'll work with it." He shoved a hand through his hair. "Harold's choosy about the people he keeps company with. You ought to be flattered."

She definitely was.

"He can sleep on my foot anytime he likes." She studied Drake in silence for a few minutes. "The life of a cowboy," she mused. "Mind if I use that for the title of my dissertation? Part of the title, anyway."

"You creative types," he replied. "You sound like Slate. He'll throw out a title for one of his movies and wait for reactions. Says he prefers first impressions." He sat down across the table, appropriated her glass of lemonade and drained it in a single gulp.

Luce didn't mind at all. They were going to be good together. He'd never pressure her, and she wasn't interested in changing him. Oh, he could use a few nudges here and there—everyone could—but a sexy cowboy had been on her life wish list, and he certainly fit the bill.

"How about 'The Life of a Cowboy: I Can Only Control What I Can Control'?"

One corner of his mouth lifted in a smile. "Shouldn't there be something in there about nosy graduate students? Let me revamp. 'I Can Only Control Certain Things in Nature, and Women Are Not Among Them.'"

Luce was really laughing now. His sardonic sense of humor was one of the things she loved about him, even when he was disheveled and smelled like saddle leather and pine forests. She shook her head. "That's a chapter in *The Cowboy Guide to a Successful Relationship.* Stay focused. We're talking about the most important thing I'll ever write."

"Yeah, guess I forgot for a second there. Let me see if Harry can watch Harold while you and I go for a ride. I've been thinking about Mrs. A-C's suggestion. The valley isn't that far. When we first met, you said you wanted to see it. Besides, I haven't been on a horse all day."

For him, astounding. Horse deficiency.

She wanted to see the place where the horses wintered, no doubt about it. Luce would've jumped up with alacrity, but Harold's head was firmly planted on her shoe. "Your mother's lending me some boots. I'll go put them on."

Drake came over to give Harold a reassuring pat and the animal lifted his head. "We'll be waiting right here."

Luce went to her room, grabbed the boots and tugged

them on. They were soft as butter, patterned with horses on the sides and totally comfortable.

Drake nodded in approval when she reappeared. "Nice job, cowgirl."

She didn't qualify for that title yet, but she was trying. "I'm learning, one day at a time, from a very qualified teacher."

He elevated his brows and gave her a devilish male grin. "I think you can hold your own. Oh, wait, we're not talking about riding, are we?"

"Watch it, Carson." She smacked his arm.

He caught her around the waist and pulled her to him. "This being in love business… I'm trying to figure it out and not getting very far."

"You're trying to make sense of something that doesn't actually make sense." Luce kissed him with a lingering pressure of her lips on his. "I'm on the same sinking ship."

"We can drown together."

"We can do a lot of things together, most of them better than drowning! Now, let's go for a horseback ride. I can tell you need an equine fix."

He ran his fingers up her arm. "And I can tell you have more confidence."

"Wait until the first time I fall off!"

"We all take a fall at some point. I've even seen Red bite the dust."

"You have?" That surprised her.

"Hell, yes."

It wasn't funny, and yet, somehow, it was. "That old cowboy fell off his horse?"

"Don't ever bring it up." Drake urged her toward the doorway. "I'd suggest not calling him old, either. He's kind of sensitive on the subject. I've also discovered that it's safer not to tell him he shouldn't do something because then he'll do it just to prove me wrong. So far he's in the winning bracket."

"I didn't mean old in a bad way."

"I know. He's a surprisingly sensitive guy about certain things. Oh, have I mentioned that you have to saddle your horse by yourself?"

He hadn't. Well, that was on her list, too. "I was hoping to bribe Ryder to show me how so I could impress you."

"I'm impressed already. No worries there."

She could live with that.

CHAPTER TWENTY-ONE

SHE WAS AN apt pupil, if a little out of practice. It didn't hurt that Grace's horse, Molly, was tolerant and patient, which, of course, was why Slater had picked her for his wife.

"Tighten the cinch again," Drake advised. "Horses are pretty smart. They'll sometimes take a breath and hold it so the saddle's loose when they let it out. Never underestimate an animal's intelligence. She's very amiable, but not all horses are the same. Always check your saddle twice."

"She's sweet." Luce stroked her silky neck.

"Remember, you're practicing on this horse, but another one might be totally different. Never presume it's going to go well if you don't know each other."

Slater's horse, Heck, wouldn't let her within ten feet of him. He was a beautiful horse but gave *feisty* a new meaning. Drake had helped Red break him, and he'd been hell on wheels. Even now, Drake was cautious around him and had ordered Ryder to leave his stall to more experienced hands. Red could do it, but Ryder couldn't handle that animal and he was a head taller than Luce.

"She likes you," he commented. "Don't get the idea that Smoke would ever allow you to get this close."

"He already has."

Drake thought fainting might severely damage his male image, so he didn't. *"What?"*

Luce acted nonchalant about it, her shoulders lifting in a shrug. *"He* came up to me. I touched him and that was it. He's as curious about me as I am about him and the rest of the horses. And he knows I'm not there to do them any harm. I don't carry a gun or ride a big horse. I just want to watch them. I walk only so close, and then I sit down and leave them alone as I make notes."

He actually took off his hat and threw it on the ground. "You *touched* a wild stallion? Are you loco?"

Luce had the nerve to look offended. "Hey, I was sitting there writing and suddenly realized he was right behind me. He sniffed my hair and I held up my hand. Here it is." She offered Exhibit A, palm up. "He didn't bite it off or anything. He smelled it and went on his way. I'm harmless. Give him credit for knowing that. You've already seen that he's gotten used to me."

Her logic worked, but she also needed to understand that they weren't talking about the placid mare he'd just helped her saddle. "He's a wild animal, and he's a really big one. Sharp teeth and hooves. There are bigger critters than us he wouldn't hesitate to go after, like that cougar."

"I didn't go up to him! I turned around and *he* was right there. Like I said, I was focusing on my notes and I had no idea he was so close."

"You are the greenest greenhorn I've met. That little interaction is exactly why you aren't going anywhere without me." He retrieved his hat and plopped it on his head.

She considered him through slightly narrowed eyes. "I seem to have survived for lo these twenty-six years. I promise you, negotiating multiple lanes of traffic in LA during rush hour is a lot more dangerous than anything you can serve up here, and I've done that many times. Are you always going to be so dictatorial?"

"I'm going to be protective, you can count on that. Now, get your very enticing behind on that horse and let's go for a relaxing ride. I'm not helping you mount this time. You work that out for yourself." He did check the saddle very quickly. She'd have to go solo someday, but if he was there, anyway, he might as well make sure she was as safe as possible.

She glared at him. "No problem."

She did a fair job of it, although part of her success was due to the patient horse. Starburst led the way, Molly followed and Drake was finally able to breathe in a deep lungful of the evening air and relax.

"Next valley over," he said. "It's a beautiful place, but I've never understood why the original homesteaders chose that spot to settle. The cabin's been there a long, long time. Since shortly after the Civil War. I'm guessing they had sheep, because you can't graze cattle there. I also think that for whatever reason, the guy wanted to be as obscure as he could. Red tells me the legend is that he came to town once a month, bought the essentials—flour, coffee and sugar— but otherwise no one saw him. Everyone thought he had something to hide. Eventually, he stopped showing up and they found the place abandoned, the door still open. No one knows if he went away voluntarily or suffered some severe misfortune. There were no papers besides the deed, but no remains, either."

"Did anyone else ever live there? Lettie mentioned that the property taxes hadn't been paid in years."

"Yeah, there was another recluse there for a while, but I don't know much about him. And he was long gone by the time we came along."

"So the real story is about the original homesteader who mysteriously disappeared…"

"Yeah. Naturally, as kids we rode over, hoping it would be haunted. Unfortunately not. Maybe Slate will get lucky with his cameras. He's putting it in the documentary, and that might help Lettie Arbuckle's plan. If anyone can pull it off, it would be her, but I still think the red tape involved will be prohibitive."

"There's nothing like a good old-fashioned ghost story to charm a girl." Luce was easier with the horse now, her hands more relaxed on the reins. "Scary. In a romantic way, I mean."

"Well, I strive to be ever the romantic. Feel free to fling yourself into my arms anytime." He glanced over at her. "However…all ghost hunting so far has proved fruitless, so maybe neither of us should get our hopes up."

"I've flung myself into your arms already—without a ghost."

"And I loved every minute of it."

Luce had the best laugh. Light and feminine. "You did?"

"Like you didn't know that."

The breeze ruffled her hair, and her smile held a hint of mischief. "I might have noticed it. That aside, you really think Mrs. Arbuckle is being too ambitious? I want to be sure I've got all my facts straight."

Oh, yes, her paper. He rode along, slowly, although he could tell that Starburst would've preferred a faster pace. "Containing the horses isn't going to be simple."

"Very few things in life are simple, cowboy."

"A night like this is." His smile was genuine. "An evening ride with a pretty girl, a fresh breeze, the mountains framing a spectacular sunset… This is a simple joy. Harry said something about steaks for dinner, along with her famous scalloped potatoes. Another simple joy."

"Is there anything Harry makes that isn't famous?" Luce tucked a strand of hair behind her ear. She really was sitting her horse more comfortably, not thinking about it so much.

"No," he admitted. "Some people are born to create wonderful paintings. Some are destined to compose music that's listened to and admired for centuries. She has a talent for making fantastic food and running a household the way a general might direct a battle plan. It doesn't hurt that she and my mother are like sisters. My mother, to her credit, is willing to step back and let Harry run the show. Harry, to *her* credit, has always kept her nose and her opinions out of any parenting decisions unless asked. I see that now as an adult, but I didn't notice it as a kid. Even when you asked her directly, tried to get her involved, she'd say, 'I think that needs to be settled between you and your mother.' She wasn't opposed to letting any of us know if we were out of line, but she didn't meddle."

"And when she was finished telling you to smarten up, she gave you a cookie." Luce smiled.

"Usually," he agreed, since she was right. "Or two. Sometimes a slice of pie if Mace didn't get there first. He's quite the chowhound."

"My impression is that he works as hard as you and Slater

do, so that might be the secret to the male Carson persona. Hard work, which equals being perpetually hungry."

"My dad was no slouch, either." He pointed. "The only real entrance to the valley is that narrow corridor up ahead. That's problem one for Lottie's relocation plan."

THE VALLEY WAS as beautiful as Drake had promised.

Steep, green, with a meandering stream running through, it was sheltered by a towering rock wall to one side. Luce immediately thought that if solitude was what you wanted, this would be the place to go. There wasn't a dramatic mountain view, but there was plenty of privacy.

No wonder Smoke brought his band of horses here for the winter. The storms coming in from the west probably didn't hit this spot as fiercely. She'd run the weather models when she'd embarked on this scientific journey, doing her best to understand how the habitat worked.

She wasn't entirely joking when she said, "I see why people might think this place is haunted. It feels strange, a bit surreal."

The cabin itself was decrepit, a relic of the long-gone past. The ancient logs and a rickety front porch had started to deteriorate, but the chimney looked sound, and there were the ruins of a barn. The last time someone had lived here was more than a few decades ago.

Drake didn't disagree with her. "It's a hidden gem. That makes Mrs. A-C's plan both good and bad. People will love that deserted old cabin and the grazing wild horses, but getting them in here is almost impossible if they aren't riding. There's no road, and I don't want one. It would have to go across Carson property."

"It doesn't have to be a road," Luce reasoned. "Maybe

just a trail—a ride to a haunted valley. Toss in a visit to the vineyard, and you'll really have something." She paused, her mind moving at warp speed. "Do you see the state agreeing to open a park? I don't know how these things work."

He'd relaxed visibly, out there in the open spaces. The thought of Drake Carson walking into a corporate office for a meeting was practically incomprehensible; he was meant for *this* life. Glimmering Western sunsets and the soft whisper of the breeze ruffling the aspen leaves—that suited him so much better than skyscrapers and concrete ever could.

Luce was starting to feel that maybe it was the same for her.

He shrugged, his answer carefully considered, as usual. "I suggest we wait to see what Lettie finds out," he began. "That woman knows how to get things done." He smiled, the wind ruffling his hair. "She reminds me of my mother, but with a lot less tact. They're quite a team—one of them will pour you a cup of tea and, while you're distracted, the other will run over you with a bulldozer. In any case, they almost always get whatever they're after."

In Luce's admittedly limited experience, that assessment was dead-on.

"Big, strong men should step back, huh?"

"Big, strong men should run for their lives." Drake grinned. "You do realize you fall into the same category as my mother and Lettie. The Unstoppable Female."

She silenced him by holding up one hand. "Pardon my grammar, but you ain't seen nothin' yet, cowpoke. Wait until you meet my sister and mother. Whoa, you're going to be in for an experience." She pretended to assess his appearance. "You might have to get your hair cut," she speculated.

He looked endearingly perplexed. "My hair? What's wrong with my hair?"

"Nothing, as far as *I'm* concerned, but Mom and Beth are big on making people over. Watch out, that's all I'm saying. If you don't, you might find yourself in a Beverly Hills salon, getting highlights or a spray tan."

"That'll be the day," he drawled.

"Oh, it's very LA," she told him solemnly. "Guys even get facials."

"Not this guy, ma'am."

"I'm joking," she said. "Beth and my mom wouldn't dream of trying to improve you." She erupted into laughter. "Not that I'm saying you're perfect or anything."

Drake gave her a mock glare, then he laughed, too. A moment later, his expression was somber again. "Listen, couldn't we just get married at the ranch? Say, on the ridge where you and I first met? A minister and a few witnesses, and we're in business. Mace and Slater could be there, and Slater's crew could take the pictures. Sound good?" He didn't wait for her answer, which was convenient, because she didn't have one ready. "That way, you'll have a wedding and I'll survive the ceremony and the reception. We can feed each other cake and fly out for our honeymoon."

Actually, Luce rather liked the idea of a simple, rustic wedding. She wasn't really the fuss-and-ruffles type, though she did want the day to be special. Not quite as "special" as their mothers were gearing up for, however. "Do you mean it, Drake? Because if you do, my sister would come out here in a heartbeat to be my maid of honor."

"Oh, believe me, I mean it."

If there was one thing she knew about Drake, it was that he said what he thought and thought about what he said; his opinions were never unconsidered. So she did the same. "I'm in favor of something romantic, memorable and un-complicated," she said honestly.

He brightened. "You are?"

"Sure." Luce nodded. She was fairly certain her mother would be disappointed; Dorothy Hale was probably plan-ning an event more appropriate to the gardens of Buck-ingham Palace than the wide-open spaces of Wyoming. Her father wouldn't be a problem, and Beth would be on her side.

Their special day would be lovely.

"I know you wanted to meet Mom and Dad before the news got out," she went on. "We could call them, if you like."

"Or," he countered, "we could see if Tate Calder or Tripp Galloway can find the time to fly us out there to pick up your sister. Think she could talk your folks into taking her to the airfield? That way, at least, I could shake hands with your dad and give your mom a chance to look me over, make sure I don't have three heads or anything."

Meeting her parents in person, prior to the wedding, seemed more important to Drake than it was to her, but she thought she understood his reasons. Like his brothers, he'd been raised rough-and-tumble, but with very good manners.

This, she suspected, was what he thought his father would want him to do. It touched her heart, the realiza-tion that he still missed Zeke Carson, after all these years, still cared about doing what would be the right thing in his eyes.

She spoke softly. "Your dad would be wildly proud of you no matter what."

Drake didn't respond to that. "Can Beth manage to get your folks to the airfield or not?" he asked.

That was truly a laughable question. "Beth's been twisting Dad around her little finger, as they say, since the day she was born. It's impressive to watch her in action. My mother and I just look at each other and shake our heads. Dad's no fool. He knows exactly what she's up to, but he can't say no."

"Talk to her. Choose a date for the wedding. I'll see what I can work out on this end."

They'd have a romantic story to tell their children, that was for sure. "I'll call her as soon as we get back."

He squinted at the sky. "Speaking of which, we'd better start back. I'm not Red, but it smells like rain to me and there are clouds rolling in. Looks like a spring storm brewing up there. You think you can handle a slightly faster pace?"

Luce nodded, trying to ignore the small flicker of panic. "I'm going to have to sooner or later, I suppose."

They almost made it before the rain came. When he lifted her from her horse, they were both laughing and soaking wet. Drake didn't let her go but smoothed her damp hair away from her face and kissed her. He said, "You did well, cowgirl. While we wait for the rain to stop, I'll show you how to unsaddle your horse and brush her down."

Facetiously, she answered, "I'm not sure California girls do that."

"If I'm not mistaken, you're about to become a Wyoming girl. Now, pay attention, and if you catch on right quick, I might even help you out of your wet clothes when we get into the house."

Would she ever be able to resist that sexy smile? Somehow she doubted it. "You have a deal, cowboy."

CHAPTER TWENTY-TWO

THEY WERE EXACTLY three minutes behind schedule when the plane touched down and taxied across the tarmac. In Drake's opinion, traveling by private jet beat the commercial airlines anytime—no security hassles, no lost baggage and no layover. The flight had been smooth, due to a high pressure system coming in, and the turnaround would be quick.

It had taken the better part of a week to coordinate everybody's schedules, but he considered it well worth the time and effort.

Luce's sister and father had arrived in a high-end luxury car that had a pedigree that would've impressed the CEO of a Fortune 500 company. His own truck regularly smelled like dried mud and horse, but no one needed to know that, since he had just flown in on a private plane. He'd opted for a regular shirt and slacks, and to his surprise, Luce had told him to go change.

"Be yourself," she'd said before they left the house.

"Wear jeans and boots. Drake, you're comfortable with who you are. That's really all that matters. My parents will respect that. It won't be news to them that you live on a ranch."

So he kept the nice shirt and gratefully exchanged the slacks and loafers for jeans and boots.

Takeoff was a little turbulent, but Tripp had mentioned it might be. They flew out of it quickly and the trip was smooth from that point on. Luce didn't talk much, but he sensed that she was nervous.

Once they disembarked, Luce rushed across the tarmac to hug a woman who had to be her mother, given the resemblance. Mrs. Hale was expensively dressed in a long white silk shirt and dark pants, her blond hair cut at chin level. Dangling earrings, high heels and a fancy leather handbag completed the overall image of sophistication. There was a second woman, Luce's sister no doubt, a much younger version of the first.

Both were delighted to see Luce, and there was a lot of happy chatter.

Luce, in comparison to her mother and sister, was different, more the outdoors type.

Perfect in every way, in Drake's opinion.

Mr. Hale waited, benignly patient, for his turn to greet the prodigal daughter. He was distinguished-looking, but clearly good-natured, too. Once he'd greeted Luce, the older man met Drake's eyes. They assessed each other in silence for a moment.

Then Drake stepped forward and put out his hand. "I'm Drake Carson," he said.

"John Hale," Luce's father responded, his voice reserved

but cordial. "This is my wife, Dorothy, and our other daughter, Beth."

Drake smiled, shook each woman's hand.

"We've met before," Dorothy Hale said with a sparkle in her eyes. "You probably don't remember, since you and your brothers were small the last time I visited Blythe—not even in school yet, if I remember correctly."

Drake didn't know what to say to that. The whole situation felt awkward and a little contrived, and he began to wish he'd taken Luce's suggestion and introduced himself by phone or over Skype.

"I've never had the pleasure," Luce's dad said cordially. "Luce speaks very highly of you, though, and God knows we both think the world of your mother."

Luce must have sensed Drake's discomfort, because she hooked her arm through his and leaned against him. "Dad, Mom—this is all about telling you, live and in person, even though you already know that Drake's asked me to marry him and I've said yes."

Drake wasn't the nervous sort, but for some reason, everything he'd planned to say had gone right out of his head. He did some mental scrambling and then said, "I love your daughter very much."

"I can see that," Mr. Hale said with a glint of amusement in his eyes. "I take it you flew all the way here to talk to us about this?" He smiled warmly. "We appreciate that, son." He paused to look around the airfield for a few minutes. "Your method seems a little unorthodox, which makes me think this was Luce's idea. And Beth's." His gaze swept from one daughter to the other, full of affection, and Mrs. Hale gave a soft laugh. "I don't know why women can't do things in a straightforward way, just call up and break the news, or come to the house. They like drama, I guess."

Drake relaxed a little, but not completely. He didn't give a damn what people thought of him, but he wanted the Hales to understand that he would be good to Luce, always. "I realize you don't know much about me, but—"

"I know your family," John broke in, "and your mother and Dorothy are close. Your grandfather's a longtime friend of ours, as well—how is George, anyway? It must have been a blow when your grandmother died."

Drake felt a pang of sorrow, thinking of his grandmother, dead some ten years now. He knew his grandfather missed his wife every moment of every day, but the old man was determined to carry on and ran his California vineyard with the energy and ambition of a much younger man. "He keeps busy and visits the ranch when he can," he said, and his voice came out sounding hoarse.

Mrs. Hale hadn't said much before then, but now she spoke up. Cut right to the chase. "We know our daughters are both smart, sensible young women, Drake. If Luce wants to marry you, and if you're anything like your mother and grandfather, you're a fine human being. You certainly have our blessing."

"Do I get to say anything?" Beth demanded good-naturedly.

Everyone smiled.

"Be our guest," John Hale said with a gesture of one hand.

"My sister is a catch," Beth said pleasantly, but in a direct way, "and if you treat her well, I'll be the best sister-in-law ever. If you don't, I'll be your worst nightmare."

Drake laughed, liking Beth, as he liked Mr. and Mrs. Hale. "Duly noted," he said.

John Hale slapped Drake on the shoulder. "Good luck, young man," he said. Then, kissing Luce, he added, "To you, too, sweetheart."

Mrs. Hale was smiling and crying a little at the same time. "I wish you could stay with us awhile, both of you," she said. "We have a lot of planning to do, Luce. It's not every day a person's daughter gets married."

Behind them, Tripp fired up the airplane's engine, and the props began to turn.

"We've got lots of things to do back at Mustang Creek," Luce said, not quite meeting her mother's eyes. "Drake runs the ranch, you know, and I'm still working on my research project."

"Lucinda can be a bit of a handful," Mr. Hale said with another fatherly smile at Luce. "It's only fair to warn you."

Drake smiled. "She'll keep my life interesting, anyway."

"I can hear what you're saying, both of you," Luce said in lilting tones. Her beautiful eyes sparkled with exaggerated affront. She rose up on tiptoe and kissed her mother, then her father, on the cheek. "Thanks for that, Dad," she teased.

"I hate goodbyes," Dorothy said, blotting her eyes with a tissue. "I'll just wait in the car."

"Women," said John, but tenderly.

"We really have to get back," Luce said.

Beth hugged her. "Come back when you can stay longer, sis," she said. Then she smiled, stood on tiptoe and kissed Drake's cheek. "Take care of my sister, cowboy," she told him in parting, "and nobody will get hurt." With that, she followed her mother.

Drake put his arm around Luce's shoulders, gave her a

gentle squeeze and extended a hand to his future father-in-law. "I don't have a lot of experience with father-daughter moments," he said, "but this sure looks like one to me, so I'll leave you to it."

John Hale's grip was firm and friendly. "We'll see you again soon," he said.

Drake nodded, caught and held Luce's eyes for a moment. She nodded back, and he turned and walked back toward the plane, where Tripp was overseeing the refueling process.

"Dad?" Luce said, full of love and benevolent desperation in her voice. "Will you do something for me? Will you please remind Mom that we really and truly want the wedding to be ultrasimple, so she shouldn't go too crazy planning the reception?"

She knew Beth had filled their parents in on the dates and the general plan and would help in Luce's campaign to keep the festivities out of overdrive, but getting her dad on board was important, too.

"Will I at least get to walk you down the aisle?" He asked the question lightly, with a smile in his eyes. Luce knew her answer mattered to this man who had always been a good father to her and to Beth, and a devoted husband to their mother.

She hugged him again, hard. Let her head rest against his strong shoulder for a moment, remembering. Appreciating. And, most of all, loving. "Of course you will, Dad," she assured him, looking up into his kind, strong face. "Although it might be more of a path than an aisle." They both smiled at that. "It's just that, well, for Drake and me, this wedding isn't about one day, it's about setting the tone for our whole future, our marriage." She paused. "And you know me, Dad, I've never been the lace-and-flounces type, have I? That was Beth's department, and when she got married, as you recall, Mom planned, organized and fussed to her heart's content."

Her dad smiled again, a bit wistfully, and shook his head. "I understand, sweetheart. And your mother will, too, with a little convincing. Don't waste a moment worrying about us, because we're on your side. This is your day, and Drake's, and we'll respect that."

"Thank you," Luce said.

He kissed her forehead. "Just be happy," he told her gruffly. "And remember, we love you."

Luce's eyes stung with sudden tears. "And I love you, Dad. You and Mom and Beth."

Holding her shoulders in a gentle grip, her dad looked past her, to Drake and the waiting airplane and probably the years ahead. "Let us know when you get back to Mustang Creek," he said. "Your mother will be anxious until she's sure you're back on solid ground."

"I'll send a text," Luce promised. Then, with a wave toward the car, where her mother and sister waited, and a soft goodbye for her dad, she turned, seeking and finding Drake, walking toward him.

Toward all they would do and be and have together.

CHAPTER TWENTY-THREE

As Luce was to discover over the dizzying course of the next ten days, there was her definition of *simple*—and then there was the Blythe Carson–Dorothy Hale version.

Dorothy and Beth, baby in tow, arrived in Mustang Creek barely a week after the hasty airfield conference, full of happy plans.

Luce, though slightly wary, was thrilled to see her mother, sister and infant nephew.

Dorothy and Blythe hugged and cried and laughed, and they were still chattering long after everyone else had retired that first night.

Luce tried to sleep—upcoming wedding notwithstanding, she was still searching for the herd of wild horses every day, albeit without success, and she'd been spending hours on her research notes, as well. She needed her rest.

Still, knowing her sister and tiny nephew were just down the hall, Luce couldn't lie still long enough to close her eyes, let alone drop off into sweet slumber.

So, barefoot and wearing pajamas, she tiptoed toward that particular guest room, blushing a little as she passed Drake's closed door.

Alas, there would be no private slumber party tonight, not with Luce's mother in the house, huge as it was. She consoled herself with the reminder that soon enough Drake's room would be her room, too.

Reaching Beth's door, Luce rapped lightly, hoping her sister hadn't already gone to sleep. Motherhood, according to Beth, was strenuous business, and the day had been a busy one.

"In," Beth called quietly. For a moment, it seemed to Luce, time shifted, and she and her sister were girls again, meeting in one of their bedrooms to whisper and giggle and, sometimes, commiserate over a boy or a bad grade or being grounded.

Luce stepped willingly into the time warp.

Beth had just gotten the baby to sleep in the antique cradle hauled over from Slater and Grace's part of the house for his use.

She smiled at Luce and held an index finger to her lips.

Luce smiled and nodded and crept over to admire the sleeping infant. His name was Ben, and he looked downright cherubic lying there, his downy hair fluffing out, his lashes resting lush on his plump little cheeks.

Luce's heart swelled with love for this child and, naturally, she thought of the babies she and Drake would have.

Was it even possible to sustain the kind of happiness she was feeling now?

Probably not, she supposed. Like everyone else, she and Drake would have their ups and downs, but the core of their relationship was solid and lasting, and that was what counted.

She and Beth moved to sit, side by side, on the edge of the bed, speaking in near whispers.

"Okay," Luce began, "let's have it. Is Mom here to see her best friend and help with the preparations, or is she planning a full-scale assault on my wedding plans?"

Beth smiled, took Luce's hand and squeezed it gently. "We're here because you're getting married, and we want to be with you. I think Dad and I have been fairly successful in persuading Mom not to go all Martha Stewart, though I can't guarantee she and Mrs. Carson aren't plotting a takeover even as we speak."

Luce shook her head, but she was smiling as she returned Beth's hand-squeeze. "Whatever happens, I'm so glad you're here. Mom, too, of course."

"Dad and Liam will be here the day of," Beth said. Liam was her husband. "In the meantime, Mom and I just want to be part of the process." She made a cross-my-heart motion with one hand. "We'll behave, I promise."

Luce laughed, very softly. "Who are you," she joked, "and what have you done with my sister?"

Beth stifled a giggle, à la the old days, when they were teenagers with silly secrets. And her eyes shone as she gazed at Luce. "I'm so happy for you, sis."

Luce teared up briefly and gave Beth a one-armed hug. "Thanks, Bethie. That means a lot to me."

They sat in silence for a little while, just being sisters, side by side, shoulders touching.

Then, with a faux wince, Beth ventured, "You do know about the wedding shower, right? I hope I'm not blowing a big surprise."

"I suspected something was up," Luce admitted, pleased in spite of her no-fuss policy. "I've caught Grace and Harry and Blythe whispering a few times, among other hints."

"So you've made friends here?"

"I haven't had much spare time," Luce answered, "but, yes, I've been meeting new people right and left. Hadleigh, Melody and Bex—they're married to Drake's closest friends—have been great to me. Being neighborly is very big in Mustang Creek."

"Good," Beth said. "I love my husband, but the older I get, the more I cherish my girlfriend time."

Another silence followed, contented and reflective. Again, and typically, Beth was the one to break it.

"Okay, so I do have one question," she said.

"Shoot," Luce responded.

"What about your PhD, and your plans to teach? It's none of my business, I know, and yet—"

"And yet it is," Luce said. "You're my big sister, after all. The answer is, I may modify my plans a little, at least at first, but I'm definitely going forward with the original idea."

"Where would you teach? Is there a college in Mustang Creek?"

"A community college," Luce replied, "with a very good chance of upgrading to a four-year institution in the next few years. They've already approached me about establishing an ecology program this fall, in cooperation with the high school, and that means I can teach while I finish my graduate work."

"And what does Drake think?"

Luce smiled and patted her sister's hand. "He's all for it. Drake is as committed to the environment as I am, if not more so, and I'm counting on his input when I start my syllabus."

Beth fairly beamed. "Wow," she said. "The man is not only hot, he's progressive."

Luce laughed. "I wouldn't go that far. Drake's hot, all right, but progressive?" She shook her head, still amused. "When he decides to dig in his heels, he can be incredibly stubborn, and some of his ideas are distinctly old-fashioned."

"Examples, please, little sister."

"Well, he can be overprotective. He opens doors and tips his hat and says 'Ma'am' when he speaks to a woman over fifty. He stands when any female enters a room and won't hear of going Dutch."

Beth made a mock-sympathetic face. "Poor you," she said.

"Yeah," Luce agreed happily. "Poor me."

Beth yawned then and, since yawns are catchy, Luce did, too. The sisters exchanged good-nights, and Luce went back to her room.

This time, she had no trouble falling asleep.

THE NEXT FEW days were busy ones. Luce saw little of Drake, but this only ratcheted up the anticipation, and when they were together, invisible fireflies lit the atmosphere between them.

As it turned out, literally every woman in Mustang Creek had been invited to the wedding shower, held in the community center, and there was a capacity crowd. By Blythe's decree, and much to Luce's agreement, nobody brought gifts; the gathering was meant to be a getting-acquainted celebration, and it was certainly that and more.

Although the no-gifts rule was observed, it apparently didn't apply to food. Luce had never seen so many cakes, pies, cookies and casseroles supplementing the catered spread. There was plenty of wine—Mace's label, of course—as well as lemonade and punch and that small-town specialty, two large urns of coffee, regular and decaffeinated.

Luce was absolutely dazzled; Melody, Hadleigh and Bex had hung streamers, and there were flowers everywhere.

Luce had a wonderful time, as did her mother and sister, though with all those new faces, she began to wish someone had passed out name tags.

The event lasted some three hours, and Luce was dizzy by the end, feeling fully welcome in her new community. There was still a great deal of food, but the women of Mustang Creek were prepared; they'd brought plastic containers of all sorts along, and they filled every one to the brim.

Much of it would be eaten later that same day, since, once a week, the community center offered free meals to anyone who showed up. By design, tonight was the night. The remainder of the largesse, mostly desserts, would be taken to the town's two nursing homes as a treat for the residents.

Luce treasured the prospect of friendship with these women, and their generosity, to the less fortunate members of the community as well as to her, was a memory she would hold in her heart forever.

WHEN THEIR WEDDING DAY finally arrived, Luce was in a strange, blissful state, and for the first time, she understood what the old cliché about walking on air really meant.

Blythe and Dorothy had done their best to restrain themselves, but only so much could be expected of the mothers of the bride and groom.

The spacious yard behind the ranch house glittered in the twilight when everyone gathered for the ceremony. Colorful Chinese lanterns glowed in the branches of the maple and oak trees, the rented folding chairs had bows affixed to their backs and a three-piece mini orchestra had set up in the gazebo.

There was an abundance of food, as there had been at the shower a few days before, but Luce knew not a scrap would be wasted. Once again the leftovers would be shared; this time two local churches had agreed to package what remained and deliver meals to every shut-in in town.

When all was ready, the ceremony began.

Luce wore a simple, ankle-length dress of white eyelet over a silky fabric; Drake, a dark suit that flattered his cowboy frame in a whole new way. The small orchestra played quietly.

Luce's father, recently arrived, proudly escorted the bride to the rose arbor serving as an altar, where Beth waited, beaming, bouquet in hand.

Drake, with his brothers at his side, stood tall and proud and impossibly handsome, facing the Carson family's long-time minister.

"Who gives this woman in marriage?" the pastor asked.

"Her mother and I," answered the father of the bride in a clear voice. Before returning to his seat in the front row, next to Dorothy, Blythe and a happily weepy Harry, he bent his head and kissed Luce gently on the cheek.

The vows were made, the rings were exchanged and Drake and Luce were pronounced husband and wife.

Drake's kiss was long and deep, and when it ended, the

guests applauded and cheered, and he whispered mischie-
vously, "There's something to be said for starting off on
the right foot, so to speak."

And Luce laughed for joy.

As MUCH AS DRAKE loved his family and friends, there were
times, during the picture-taking and the cake-eating and
the exuberant congratulations, that he wished they'd all
vanish, temporarily of course, into some parallel universe,
so that he could be alone with his wife.

It seemed to him that the fussing and the eating and the
making of toasts would never end. Drake choked up as he
watched his bride and her father share the first waltz.

God, Luce was so beautiful.

And she was his wife.

When it was his turn to dance with the bride, Drake
forgot everything but the way it felt to hold this woman
in his arms, to see her smiling up at him, her eyes alight.

Eventually, the long-awaited cue came. Slater gave the
prearranged signal to take Luce and slip away—a raised fist.

Finally, finally, the honeymoon could begin.

Drake grabbed Luce and led her to the refurbished buck-
board awaiting them. Red was at the reins, all spiffed up in
his best suit, reserved for weddings and funerals, and grinning from one ear to the other. He jumped down, nimble
for a man of his age, and watched proudly as Drake lifted
Luce up into the seat, then followed, taking the place Red
had occupied.

There were more cheers and good wishes, and then Mr.
and Mrs. Drake Carson were on their way.

The honeymoon would be an unconventional one,
Drake supposed, at least in terms of location, but it was
exactly what both he and Luce wanted.

Earlier in the day, with the help of his brothers, Drake had set up a tent in the private spot where he and Luce had made love the first time. A campfire was laid, and there were fancy provisions, but just then, Drake didn't care if he ever ate again.

Luce sat close, leaning against him, her arm hooked through his.

"I can still arrange for a hotel, if you've changed your mind," he told her, raising his voice a little to be heard over the two-horse team and the creaking harnesses.

"Not a chance," Luce said. "This is perfect."

The words proved prophetic.

When they reached the campsite, the tent, just big enough for an air mattress equipped with a double sleeping bag, glowed like a palace in the star-spangled moonlight.

For a touch of elegance, there was a small portable picnic table, so they wouldn't have to eat breakfast sitting on the ground. If they ever got around to breakfast, that is.

Luce drew in an audible breath. "Oh, Drake," she whispered. "This is lovely!"

Her pleasure was his pleasure, and not just in bed.

Drake secured the wagon's brake lever, wrapped the reins loosely around it and climbed down. When he reached for Luce, she wrapped her arms around him and slid her body along the length of his as she descended.

He kissed her, long and hard and deep.

"Happy?" he asked when he caught his breath.

She smiled. "Yes," she replied, "and about to be a whole lot happier still."

Drake laughed and swatted her lightly on that delectable backside of hers.

"Like any good frontier husband," he said, "I've got to look after the horses before I can do anything else."

"Then I guess you'd better hurry, cowboy," Luce purred, her eyes dancing.

With that, she headed for the tent, disappeared inside.

If there was a God in heaven, Drake thought, with a silent apology for irreverence, she'd be out of that dress by the time he joined her.

IT WAS DELICIOUSLY DARK inside that small tent, and Luce wasted no time wriggling out of her wedding dress and panty hose and bra. Since there was no place to put the discarded garments, she tossed them through the narrow opening and stretched out to wait for her husband.

He was in the process of stripping when he entered their honeymoon hideaway.

Luce was more than ready for him, and there was no question that he was ready for her.

They'd made love before, of course, but somehow that night was even better. In fact, it was transcendent.

They touched each other everywhere.

They kissed and withdrew, not to tease, but because they needed to catch their breath.

They drew out the foreplay until neither of them could bear the wait any longer, and when they came together, they felt their souls mate along with their bodies.

Intermittently, they slept, satiated, and then woke to love again.

For a solid forty-eight hours, they were alone in their singular world of grass and trees and snow-capped mountains.

Then, inevitably, it was time to go back.

"Could we do this again?" Luce asked. This morning, she was wearing shorts, hiking boots and a tank top from the suitcase they'd brought along in the back of the wagon.

Drake, busy hitching the horses to the wagon, paused long enough to kiss her thoroughly. "I was thinking," he said, working again, "that we ought to build a house here. What do you think, Mrs. Carson?"

She turned him around, flung herself at him, arms around his neck, legs around his hips. "I think you're a genius, Mr. Carson," she cried, and then she kissed him just as deeply as he'd kissed her before.

NO HONEYMOON LASTS FOREVER, Drake reminded himself when they drove up to the ranch half an hour later and found Red waiting for them with a solemn expression on his grizzled old face.

"He doesn't look happy," Luce observed, perched beside Drake on the wagon seat and sounding worried.

"He never looks happy," Drake said.

Luce didn't wait for him to help her down from the wagon this time. She marched over to Red and asked, "What's wrong?"

Red chuckled. "See you're takin' to bein' a ranch wife right off the bat," he remarked, not unkindly.

"You looked so serious," Luce persisted.

"I ain't what you'd call expressive," Red told her. By then, Drake was out of the wagon, coming toward them.

"Stop stalling and spill it," he said.

"Look, I didn't mean to get you all riled up. I just wanted to welcome the bride and groom home proper like, that's all. Let me deal with this wagon and these horses and we'll talk business."

Knowing Luce wanted to take a shower and then drink coffee that hadn't been boiled over a campfire, Drake said, "Go on inside, Luce. Mom and Harry are probably waiting to make sure you're still in one piece after a wilderness honeymoon."

Luce smiled, but she didn't budge. "In a minute," she said. "If this is about the mountain lion, or the wild horses, I want to hear it."

Red looked a little surprised, but he didn't offer an opinion. In his era, women didn't talk back to their husbands.

Drake felt a little sorry for Red's generation, because this particular woman was worth listening to.

"The BLM and the Fish and Wildlife people are all over this," Red said as stolidly cheerful as ever. "They plan to tranquilize the cat and relocate it farther north. If they can find it, anyhow."

Drake was relieved. Relocation was ideal in a case like this, but it wasn't always possible for a variety of reasons, including budgets and manpower.

"Just goes to show change isn't always bad," Red agreed. "Back in my day, they solved problems like this one with a bullet."

"Change isn't good or bad," Drake said. "It just is. And this is *still* your day, Red."

"As long as my eyes open every morning, I reckon that's true." Red scratched his chin, his tone jocular.

"What about the wild horses?" Luce asked.

"No sign of them," Red replied with regret.

"In that case, I'm going inside." Luce stood on her toes and kissed Drake's cheek. "See you around, cowboy," she said, and then she was moving away, headed for the house.

A glint appeared in Red's eyes the moment Luce was gone.

"You've got more to say," Drake prodded. "So say it."

"All the weddin' visitors are gone," Red replied, "but you have some company coming your way."

Given the topic of conversation, the incoming person had to be none other than Lettie Arbuckle-Calder. "Does she have a hyphenated last name by any chance?"

"You got it." Red practically chortled. "She ain't alone, either. Two lawyers and some other fella's comin' with her. They ought to be here any minute now. Your mother told me to send you in to talk to her soon as you and Luce got back."

Luce was on her way to the shower. If Drake went inside now, he ran a definite risk of following her upstairs. And if that happened, he'd be late for Lettie's meeting.

If he got there at all.

"Damn," Drake muttered. "I hope this doesn't mean Lettie and her bunch have filed some sort of injunction to keep me from capturing that stallion and moving him off this ranch. If that happens, I'll never get my mares back."

"Seems to me you ain't made much headway in that direction anyways," Red said wryly.

"Thanks for pointing that out," Drake retorted. "For a minute there, I'd forgotten."

Red busted loose with one of his gap-toothed grins. "Look on the bright side, son. In a roundabout way, that stallion landed you a beautiful wife." He hoisted his rickety old carcass up into the wagon seat and took the reins. Looking down at Drake, he went solemn again. "Just simmer down and listen to what these folks have to say. Like as not, they want the same thing you do, just for different reasons. And Lettie Arbuckle might be a lot of things, but stupid ain't one of 'em."

Drake didn't answer. He just went around to the back of the wagon, lowered the tailgate and pulled out Luce's suitcase and his leather overnight case.

Soon as he raised the tailgate again, Red drove off.

DRAKE HEADED FOR the house. No sign of anybody.

Not daring to join his wife upstairs, Drake found clean jeans and a shirt in the laundry room, then used the adjoining shower, reserved for men who might dirty up Harry's clean floors or get dust on the furniture.

While he lathered up, he thought about Lettie. She could be pushy as hell, but he'd served on the board of the county humane society with her, and he knew her concern for the welfare of animals was genuine. If she was on the annoying side, well, her heart was in the right place.

Fifteen minutes after he'd gotten dressed and poured himself a cup of coffee, the Lettie Arbuckle–Calder contingent showed up in a caravan of luxury vehicles.

Harry and Blythe instantly reappeared, greeted him cordially and proceeded to welcome their guests.

Everyone gravitated to the dining room and seated themselves around the big table, conference style.

Luce joined them while they were still getting settled, and another round of good wishes ensued.

While Harry bustled off to the kitchen to brew a gallon or two of coffee and arrange the inevitable baked goods on platters, Lettie stated her business.

"We've come to outline our plan concerning that stallion and his band," she said, and her tone was decisive. "Those beautiful, majestic creatures must be protected at any cost."

Harold, who was now recovered to the point that he

could get around, ambled in and settled himself as close to Drake as he could manage, and Violet soon arrived, too.

All eyes swung to Drake, as surely as if he'd bolted to his feet and roared an objection.

Before he could lodge an opinion, before he really *had* an opinion, however, Harry rushed in from the kitchen, clearly panicked. "I just heard from Grace over the intercom," she blurted. "It's time!"

Luce went pale and rushed toward the wide doorway. She turned back to him. "Come on, Drake," she said urgently. "Slater's off on location somewhere, and we've got to get Grace to the hospital!"

Call him slow, but Drake hadn't made the leap from Harry's "It's time!" to the fact that Grace was about to give birth.

Blythe, too, was on her feet, apologizing to the group assembled around the table.

Luce waited impatiently. "You get your truck," she told Drake, "and I'll get Grace. Hurry!"

"I'll call Grace's doctor and let Slater know," Blythe said.

"Oh, dear Lord," Harry said, looking faint.

Somebody led her to a chair and sat her down, made her put her head down low.

Drake ran to the kitchen, grabbed his keys from the hook next to the back door and hurried outside to fire up the rig.

When Luce appeared, Lettie was with her, and they were supporting Grace between them.

"Get her in the truck," Lettie ordered.

Drake obeyed, hefting a bulky Grace into the backseat.

Harry, apparently recovered, ran outside with a stack of clean towels. "You might need these!"

"I hope to God you're wrong about that," Drake muttered.

Luce bounded into the passenger seat and buckled her seat belt. "Go!" she told Drake.

Grace moaned softly.

Drake laid rubber.

"Why didn't you tell someone you've been having contractions all day?" Luce asked her sister-in-law, sounding surprisingly calm.

Drake was anything but.

"They *were* far apart," Grace protested. "And I get them all the time!"

Another moan, this one deeper and slow to end.

"Well, they sure aren't far apart now," Luce said.

"I'm not sure we're going to make it to the hospital," Grace groaned.

"Don't worry," Luce told her. Easy for her to say, since she wasn't the one fixing to have a baby in the backseat of a pickup.

Drake said nothing. He just drove.

And he prayed.

"If necessary, Drake can fill in for the doctor," Luce went on merrily. "It can't be that different from delivering a calf."

Drake swore under his breath and kept the pedal to the metal. Checking the rearview mirror, he was relieved to see Harry and his mother barreling along behind them in Harry's old station wagon.

Lettie and her bunch followed, on their way back to wherever they'd been before they showed up at the ranch en masse.

It was quite a procession. Grace gave an apologetic little scream.

Holy shit, Drake thought.

"Hold on, Grace," Luce said, rifling through her purse. How was it that, no matter what the emergency, women always managed to have their handbags with them? Triumphantly, she held up a small bottle of hand sanitizer. "Voilà!"

"I can do this," Grace said, panting the words. "I can do this."

That was Grace for you.

"How far to the hospital?" Luce asked, digging in her purse again.

"A lot farther than I'd like," Drake said tightly.

"Everything's going to be all right," Luce said in a sing-song voice. She'd extracted a pair of nail scissors and a package of dental floss by then.

Grace wasn't fooled by Luce's eager reassurance. She was, after all, in pain and possibly on the verge of giving birth to her first child in a truck. "An epidural would be good right about now," she answered, shutting her eyes.

The next thing she said was "Oh, my God, the baby's coming—now!"

Drake was about to whip over to the side of the road, shut off the truck and take care of business, but before he could, Grace spoke again.

"Or not," she said happily. "Whew. That was a bad one."

They made it, after all.

Just barely.

In the end, an emergency-room doctor delivered the baby in the backseat of the truck, right there in the hospital parking lot.

At least Drake had dodged *that* bullet.

Luce loved the fact that he would've done whatever he had to, though. It gave her a greater sense of his brother's vision of life in a place like this. His documentary about this area showed how people used to rely on one another. In the old days, with no hospitals handy, midwives, the occasional doctor or sometimes stalwart husbands had to make do. "You almost had to deliver the baby," she said.

Hours had passed, and they were back home in their room.

"*Almost* is good." Drake sank down on the bed and fell back, crossing his arms behind his head. He was wearing jeans, but no shirt and no boots. "I can deal with that. And, by the way, there is a major difference between delivering a calf and delivering a baby."

Luce smiled winningly, stretching out beside him, running a hand lightly over his chest. "You can do anything," she said.

"Thanks," Drake replied wryly, "but there may be a few flaws in that theory."

"The important thing is Grace and the baby are both doing well."

"You're right. That *is* what's important. Of course, Slater may need treatment for heart failure, now that he's heard the story."

"Poor Slater," Luce agreed, still stroking Drake's chest. "All the way up in northern Alberta. He must be beside himself."

"By now, he's on his way home," Drake said.

"If you're away from home when I have our first baby," Luce said, "I might have you horsewhipped when you get back."

Drake laughed. "I'll keep that in mind."

"Good."

"And if you don't stop doing what you're doing, that baby might come sooner than expected."

Luce kissed him. "Promises, promises," she murmured. "Are you just talking, or do you plan to put your money where your mouth is?"

"I definitely plan to put my mouth in a few places," he answered. "Forget money."

IT HAD TAKEN eight of them that morning, and a carefully orchestrated dance of experienced horsemen, not to mention a whole lot of luck, but they'd accomplished their mission.

They'd tracked down the stallion, finally, and cornered him, along with his band, in a canyon.

Cutting out Drake's mares wasn't easy, but with some fancy riding and even fancier roping, they'd gotten the job done.

The stallion was outraged, naturally, and he'd get the mares back if he got the chance.

It was Drake's job to make damn sure that didn't happen.

Two riders had kept the stallion and his following boxed in until the mares, some with foals, were well away.

Back home, he and the others put them in stalls, fed and watered them.

When Luce appeared, Drake pointed at one of the stalls. "Take a look," he said.

Luce gave him an uncertain glance but went to peer over the top of the stall door. The look on her face made it all worthwhile. "Oh, Drake! He's beautiful!"

The colt was truly a fine-looking little horse. The spitting image of his sire, right down to the way he left his mother to come and stare up at Luce, nickering quietly.

"You said you wanted a horse of your own," Drake told her. "You'll have to sweet-talk Red into starting him when that high-spirited colt gets old enough. The old man has a soft spot for you, so that should work out."

"He's gorgeous." She whispered the words, marveling. So was she.

There was nothing ordinary about her, including the fact that she'd decided to study wild horses even though she'd been skittish about riding at first.

She was made for ranch life.

God, how he loved her. She'd spent her honeymoon in a tent and delighted in every minute of it. She'd jumped into a truck and driven country roads with a pregnant woman about to deliver in the backseat.

Oh, yes. She was his kind of woman.

"This horse is going to be magnificent when he grows up."

"He'll have to be gelded," Drake reminded her.

"You really surprised me this time," she said, and her eyes were alight.

He was fairly sure he'd fallen for those eyes first. The minute she'd stormed at him through that meadow. He couldn't forget her tempting body, either...

But it wasn't only physical. Her adventurous spirit had moved him from the beginning and so had her innate kindness. He searched for the right answer and found honesty the only option. "It might have been," he admitted. "Did it work?"

She smiled and rose on tiptoe to kiss him. "You'll find out tonight."

★ ★ ★ ★ ★

Keep reading to enjoy an insightful—
and delightful—personal essay from Linda Lael Miller,
the queen of Western romance!

GROWING UP WESTERN

IF I'VE BEEN asked once how I came to understand the West, both old and new, so well, I've been asked a million times. It's a question I never tire of, unlike "Where do you get your ideas?" (my standard and admittedly snarky reply is usually "I go to ideas.com. I'm a subscriber.") and the ever popular "How much money do you make?" (Answer: "How much do *you* make?") Since Skip and Hazel's baby girl was raised up right, as we say out here, I am much more polite to the elderly and the obviously well-intentioned but naive. With them, I simply counter sweetly, "Now, why would you ask a question like that?"

The most accurate answer, as far as I know, is this. I grew up in the old West, as well as the new. I lived it, sometimes vicariously, often straight up, like a shot of whiskey.

For instance, one of my earliest memories is of our first home, affectionately referred to in Lael lore as the Van Horn. (Probably the surname of the good folks who owned the property before my grandfather Jacob Daniel

Lael bought a big chunk of land and gave some of it to my father, Grady "Skip" Lael, and some to my uncle, Jack Lael.)

Our "house" would have made the cabin in *Little House on the Prairie* look like the Biltmore Estate. In actuality, it was, I'm told, a converted chicken coop, with no insulation and certainly no indoor facilities. Since I was only about two when my memory kicked in and commenced taking notes, I didn't feel at all deprived. After all, the only other houses I frequented did not seem significantly different.

There was no running water; a daily supply had to be scooped from the nearby creek in buckets and carried back to the house, where, if it was meant for anything besides drinking from the trusty dipper, it would be heated on the potbellied stove. Amazingly, Mom did all the cooking on that little stove, with its crooked chimney poking out of the wall.

Dad, recently discharged from the United States Marine Corps, where he served bravely on Iwo Jima, among other terrifying places, was a resourceful man. He knew we would need insulation, come those cold eastern Washington winters, but he probably didn't have the proverbial two nickels to rub together. He paid a visit to the funeral home in Colville, some forty miles away, and talked the proprietors out of a stack of large cardboard cartons, which had originally housed spanking-new coffins.

He brought the flattened boxes home, trimmed them to fit his purposes and nailed them to the thin board walls of the chicken coop, with all their cracks and knotholes, and lined the inside of the roof, too, since there was no ceiling. He was very careful, he always said, with a twinkle in his blue eyes, to keep the printed side to the wall. That first night, he lay down in bed, pleased with his industry, and there right above his head in bold print were the leg-endary words *Sunshine Coffin Company.*

Dad owned (and deeply loved) a bay gelding called Pea-nuts. He used the horse to herd our very few cattle, among other tasks. Mainly, I suspect, he just liked riding, being a cowboy at heart with a history of rodeos behind him. He was, back in the day, a bull rider and traveled widely with his older brother, Jack, who was a serious contender in every rodeo he entered. Known from Northport, Wash-ington, to Madison Square Garden in New York City (we would have pronounced NYC the way that guy in the salsa commercials did) as "Jiggs" Lael, my uncle was the classic bronc-buster. Elvis-handsome, he won numerous buckles and got to kiss Miss America twice—two different Miss Americas on two different occasions—for placing first in the bareback ridin', as we termed it.

In their travels, Dad and Uncle Jack had plenty of ad-ventures, and I've woven several of them into my books over the course of my career. A particular favorite is the tale of a bar fight in a run-down Montana establishment, involving a couple of cowboy brothers sent by their mother to fetch Pa home for supper. Pa was roundly drunk and scrawny as a baby bird, while his sons were big as upended boxcars. One of the cowboys whispered mildly to Dad and Uncle Jack, "Now, friends, you need to stay out of this. It's a family matter."

They stepped up to Pa's bar stool and each gripped one of his arms, hoping for a peaceable departure.

Well, Pa might have been little, but he was mighty, and he wasn't through with the day's drinking, either. He put up one hell of a fight and did some damage to his tough sons before they managed to haul him out of the saloon and home to Ma. A version of that story turned up in my novel *The Bridegroom* years later.

I often went riding with Dad on Peanuts, from the age of two. He called our forays "cuttin' brush," which meant we were chasing stray cattle hither and yon, and he said I sat that saddle like a pro, even then. Today, thanks to a great deal of effort on my brother's part, I own that very saddle, battered and worn, the canticle inscribed with the name "Skip Lael," and it is my most prized possession.

Still more immersion in the Western culture came through our neighbors and dear friends, the Wileys—we're at four generations and counting—where my brother and I spent a lot of time growing up. The Wileys were not blood relations, but Guy Wiley, the mischievous patriarch of the clan, was "Grampa" to us, and his wife, Florence, was "Gramma."

Compared to the Van Horn, the Wiley ranch was J. R. Ewing's Southfork, although in actuality, it was and is a very small, never-painted house, downright tiny by anybody's standards. It never felt cramped because there always seemed to be room for one more, and the place was often filled to the rafters with cousins, neighbors and stray kids in need of a place to be. Guy and Florence raised five children in that two-bedroom house, and several generations have grown up there since. I'm only one of many, many people with fond memories of that house and the kindness of the Wileys.

My favorite part of the ranch house was the kitchen, not just because of the delicious pies, fried chicken, creek trout, venison roasts, garden vegetables and fresh and preserved fruit that were served at the venerable old table over by the windows. I liked the kitchen because Gramma Wiley was always there, doing something at her big old wood-burning cookstove and, better yet, telling stories.

Gramma had so many stories. Her mother, who lived with the family until her death at a very great age, was the widow of an honest-to-God Civil War soldier. As the tale was told, the older of the two Gramma Wileys had been married to a young man serving on the Union side. He'd marched off to war with his best friend, from whom he extracted a solemn vow that if he fell in battle, the best friend would take care of his wife and small children when the fighting was over. The husband did perish, like so many others, and the best friend was as good as his word. He went back home when the war ended, married the widow and fathered several more children, including Florence. This man, whose last name was Heritage, a fact that seems strangely fitting, was definitely ahead of his time—but I'll get to that.

Eventually, the couple bought a farm outside of Coffeyville, Kansas. In those days following the Civil War, Kansas was still the Wild West, and it wasn't called "bloody Kansas" for nothing. Before, during and after the great conflict, there were plenty of differing opinions, and a lot of them ended in violence. Bands of outlaws—most of them displaced veterans from both the Union and the Confederacy—roamed the countryside, robbing banks, rustling livestock and shooting up saloons. It was a very dangerous time.

Mr. Heritage, however, was a man of peace. He didn't even believe in spanking his children, and I'd be willing to bet that he'd seen all the killing he cared to look upon during the war. Still, a farmer with a family to protect, and to feed, he would have owned a gun or two, for hunting and personal defense.

One day, when Gramma Florence was a very small child, gunshots sounded in town, and repeatedly, audible even from the farm, which was some six miles from Coffeyville. Of all the stories she told me, in the heart of the Wiley ranch house outside Northport, clattering the lids of her cast-iron, chrome-trimmed Kitchen Queen all the while, this one is my second favorite.

Her father did not go to town to participate in the melee. As I said, he was a man of peace.

Word soon reached them, probably via a well-informed neighbor passing by on the road, that the Dalton brothers, a famous outlaw band of the day, had intended to hold up the bank in Coffeyville. Banks weren't federally insured in those days, so if the money was stolen, it was just plain gone, for good. Folks would be ruined, perhaps see their children go hungry, if the thieves succeeded.

The men of the town, along with ranchers and farmers from the surrounding area, had gotten wind of the plan ahead of time, and they were ready and waiting, sprawled on rooftops, hidden in the narrow spaces between storefronts, crouched behind horse troughs, with their rifles and pistols cocked, when the Daltons rode up and reined in right in front of the bank.

The locals opened fire, releasing a literal hail of bullets.

The Dalton brothers were dead before they could dismount, probably before they realized what was happening.

The townsfolk decided to bring home a salient point: the wages of sin is death, as the Bible rather ungrammatically puts it. They strapped those dead outlaws to boards and doors ripped from their hinges and set them upright along the street, right there on the wooden sidewalk. People came from far and wide to look at them, bloody and fly-specked, and they brought their children, too. The message was abundantly clear: this is what comes of the criminal life. Aspiring outlaws, beware.

There were so many visitors trooping past the bodies, I was told, that guards had to be posted to keep folks from stealing buttons off the dead outlaws' coats or snipping off a lock of hair for a souvenir. Photographs were taken, and can still be seen in books and online, and the images are grim indeed.

Mr. Heritage was having none of the spectacle, morally instructive or not. He was not about to march *his* children past a bunch of bullet-riddled outlaws, and that was that. They didn't go into town that day or any other day, until the Daltons had been taken off display and decently buried.

I've always admired Mr. Heritage for his sensitivity, among other qualities. As I said before, he was an unusual man, especially in that time and place.

Still, Gramma Florence remembered that day as vividly, all those years later, in her plain kitchen, with me listening raptly, as if it had happened the previous week.

That being my second favorite story, I will now tell my first.

One day, on that same farm, at about sundown, supper was cooking and Mr. Heritage was outside, probably chopping wood or pumping water, when a rider approached his gate. The stranger wore a long, dusty overcoat and his hat was pulled down low over his eyes.

Mr. Heritage went to the gate to speak to him, that being the neighborly thing to do. He spoke quietly with the man for a while, then, as later reported, invited him to come on in and join the family for the evening meal.

The stranger thanked Mr. Heritage, kindly and quietly, but declined. Mr. Heritage directed him to the barn, where he and his tired horse could pass the night with a roof over their heads. It's pertinent to mention here that, although hospitality was a way of life in those days, especially on lonely farms and ranches, where any visitor was an event, no unknown caller would have been asked to spend the night in the house, because of the women and children.

Presently, Mr. Heritage came inside, where the family was fairly bursting with curiosity. Why hadn't the man seen to his horse and come in to join them at the supper table? He surely looked like someone in need of a hot meal and some pleasant conversation.

Mr. Heritage, probably washing up at the basin prior to sitting down to the meal, was thoughtful. He'd offered, he told his wife and children, but the man had refused, saying he didn't want to endanger them by getting too close.

He was, he had admitted, a fugitive from the law, wanted dead or alive.

And his name was Jesse James.

The notable outlaw was a kind of Robin Hood figure to ordinary folks. He never stole from them, or shot at them. Indeed, he'd been known to meet their mortgage payments, supply food when they might have gone hungry otherwise and protect them from other outlaws.

A little research into Jesse James's life will show that he was, for all practical intents and purposes, a cold-blooded killer and a clever thief, an outlaw in every sense of the word. Growing up on a hardscrabble farm himself, he and his family had suffered greatly at the hands of renegade

Yankees, had their crops trampled and were terrorized to the extent of a mock hanging that left Jesse's beloved step-father a broken man. From that day until he was shot in the back while hanging a picture in his own living room, James hated the United States government and, by extension, all officialdom, as did his brothers.

The law was probably relieved when the infamous Mr. Howard gunned Jesse down, since it saved them the trouble of hanging him. To the common folks, however, Jesse James died a hero, and he was widely mourned, the subject of song and story.

And he'd spent a night in the Heritage barn, this very man, feeding and watering his horse, grateful to bed down in the hay and straw, probably full of the generous supper Mr. Heritage almost certainly brought out to him on one of his wife's own Blue Willow dinner plates. The next morning, most likely before sunrise, the visitor saddled up and rode on.

I like to think he tipped his hat in farewell as he went.

As an avid student of American history, I'm familiar with the life of Jesse James, and I still marvel at the mysterious complexity of human nature. Truly, with a few notable exceptions, everybody is some combination of very good and very bad, with a great deal of both blending in the middle.

These two stories were integral to my formation as a writer, and I'm sure there were many more, lost to present recollection.

Ranch life was still rustic, even in the 1950s and early '60s, so my immersion continued. Cattle had to be rounded up, fed, watered or milked. There was no branding on the Wiley ranch; they used ear tags to mark their livestock. Kindness was the Wiley way, and animals benefited as well

as humans. Gramma, like her own father, would not coun-
tenance spanking, and fistfights, a sport on other farms and
ranches, were strictly forbidden.

The chores were endless. Water had to be pumped and
carried in, eggs gathered, cows milked, cream and milk
separated, cream churned into good country butter, with
no additives except for a tiny pinch of salt. (Too much salt
was considered a dirty trick, since it made the butter set
up considerably faster.) The women made quilts—by the
light of kerosene lanterns when I was very young, and later
by the unreliable light of a single bulb dangling over the
kitchen table—and sewed shirts for their men, complicated
Western styles with fancy yokes and snap buttons, stitching
the seams either by hand or on Gramma's ancient treadle
sewing machine. They didn't go to town for fancy store-
bought patterns, these necessarily resourceful women; they
took measurements and cut the pieces from old newspa-
pers, pinned those to the cloth and snipped out shapes that
went together perfectly.

They conjured up hot biscuits, fried chicken (or grouse
or rabbit or venison or, very rarely, beef from the family's
own herd), and coffee that would, as the men liked to say,
put hair on your chest. They grew vast gardens, baked loaf
after loaf of delicious bread and put up preserves for the
long, hungry winters, all without running water or electricity. We kids had chores to do—carrying wood for the
stoves, weeding and watering the garden, digging potatoes, shelling peas and stringing beans. The cousins milked
cows—I never got the knack—and we also gathered eggs
and fed the chickens. The coward in the lot, I was scared
of roosters, not to mention bulls, and I couldn't "buck"
bales (of hay) to save my life.

Still, we lived in a magical world, those days on the ranch, wading in the ice-cold creek, trying to catch fish, riding far and wide on horseback. If the chores were done and there was no hay to cut, load and haul, we were free to mount up and take off. In those days, nobody worried about us unless a horse came back riderless or we were, God forbid, late for supper.

The girls did the dishes after a meal, in basins, the water heated on the Kitchen Queen. The boys lugged buckets up from the creek and split firewood to kindling, because the cookstove was always hungry, even in the heat of summer.

In the evening, Gramma liked to sit in her rocking chair, reading by the light of a kerosene lamp, sewing or darning socks, or playing solitaire with cards bent and nearly colorless with age. At the time, it all seemed normal. In retrospect, I wonder how on earth the woman did so much work, so cheerfully.

We were poor, by most people's standards, but none of us had a clue. Life was real and rich and full of stories.

About the time I was ready for kindergarten, the bottom fell out of the beef market, and we moved into Northport, population five hundred, give or take, but along with my brother and numerous cousins, we still spent lots of time on the Wiley ranch, especially during the summers.

Dad's faithful old horse, Peanuts, had died by then. He'd gotten into some squirrel poison, and I remember Dad spending at least one entire night out in the barn looking after his range buddy. Until he passed away, at eighty-one, my father would still choke up whenever Peanuts was mentioned.

Dad became the town marshal, and I think he took his cues from Matt Dillon on *Gunsmoke*, because he always hurried home to catch the new episode, even when he was on patrol. Besides serving as marshal, he was also the street commissioner (which meant he plowed snow and graded the roads constantly) *and* the water commissioner, a job that entailed digging through frozen ground to repair North-port's century-old wooden water pipes when they were clogged, iced over, or had simply crumbled. All this for the princely sum of five hundred dollars a month, without benefits. In addition, Dad grew a garden and, later on, he and Mom ran Lael's Motel. Admittedly, most of the motel work fell to Mom; we had a total of four rooms, and we practically sang "Happy Days Are Here Again" whenever they were all rented.

By this time, the Western mind-set was firmly implanted in me, and in my brother, too.

Oddly, since I believe I was born to be a writer, I was a slow reader, early on. In retrospect, I realize that the main problem was undiagnosed ADD. The condition was un-known in those days, so my report cards said things like, *Linda daydreams a lot*, and alas, *Linda talks too much*. I didn't much care for books, since concentration was and still is difficult for me, but I loved wandering in my imagination, and I could spend days doing just that.

It was my voracious reader of a mother who turned the tide where reading was concerned, God bless her forever. I was home sick, and it was her day to work at the town's tiny library, which offered only donated books and was open on Tuesday afternoons, period. When she came home, I was whining on the couch, tired of daytime TV.

Mom handed me a stack of Nancy Drew books, sug-gested I give them a try and heated up a medicinal can of Campbell's chicken noodle soup.

I must have been bored out of my skull, because I leafed through those thin volumes, worn and dog-eared by previous readers, settled on one that didn't seem too terrible and read a page or two.

It was a eureka moment, for sure.

Here was Nancy Drew—a *girl*, no less—who drove a snazzy "roadster," a convertible to boot, and solved genuine mysteries without adult interference. She and her two girlfriends, George and Bess, investigated crimes *and* saw that the perpetrators were brought to justice. Nancy had a good-looking boyfriend, Ned, but she and George and Bess didn't need him to rescue them; he was window dressing, not muscle.

I was enthralled. Hooked. In for the duration.

After those Nancy Drew books, I read Cherry Ames, Student Nurse, the Hardy Boys, everything the Tuesday-afternoon library had to offer. Then I began to borrow books from the loaner shelves at the grade school. (Only the high school had a library then.) I devoured biographies—Annie Oakley, Abe Lincoln, George and Martha Washington. I gobbled up the Little House stories. I read about astronauts and planned on becoming one, until I found out that astronauts had to be wizards at math and science.

Drat. So much for space travel.

For a while, I wanted to be Annie Oakley, as seen on TV. She wore a great fringed cowgirl outfit with a vest, was a sharpshooter and a trick rider. Furthermore, she rounded up outlaws right and left, just like Nancy Drew, only with more action.

Alas, it finally occurred to me that the job of being Annie Oakley, either the real one, long dead, or the one on TV, with the blond pigtails and the great horse, was filled.

I was stuck with being plain old me, and I wasn't very happy about it, either.

Then, one Saturday night when I was nine, I got my first look at Little Joe Cartwright, of *Bonanza* fame, in glorious black-and-white. The crooked grin, the curly hair, the pinto horse—I was in love. (And, all these many years later, I am *still* in love with Little Joe. A portrait of him, done by my friend, actor/artist Buck Taylor, hangs above my living room fireplace.)

My imagination went into overdrive. I began to daydream in earnest, creating scenarios in my busy little brain for hours, even days, at a time. Usually, I was a long-lost Cartwright sister, riding the range with my handsome brothers and Pa. As puberty commenced, I changed roles and became Little Joe's girlfriend, or his bride. Anyone who remembers *Bonanza* will tell you, marrying Little Joe was a dangerous business. The poor woman was doomed, destined to die tragically, not to mention dramatically, in her heartbroken lover's arms. Never, ever did she survive longer than two episodes. Today, ironically, one of those ill-fated brides, the actress Jess Walton, who still plays Jill Abbott on *The Young and the Restless*, is a good friend.

I began to set some of my stories down on paper. They were fevered and brimming with purple prose and lines like, "Breathe, damn you!" and I absolutely loved writing them.

One day, in fifth grade, the teacher, a man named Bob Hyatt who had the distinction of having served in the army with Elvis Presley, handed back papers we'd written as part of an English lesson. I, the daydreamer, was astonished to see that I'd not only received an A, but Mr. Hyatt had graciously written something underneath the grade, along the lines of *You have real talent. You could be a writer.*

I had never been good at much of anything, except getting out of doing farm chores so I could stay inside and listen to Gramma Wiley's wonderful stories.

I could be a writer.

Seriously? Writing was an actual *job*? It paid real money? And I was good at it?

I was blown away. Ten years old, and I was off and running. I wrote and wrote and wrote, frenzied with the pure joy of it. I turned out plays, which I also directed and starred in. I scribbled stories, usually *Bonanza*-themed, and passed them in class the way most kids passed notes.

I remain the only person I know who was sent to the principal's office repeatedly for passing around—or writing—stories when I was supposed to be studying. Or listening. Or reading something educational.

From that long-ago day in fifth grade, I can honestly say I never looked back. I was a writer. In real life, I couldn't be Annie Oakley or an astronaut, but in stories—joy of joys, thrill of thrills—I could be *anyone I wanted*.

In high school, I wrote an entire novel, by hand and in pencil, filling some twenty-six spiral notebooks with what I thought was deathless prose. From my present vantage point, I know I should probably have driven a stake through those notebooks and exposed them to unrelenting sunlight. The title of this tome was *Sea of Faces*, and it was a coming-of-age story—sappy, improbable and surely as bad as anything Jo March wrote in the early chapters of *Little Women*.

Most likely, it was worse.

Now I wish I'd saved that manuscript, along with a few

others that were only marginally better. I could have read a few pages aloud at writers' conferences, to show just how bad a writer can be and still find herself making a respectable living at the trade years later. Or it might have come in handy as a replacement for the Sears catalog in the outhouse at the ranch.

Looking back, I can certainly see the wisdom of the old adage about being willing to write a whole heap of lousy stuff before it's even remotely possible to write well. I certainly did my homework on that score.

I was still a Western girl, riding horses when I had the opportunity, attending the Colville rodeo and the now-defunct Diamond Spur event in Spokane, then regarded as the big city with the bright lights. I was the original *Bonanza* freak, but as the years passed, I added *The Big Valley*, *The Virginian*, *The High Chaparral* and several other TV Westerns to my watch-list. I also shamelessly stole the characters and settings for stories of my own, and when the Beatles came along, I added them, too, even though they weren't cowboys.

I'd taught myself to use punctuation long before we covered it in elementary school, since I read so much, and I learned the concept of scenes from watching my beloved TV Westerns. I clued in that something had better happen at the end of a scene to make the reader/viewer want to come back and find out what happens next.

I married at nineteen, and I continued to write, brave enough now to make up characters of my own. I wrote another bad novel, about a family called Corbin, though by then I owned a portable Smith-Corona—electric, no less. I worked at office jobs, and in my spare time, if I wasn't writing, I was reading.

I had zero money and probably owned a total of four books, one of which was a Bible, but I was living in the big city of Spokane, and the libraries were not only well stocked, they were open five and a half days a week. I consumed books by the stack, especially historical novels by Taylor Caldwell, Lloyd C. Douglas and Janice Holt Giles, and checked out as many back issues of *The Writer* and *Writer's Digest* as the rules allowed. I read every article, took notes, tried to apply what I'd read to whatever project I was banging out on my Smith-Corona at the time. Eventually, I wore that little machine out.

I had—and still have—an insatiable appetite for words, words and more words. These days, I tend to favor audiobooks, if only because my eyes are tired by the end of a writing day, and listening is easier. Also, since I still have ADD, I like to be mobile.

Somehow, my now-ex-husband and I managed to scrounge up the funds for more typewriters—and I wore those out in turn. I wasn't making a dime, or publishing anything, but I was undeterred. Now, looking back, I marvel at my own bullheaded persistence.

I don't think I ever doubted that, one fine day, I would earn a living doing what I loved most—writing.

It's a good thing I was raised by people who could get an old truck running on a freezing day, work eighteen-hour days for practically no money and haul cows out of chest-deep mud, because I still had a long road ahead of me.

I just never learned to quit, a trait that hasn't always worked in my favor, but certainly served me well in this case.

In the early 1980s, I managed to place thirty-seventh in a short story contest run by *Writer's Digest*, and damn, I was proud of that. Soon after, I placed another short piece in a literary magazine. I didn't get paid, but there was my story in print, with my name under the title.

I needed no more encouragement than that.

I wrote another novel and actually submitted it. It was rejected everywhere, but one kindly editor enclosed a letter, expressing regret at having to turn the story down. She said I had talent and went to the trouble, bless her diligent heart, of describing all the things that were wrong with the book.

I put both the manuscript and the letter away and turned to other things. I took the *Writer's Digest* short story course by correspondence, and that was a turning point. My instructor was a woman named Nan Schram Williams, and she was a ghostwriter, composing autobiographies for famous people, but she also wrote "confession" stories for magazines like *True Romance, True Story, True Confessions,* etc. She made either five or three cents a word doing that and advised me to give it a shot.

Even now, I chuckle when I remember this, because my mother wouldn't allow me to read "those magazines" as a girl. The titles were wild and, as Mom put it, "suggestive." Hesitant but determined, I skulked into the grocery store and bought a few copies, soon discovering that while the titles were attention-grabbers, the actual stories were sweet little pieces, almost always about love. Although they were written by freelancers, there were no bylines, as the stories were supposed to be "true," set down on paper and submitted by the people who had experienced them. As such, they were always told in first-person.

I decided to try my hand at one. I wrote a gentle story about a young widow falling in love again, mailed it off to *True Romance* and forgot about it. Imagine my delight when, weeks and weeks later, I received a letter offering to buy the story for a future issue. By the time the check arrived, more weeks and weeks later—a whopping one hundred and thirty-five dollars—I'd written and submitted several more heartfelt confessions. We used the money to replace the windshield in our car.

I sold over thirty of these torridly titled tales and even placed a story with *Women's World*, which paid a mind-blowing twelve hundred dollars, a fortune to a young wife and mother.

Encouraged, I got out my rejected novel, reread the editor's thoughtful letter and applied her suggestions to the manuscript. I sent it off and received another round of rejections for my trouble, but one fine day, I spotted a blurb in the marketing section of *The Writer*. Pocket Books was starting a new line of historical romances, called Tapestry, and they were looking for stories.

I figured I didn't have much to lose besides the postage and sent three chapters and an outline off to Linda Marrow, then an assistant editor at Pocket. She called a week later—be still my beating heart—and asked for the rest of the book. As this had happened once before, and the resulting rejection had devastated me, I tried not to get too excited. I sent the book.

On Valentine's Day, 1983, Linda's boss, Kate Duffy, called and made me an offer. The book came out in August of that same year, and I've been gainfully employed ever since, with my total number of published novels somewhere in the range of one hundred and fifty.

What does all this prove?

Never underestimate a cowgirl from Northport, Washington. They just don't know how to quit.

Turn the page for an excerpt from
FOREVER A HERO,
the third book in the
CARSONS OF MUSTANG CREEK *trilogy,*
coming to HQN Books March 2017.

CHAPTER ONE

MACE CARSON BRAKED, nice and easy, when he saw the car up ahead fishtail on the rain-slicked pavement and then go into a slow-motion spin. After a full three-sixty, the vehicle came to rest at a precarious slant, with the passenger's side tilted downhill, ready to slip in the mud and roll over the steep slope beyond.

The car's engine was still running as he steered his truck to the roadside, flung open the door and jumped to the ground. He hurried forward but could barely make out the driver through the steady drizzle; he saw only a form sitting rigidly upright behind the steering wheel, probably gripping it for dear life.

Up close, he saw her, and something flickered in the back of his brain, something to do with ghosts, popping out of the past and smack into the present, but he didn't pursue the thought. Priority one—get the woman out of the car.

He reached for the handle and, at the same moment, she

came out of freeze-frame long enough to unsnap her seat belt and try to push the door open from her side.

Neither of them was getting anywhere with the effort, since the car was still in Drive.

"Put it in Park," he mouthed.

She stared at him for a few seconds, her face a pale oval behind the rain-specked glass of her window, while he registered that the air bag hadn't deployed.

That was good, anyway, Mace thought, continuing to pull at the door even though he knew the locks were engaged. She probably wasn't hurt, and she didn't look as though she'd been drinking. Still, she might be in shock.

The car lurched a foot or two sideways, farther into the ditch. The woman's eyes rounded, and he saw her gasp.

"Park!" he repeated, only this time he yelled the word.

She finally got the memo and shifted gears. The locks popped.

Mace yanked open the door, gravity working against him, while she pushed desperately from inside. As soon as he could, he took her by the arm and hauled her out. She slammed against him as the sodden earth on the other side gave way again, and the back of the car slid down the slope to stand on end.

Trembling, the woman clung to him, murmuring into his shoulder.

"You all right?" he asked, in no hurry to turn her loose even though the danger was past.

He felt her head bob in an apparent "yes."

Conscious of the rain again, Mace hustled her to the passenger's side of his truck and hoisted her unceremoniously onto the seat. Obviously disoriented, she looked at

him blankly at first, then with a start of what seemed to
be recognition.

"I—I'm okay," she managed, after a few stammered at-
tempts to get the words out.

"You're sure you don't need a doctor?"

She shook her head, smiled tentatively. "No," she said.
"I'm not hurt. Really." She swallowed visibly. "Just shaken
up, that's all."

Mace nodded, let out a long breath as the rush of adrenaline started to subside. The rainstorm had been a sudden
drenching torrent, but it was hardly more than a sprinkle
now. All the same, rivulets cascaded off both sides of the
road.

He stood there for a while, staring at her like a damn
fool, oddly stricken and more than a little off his game.
He had the distinct feeling that he knew this woman from
somewhere, but he couldn't place her.

"Thanks," she said, and something in her expression—
curious, grateful, mildly amused—reminded him that he
was standing in the rain.

Mace walked around the truck, climbed behind the
wheel and reached for his cell phone resting beside the
gearshift. "What happened?" he asked.

"One of the front tires must have gone flat," she replied, still smiling slightly. "There was this awful shimmying, and then I lost control of the car. Next thing I knew,
I was facing the wrong direction and halfway down the
embankment."

He frowned, reviewing the events of the last few minutes. Driving behind her, he hadn't seen the tire blow, or
noticed the shimmying. She'd been rolling along at a good
clip, a few miles over the speed limit, maybe, but she hadn't

been driving recklessly. So why did he feel like reading her the riot act, lecturing her about unfamiliar roads and slick surfaces?

He shoved his fingers through his hair and took another deep breath.

Then, with his free hand, he offered her the cell phone. Her purse, if she had one, was still in the car.

She blinked once, then accepted the phone. He wondered if she was in shock, since she didn't seem to know what to do with the thing.

Mace finally got a grip. Sort of. "You're *sure* you're all right?"

She nodded, glancing from the device in her palm to his face.

He worked the gearshift, then decided he wasn't ready to drive quite yet. Maybe *he* was the one who ought to make a pit stop at the ER.

Mace wasn't much of a talker under any circumstances, but now he thought a bit of idle chitchat might be called for, if only to let his blood pressure trip down a few notches. He'd driven these roads so often, in every conceivable kind of weather, that he could navigate them on autopilot, but the lady, vaguely familiar or not, was new to Bliss County. If he'd met her before, and he was sure he had, the encounter had taken place somewhere else. "That's a bad curve for a flat," he said.

She flicked him that cautious smile again and raised her eyebrows, as if to say, "Duh."

Mace was still spinning his mental wheels; he couldn't seem to get any traction. "You'll need a wrecker," he said, the soul of wit and wisdom, and pointed at the phone.

"It's a rental car," she said, trembling again. "And I'm not from around here, so I don't know who to call."

He reached out, pushed a button on the dashboard to ratchet up the heat, wishing he had a blanket or at least a jacket to offer her. Shock victims had to be kept warm, didn't they?

She looked down at the phone, her lower lip wobbling. *Don't cry*, Mace pleaded silently.

He moved to take back the phone, make the necessary call himself, then changed his mind. Along with his two older brothers, Slater and Drake, he'd been raised to get back on the horse when thrown, on the premise that action was always better than hesitation. "Dial 911," he said, surprised that he sounded so calm. "You'll get Junie at the sheriff's office. Tell her what happened and ask her to send out a tow truck." He gave a brief twitch of a grin. "While you're at it, you can ask if it's safe to get into a car with me. My name is Mace Carson." He saw that her color was coming back, and her eyes were brighter. "I'll drive you into Mustang Creek."

She recovered some of her composure, straightening her shoulders, lifting her chin. "I just came through Mustang Creek," she informed him. "I'm headed somewhere else actually." She paused, and mischief danced in her aqua-blue eyes. "And I knew who you were as soon as I saw you, although I appreciate the introduction."

He was taken aback, but not really surprised. After all, there was that déjà vu thing going on.

The rain was still coming down; he hadn't switched on the interior light, and it was getting dark out. He realized his impressions of the damsel in distress had been visceral, intuitive ones, more about essence than physical details.

Now he looked more closely, took in her blond hair and compact, womanly shape, noticed that she was wearing a midlength skirt and a filmy loose blouse over a camisole.

Finally he asked, "Have we met?" The question came out sounding raspy, made him want to clear his throat.

"We sure have," she replied cheerfully. "Ten years ago, in California."

The experience eluded him. He had a decent memory, or so he'd thought until now. The recollection stayed just out of reach, and that was frustrating. He'd gone to UCLA and later served an apprenticeship of sorts at his grandfather's winery in the Napa Valley. "In college?" he guessed. "Did we have a class together?"

"No."

He studied her for a moment. "Wait a minute. You're Kelly—the girl that night on campus…"

She seemed pleased, but mildly discomfited, too. And little wonder—the memory was probably still traumatic. "Yes," she answered, so softly that he almost didn't hear her. "I'm Kelly Wright."

It all fell into place then. He was thirty-one now, and a decade had gone by, so he supposed he could be forgiven for not remembering right away; a lot had happened since that night, and he hadn't seen her since.

It had been dark then, too, but warm and sultry, and she'd been in real trouble, scared and upset. Spinning off the road in a rainstorm must seem tame, by comparison.

And now she was here, of all places.

What a weird coincidence. If it *was* a coincidence.

Another tremulous smile surfaced, and she'd stopped shivering. "You do remember me, then," she said. She waggled the cell at him. "No need to ask this Junie person, whoever she is, if it's safe to get into a car with you. I'll call to have the car towed, though. She'll take care of everything? Don't I need to file an accident report or something?"

"She will." Mace peered through the windshield, but the vehicle wasn't visible in the gathering gloom. She wasn't going to be able to drive it out of that ditch, but he needed something to look at, besides Kelly, while he regained his balance. "The accident report will keep till morning." He managed to meet her eyes again. "Where were you headed?"

"There's a resort nearby, on the Bliss River. I have a reservation."

Since his sister-in-law, Slater's wife, Grace ran the resort, he knew where to take her, knew she'd be comfortable there. By morning, she'd be good as new. "I'll take you there," he said. He thought he could drive now, so he pulled onto the road to test the theory and gave the rig some gas. "What brings you to Wyoming?" he asked, once they got rolling, figuring that long-ago night in California wouldn't be the best topic of conversation to start with, since she'd already been shaken up enough, going off the road like that. "A vacation?"

He sounded like a half-wit—resort, vacation, no big leap of logic there—but he couldn't seem to help it. It was a jolt, running into Kelly after all this time, and in about the last place he would have expected.

"I have a business meeting tomorrow afternoon." She swept back her hair, and the jerky motion of her hand betrayed the fact that she was still unsteady but trying hard to pull herself together. Then, in the space of a heartbeat, she seemed to gather all her resources, aim them at casual good cheer. "Would you like to have dinner with me to-night? The online reviews of the restaurant at the resort are stellar, as you probably know, and I promise we won't talk business."

Talk business?

Then the light dawned. Oh, yeah. Business meeting. Tomorrow afternoon.

He had a meeting scheduled for the next day himself. Duh.

"I'd like that. Dinner, I mean. Stefano is the best chef in three states." He hurried through that part of the discussion, hell-bent for the next one. "You're the representative from the California distributor and your meeting tomorrow is with me. I guess the name didn't click before. Kelly Wright. When we met, you were Kelly Arden."

"Yes. I'm divorced. It seemed easier to keep my married name after my ex and I called it quits." She sounded tired, sad. He wondered how long the marriage had lasted, and if the split had been relatively amicable.

Probably, he decided. Otherwise, she wouldn't be using the guy's name anymore.

Anyway, her marital status was none of his business.

"What are the chances?" he asked, thinking aloud. "Of our running into each other as business associates? It's a big world out there."

There was a smile in her voice. "Chance had nothing to do with it, Mace. My coming here, that is. When I saw your name in a trade magazine a few months ago, touting you as an innovator, an award-winning winemaker, it seemed like synchronicity. It wasn't hard to track you down." Another pause, sort of fragile. Mace kept his eyes on the road as she went on. "I'm sure you can understand why I remember *you* so well."

"Yes," he said, sounding grim. He rarely thought of that night on the UCLA campus, but he'd never really forgotten it, either. And he'd never expected to see her again. He felt a strange combination of reluctance and relief, as if he'd misplaced something valuable and then found it when he was no longer even searching for it.

Silence fell while she examined his phone, punched in three numbers and spoke to Junie, identifying herself, describing the accident and asking for a tow truck. She said she'd be at the resort until further notice, then "Thank you" and "Goodbye."

She dropped the phone into the little well by the gearshift.

And then she just sat there, not saying anything at all.

Mace—who loved silence, thrived on it, in fact—suddenly wanted to hear her voice again. Failing that, he'd settle for his own. He turned his head in her direction for a moment, raised both eyebrows. "Dinner sounds like a good idea," he said. Then, "We have some catching up to do, Kelly."

MACE CARSON HADN'T changed all that much. He was older, of course, and more solid, but he was still the same quiet, down-to-earth man Kelly had encountered that night in Los Angeles, the kind who showed up at just the right moment, fought off the fire-breathing dragon and didn't expect credit for his actions. For her, the incident on campus, all those years ago, occasionally curdled ordinary dreams into nightmares, even now. Every aspect of it was etched into her psyche, waking or sleeping, but in the daytime, at least, she could keep all the terrible might-have-beens at an acceptable distance.

Bottom line—if Mace hadn't come along when he had, hauled her attacker off her and basically kicked the crap out of the scumbag, she would've been raped and possibly murdered.

Telling herself that Mace *had* come along at just the right moment, and that it was foolish to dwell on things that could've happened but hadn't, made sense when she was feeling rested, confident, in control. And with all those years of practice, that was most of the time.

Tonight, though, tired and still shaken from the near-miss on the highway, she was particularly vulnerable.

Her very cells remembered the throat-closing sensation when she'd realized she was being followed that moonless night as she walked back from a friend's apartment, taking a shortcut through an alley. And the way her breath had caught when she'd turned around to see that she *wasn't* imagining things, that someone was there. She'd picked up her pace, breaking into a run.

She hadn't been fast enough.

Suddenly, she'd felt the impact of another body slamming into her from behind, sending her hurtling, crashing to the ground. Then came the hard weight of a stranger's hands on her, the explosion of pure, primal fear, the scream that knotted in her throat and throbbed there, painful and without sound. She'd struggled wildly, desperately and completely in vain.

She wasn't going to get away.

But she'd fought, just the same. If there was one thing she knew, it was that she *had* to fight if she wanted to survive. Dear God, she wanted to survive.

Abruptly, remarkably, the tide turned. There was a grunt, and the crushing weight of her attacker shifted, then fell away.

Kelly had sat up, scooted backward, every instinct screaming at her to *run*.

She hadn't run, though, because she'd known her legs wouldn't support her. Instead, she'd watched, half-hysterical, sobbing, as a man in jeans, Western boots and a T-shirt dropped her assailant to the sidewalk with one well-aimed punch.

A cowboy, she'd thought stupidly. *I've been saved by a cowboy.*

The would-be rapist was unconscious when the cowboy got out his phone and called the police, and when they arrived, minutes later, the would-be rapist was still down, bleeding copiously from the nose and mouth, although he'd come around enough to whimper and whine.

Mace Carson had kept an eye on the attacker as he extended a hand to Kelly. "You okay?" he'd asked, just like he had a few minutes ago, after he'd pulled her from a car about to slide—or roll—into a deep ditch at the side of the highway.

He'd gone with her to the police station after the attack and gotten her back to the dorm when all the questions had been asked and answered. The man who'd come after Kelly like a runaway train had a rap sheet, it turned out, and he was a person of interest in several similar assaults, including at least one brutal rape. He was arrested that night, held without bail and eventually tried and convicted.

Kelly's horrified parents had insisted she leave school temporarily and come home to Bakersfield, where they could look after her. By the time she'd returned to UCLA, the "temporary" break having stretched to cover two full semesters, Mace had graduated and gotten on with his life elsewhere.

She hadn't known about the big ranch in Wyoming back then, although it wouldn't have surprised her, given the jeans and boots and whole-body dexterity.

Kelly hadn't expected that they'd become lifelong friends or anything like that. She'd simply wanted to thank Mace for helping her, both the night of the attack and afterward, when he'd returned at the request of the Los Angeles county prosecutor's office to testify.

Yes, she'd blubbered some incoherent version of "thank you" at the police station immediately after the incident, but in retrospect, that had never seemed like enough. She could've tracked him down during the decade since, of course, and expressed her gratitude in an adult, rational way. But another part of her had flatly refused to make contact, wanting to put the whole thing behind her for good, to move on, to forget.

And that part had won out.

Kelly *had* moved on. She'd gotten a degree in business, made new friends, dated a variety of guys, worked hard, continued to learn and built a career she loved. She'd been through the appropriate therapy and attended support groups for PTSD, and she'd had a white-lace-and-promises wedding, too. The marriage hadn't lasted, it was true, but she'd honestly tried to make it work.

She had her problems—didn't everyone?—and yet she'd made a good life for herself, a life she was proud of, even if it wasn't perfect. Even if she hadn't forgotten, not entirely.

It had been naive, she supposed, to believe that was possible. Traumatic experiences, especially life-threatening ones, didn't just vanish from a person's memory, but they could be managed, coped with, put in perspective. And maybe that was all anybody ought to expect, since living was a complicated and sometimes messy business.

Now, as she and Mace traveled over country roads in the warm semidarkness of his truck, Kelly had a chance to refresh her memory, at least where his appearance was concerned, without openly staring at the man. His thick, longish hair, like before, wasn't exactly brown or exactly red, either, but a mixture of the two, a rich auburn or chestnut, probably lighter in summer. His shoulders were broader, but he was still lean, and he still wore jeans, boots and a T-shirt, faded with wear.

The confident, no-nonsense attitude was in evidence, as well. Mace was clearly the take-charge type, just as he'd been in college.

Beyond these observations, though, and the things she'd read about him in the article and on a few websites, he was still a mystery.

He'd come to her rescue twice, like some cowboy-knight, and it did seem serendipitous that he'd been right behind her on the road when she lost control of her car. On the other hand, this was his home turf, his territory.

"I'm glad I took the extra insurance option when I rented the car," she heard herself say.

Mace grinned, looked her way for a moment, then turned his attention back to the road. "Yeah," he agreed. "There's bound to be some damage."

"The keys are in the ignition," Kelly recalled, fretful now. "You don't suppose somebody would—"

"Steal your car?" He sounded quietly amused. "That would take some doing, I think."

She blushed, feeling foolish. "Right," she said, glad he couldn't see her face. Now that she'd calmed down a bit, potential problems kept coming to mind. "My suitcase is in the back, along with my laptop and my purse."

"Your stuff will be safe until tomorrow," he said.

In her mind, Kelly went on cataloging what she'd need tonight, not tomorrow. Such as her nightgown, her toothbrush, her makeup case, her cell phone. She didn't have to call anyone in particular, but she was addicted to a certain game app, and she doubted she could sleep without listening to part of an audiobook.

And what about clean clothes to put on in the morning?

Mace seemed to know what she was thinking, because he chuckled and said, "The spa has everything you could possibly need for the night. Junie will make sure you get your luggage bright and early. The woman is an organizational genius."

Kelly allowed herself to be reassured. She'd made the reservation at the resort well in advance, using the corporate card, so her payment information would be on file. As for her favorite presleep distractions…surely she could get through a single night without them. If necessary, she'd buy a paperback in the gift shop, provided it was open, and charge the purchase to her room. Or catch a movie on TV.

"Good," she said in belated answer. "Everything's good, then."

She must have sounded hesitant, though, because Mace said, "You'll feel a lot better after a hot meal and a night's sleep. In the meantime, don't worry about your car or your things. Around here, most folks are not only honest, they'll go out of their way to lend a hand."

Kelly was from the big city, and his remark made her

feel somewhat wistful. "Must be nice, knowing almost everybody in town."

Mace laughed quietly. "No 'almost' about it. I also know the names of their cats, dogs and horses. Of course, that kind of familiarity works both ways. By tomorrow morning it'll be common knowledge, from one end of Bliss County to the other, that I had dinner at the resort with a lovely young woman from California after she had an accident involving a blown tire. That pretty much sums the place up."

Kelly hadn't missed the compliment tucked away in the middle of that statement, and it warmed her. "So you never thought about living anywhere else?"

His shoulders lifted in a shrug. "Not really. Mustang Creek is home, and it isn't as if I haven't been to plenty of other places. Most people who grow up here either stay put or come back after college or a hitch in the service. You can't beat the scenery, and there's a lot to be said for small-town life." He looked her way again, signaled for a right turn when they came to a crossroads. "Like most roads in this part of Wyoming, the one where you ditched your car is quiet, but I'd bet next year's profits that nobody would have driven by without stopping to help. That's just how it is around here."

Kelly wasn't inclined to refute that, although she hadn't seen another car, except for the truck she was riding in now, which she'd glimpsed in her rearview mirror, since she'd driven out of Mustang Creek. She might have had a long wait if Mace hadn't been around. For one thing, she wouldn't have had the strength to shove open the driver's-side door, because of how the vehicle was tilted—and, for another, she might've been hurt when the ground gave way.

There it was again, that habit of focusing on what *might*

have happened. Annoyed with herself, she shook off the thought. "You do seem to show up just when I need help," she said too brightly.

"Ah, shucks, ma'am," he teased. "T'weren't nothin'."

She laughed at the late-show cowboy line, and he grinned.

They made the turn, and Kelly spotted the lights of the resort up ahead. "Almost there," Mace said. "We'll get you checked in, then you can have a nice glass of wine while you look over the dinner menu." A few seconds passed and, once again, she sensed that he knew what had been going through her mind. "Everything's okay, Kelly Wright. Time to kick back and relax."

Easy for him to say, she thought without rancor. He was probably right, though.

He'd certainly been dead-on when it came to the beauty of their surroundings. She'd been awestruck on the drive, before the wreck, before nightfall, drinking in the Grand Tetons, the rushing Bliss River, the open spaces interspersed with groves of aspen trees. Even the rain hadn't marred the view. "Are you always so philosophical?"

He grinned again. "No," he said, straight out.

"What's your family like?" She didn't know why she'd asked that question. They'd almost reached the resort, so the curious intimacy of riding together was about to end.

He answered easily. "I have two brothers," he said. "Drake is the practical one. He raises cattle, with the help of a dozen or so ranch hands. Slater is the firstborn, which means he's bossy as hell. He makes documentary films about the West, new and old. Me, I'm the kid brother, so I have to work twice as hard for half the glory. Slater and

Drake, well, they can't figure me out, most of the time. I do get some pretty wild ideas."

"For instance?" Kelly prompted, maybe a touch more interested than she should've been.

Mace glanced at her, as if the question left him slightly bemused, then replied, "Last year I decided to try making corn wine. They all thought I was crazy, gave me a lot of guff about turning into a moonshiner. Red—he's the oldest living ranch hand on the planet—said they must've brought Prohibition back and he'd missed it, and wanted to know where I'd hidden the still." He shook his head, smiling. "He loves a bad joke, that old man, and he had a fine time with the white-lightning routine."

They'd reached the big circular driveway in front of the resort by then, but Kelly wished they could stay in Mace's truck awhile longer.

"But your experiment worked," she said as they drew up at the end of a line of cars, waiting for valet service. She'd tasted his blends, as had everyone she worked with, wine snobs all of them. The cautious consensus had been that Mountain Vineyards had potential, and she agreed, although her own assessment had been considerably more enthusiastic. She wouldn't have been in Wyoming otherwise, despite the debt of gratitude she'd owed him for so long.

"It worked," he confirmed, referring, as she had, to the corn wine. "It has to age awhile before I'd feel right about putting it on the market, but just about everybody who's tried it says it's damn decent."

A young man in slacks, a crisp white shirt and a vest rapped at the driver's-side window, his smile eager and toothy.

Mace sighed good-naturedly and lowered the window.

"What are you doing in the valet line, Mace?" the boy asked, apparently delighted. "You usually park in the main lot."

"Tonight, Phil," Mace answered cheerfully, "I feel like living high on the hog, availing myself of your expert services. Besides, the lady here has had a hard day, and I doubt she's up for a hike through the rain."

Phil peered around Mace, clearly trying to get a look at the lady in question, reacting with wry resignation when his view was blocked by a pair of wide shoulders.

"Just park the truck, Phil," Mace said. "And God help you if I find any new scratches or dents when the sun comes up tomorrow morning."

CHAPTER TWO

THE LOBBY OF the resort was as magnificent as the outside. Kelly was used to good hotels, even excellent ones, since her high-profile job required a lot of travel, but in this place, grand as it was, the warmth was almost like an embrace. And here she was, with no luggage and no credit cards, probably looking like the proverbial drowned rat, escorted by one of the hottest men she'd ever seen.

Thank God Mace was a local, and willing to do all the explaining, because Kelly felt off-kilter, damp from head to foot, her skirt and blouse clinging, her expensive shoes caked with mud, the light makeup she'd applied that morning in the bathroom of her LA condo long gone. She wished she'd looked into the side mirror of Mace's truck, made sure her mascara hadn't migrated from her eyelashes to lie in smudged streaks on either side of her face.

And then there was her hair.

Silently, she commanded herself to stop being so silly.

To distract herself, she watched Mace charming the clerk

at the fancy reception desk, gesturing once or twice in Kelly's direction, explaining the situation. The pretty young woman basked in his smile the whole time, fingers busy on the keyboard, well-coiffed head nodding at intervals. When she got the chance, the clerk homed in on Kelly, and the pleasant upward curve of her mouth faltered briefly.

So much for distracting herself.

If Mace hadn't been handling the check-in process, Kelly thought with an uncharacteristic lapse of self-confidence, the woman might have called security to have the homeless person discreetly removed.

Soon enough, though, Mace was turning, walking over to Kelly. Even here, in this upscale resort, among guests clad in designer clothes, he seemed completely at ease in his jeans and T-shirt.

He was smiling, and as he came toward her, Kelly could have sworn that time froze for an instant. Sound, too, was suspended; the soft music, the voices of the other people, the chime of elevator bells, all faded into a strange, pulsing silence.

Kelly simply looked at Mace Carson, marveling. Rugged as he was, his features were classic, almost aristocratic. Slap that face onto a Renaissance painting—she'd minored in art—and it would fit right in, five-o'clock shadow and all. His eyes were a remarkable shade of blue, and so expressive that he probably could've gotten any point across without opening his mouth.

There were men, she thought, and there were *men*. Some were just plain handsome, and Mace certainly qualified, but he was attractive for deeper, less definable reasons. Intelligence, sure. Sense of humor? Absolutely. And yet there was more to him, and still more beyond that, an infinity of qualities and secrets to explore.

By degrees, the strange spell began to subside. Kelly was both relieved and saddened by the shift.

Mace reached her. He was smiling, but concern flickered in his eyes. "All set," he said, and Kelly noticed that he wasn't holding a key card. Reading her curious glance correctly, he added, "Your room will be ready by the time we've finished dinner. A tour group checked out late, and the housekeeping people are hustling to catch up."

Kelly's knees wobbled, and she ordered them to hold her upright. "But...they have my reservation, right?" It wasn't like her to be so uncertain, she fretted to herself, not even after a stressful day. What the heck was going on?

"Yep," Mace said, taking a firm but gentle hold on her elbow. "Come on. You need food and at least one glass of wine—the sooner, the better."

He led her toward the restaurant entrance on the other side of the lobby. She recalled from her research that there were several eating establishments in the resort; however, this one was the main attraction.

Kelly might have balked, bedraggled as she was, but Mace was on a direct trajectory, and besides, she was hungry. Starved, in fact. She would have opted for room service, given the choice, but she didn't actually *have* a room yet, so that was out.

They were greeted warmly at the door and seated right away at a quiet table in a cozy corner of the large room. Along the way, Kelly saw that the other tables were all occupied by well-dressed, smiling people, and Mace paused a few times for a friendly word and a handshake when one of the diners called his name or waved him over. Each time, the hostess, sleek in a feminine version of a tuxedo, waited patiently, her smile wide and genuine.

Aware of tailored suits, glamorous evening gowns and jewelry usually stored in safes or bank vaults, Kelly wished she could teleport herself—and Mace—to a fast-food place. Or an ordinary diner with a counter and stools, tables with mismatched chairs and vinyl booths.

Evidently, she reflected ruefully, the dress code, ranging from smart casual to out-and-out formal, judging by the fashions on display tonight, didn't apply to Mace Carson.

Kelly was relieved when they finally reached their table. Mace pulled back her chair, and she practically collapsed onto the seat.

The hostess handed them each a heavy, leather-bound menu, announced that their server this evening would be Danielle and cheerfully instructed them to enjoy their meal.

Kelly studied the impressive offerings for that evening, handwritten in lovely copperplate, and discovered, to her embarrassment, that she was incapable of making a decision, famished though she was.

Once again, Mace stepped up. "Mind if I order for both of us?" he asked.

"Please," Kelly replied with a nod and a wavering smile.

The server, Danielle, materialized beside the table. "Hey, Mace," she said, neatly including Kelly with a nod. Danielle was attractive, but there was an air of anxiety about her, which she was obviously trying to hide.

"Hey, back at you." Mace introduced Kelly as a business associate and Danielle as an old friend.

Kelly *was* a business associate, of course, but she felt a pang of disappointment at those words, just the same. She even went so far as to wonder what *kind* of friend Danielle was, which was none of her damn beeswax, any way you looked at it, and was instantly annoyed with herself.

Mace ordered prime rib for both of them, along with a rich merlot, and Danielle collected the menus and walked away, returning shortly with a bread basket and a bottle bearing the Mountain Vineyards label. Danielle uncorked the wine expertly, filled their glasses and asked if they wanted ice water.

Mace nodded, and they were alone again, unless you counted the hundred or so other diners in the place. For Kelly, those people were drifting into a haze, just as their counterparts in the lobby had minutes before.

Mace lifted his glass, and Kelly raised her own. The rims clinked.

Kelly took a thoughtful sip, savored it for a moment, then widened her eyes at Mace. "Impressive," she said.

He smiled, clearly pleased. "Thanks," he responded, "but we're dangerously close to talking business, and I think we agreed not to do that tonight."

"So we did," Kelly said. "This is a really nice place, isn't it?"

"Yes," Mace answered. "And you're so worn-out you might fall asleep in your salad plate."

"I'm not usually so—"

"Tired?" he finished for her.

The haze dissolved. "Self-conscious," she confessed.

"Self-conscious?" He looked baffled, then apparently something dawned on him. "You do realize you're the most beautiful woman in this restaurant?"

"If that's a line," Kelly replied, smiling over the rim of her wineglass, "it's a darned clever one."

Mace's eyes danced, and he ducked his head, as though taking a bow. "Better yet," he said, "it's true."

Kelly was unsettled, in ways that had nothing to do with their very brief but memorable history. "I think I'd be more comfortable talking about wine," she said.

Danielle brought their salads, lovely crisp Caesars with croutons, and vanished again.

Kelly, who had restrained herself when the bread basket arrived, fairly dived into her salad, which was delicious. And it took the edge off her hunger—a good thing, since she might have consumed her prime rib, when it was served, with the manners of a peasant feasting at a medieval banquet.

Plus, eating salad kept her too busy to blurt out something stupid like, "So. Tell me all about Danielle. Just how well do you two know each other?"

Between the removal of the salad plates and the delivery of the entrée, she finished her first glass of wine and started on the second as soon as Mace finished pouring it.

"My expertise on corn varieties is nonexistent," she said, returning to their earlier conversation. "I thought there was field corn and sweet corn. Period."

Mace's brow furrowed in confusion, but he was quick on the uptake, this ridiculously attractive cowboy vintner, and picked up the conversational ball right away, as smoothly as if there hadn't been a half-hour gap between their corn-into-wine discussion in his truck and the remark she'd just made. "I have a friend who's a fourth-generation farmer, out in Indiana. I called him and he said the Silver Queen variety was the best option for what I had in mind. Sweet corn is his favorite, and he knows what he's talking about."

"Maybe if you didn't label it corn wine," Kelly mused,

in her element again and very glad to be there. "What if you called it Midwestern Blend? Or Heartland Varietal?"

He looked amused. "What about Hayseed Special Vintage? I kind of had that in mind."

Kelly laughed, for real this time, without awkwardness or restraint. "Colorful, but I don't think it'll fly in today's sophisticated marketplace." She felt so much better now that they were back on common ground.

"Spoken like a true sales guru. And forgive the reminder, but I thought we weren't going to talk business."

"I can't help it," she admitted airily. "I find the whole process fascinating, from growing the grapes right on through to store displays and shelving for ideal impact on the consumer."

"Seriously, the corn thing is still in the experimental stage. Truth is, I'm so busy with production now I can barely keep up."

Kelly might have said he'd be even busier if tomorrow's meeting went the way she hoped, but she kept that to herself. The notes for her presentation were on her iPad, anyway, and that was in the rental car, along with everything else she'd brought, besides the clothes on her back and the shoes on her feet. She'd spent days preparing the charts and spreadsheets she intended to show him, and she wanted to be in fine form when she made her pitch.

"I think the rain stopped," she observed, squinting through the window next to their table.

Their dinners arrived, and Kelly managed to eat sedately, enjoying every bite.

"According to the weather reports," Mace said presently, "the storm is headed east. We should see blue skies and sunshine tomorrow."

"Dawn will probably be spectacular," Kelly said. As if she had any intention of being awake in time to see it. "See, I'm taking your advice and looking on the bright side, so to speak."

"Good to know," Mace said, suppressing a grin.

"I'm doing my best." She sighed and looped a lock of hair behind her ear; it was a habit she'd been trying to break, but she was starting to feel nervous again. Why was that? "I was hoping we'd meet again one day, so I could thank you for what you did for me, but I didn't figure blowing a tire and winding up in a ditch into the equation."

Too soon, warned a voice in Kelly's head. *Too soon. First and foremost, you're here on business, not a personal mission. Stay on track.*

"Well," he said easily, "we've met again, haven't we?"

"Guess so," Kelly said and felt utterly inane.

"You thanked me before," Mace reminded her. "That was good enough. I only did what any red-blooded cowboy, or any guy with a shred of decency, would've done. That particular creep is still in prison, you and a lot of other women are safe, from him, anyhow, and that's all that matters, in the end."

"You really are noble," Kelly told him solemnly.

He held up both hands, palms out. "No," he said. "I'm just a man who happened to be around when somebody needed help."

"You're way too modest, Mr. Carson."

"And you're giving me way too much credit."

"My prerogative," Kelly said.

"Finish your dinner."

"I'm full."

He sighed, leaning back in his chair. He might've been

sitting at the table in a ranch-house kitchen instead of a five-star restaurant, he seemed so relaxed. "Me, too."

Danielle stopped by, asked if they were ready for dessert and coffee and carried away the debris when they both said, "No, thanks." Mace watched the other woman leave, his expression serious, and Kelly refused to let that bother her.

Danielle returned with the check, setting the small leather folder in front of Mace, and looked mildly surprised when Kelly reached across the table and picked it up.

For a couple of minutes, Kelly and Mace engaged in a friendly stare-down.

With a nearly imperceptible shrug, Danielle walked away.

Kelly didn't give an inch; this was a business dinner, and besides, Mace had helped her out of the rental car, where she might've been trapped for hours, brought her here and taken over the registration process. "Did you get my room number when you spoke to the receptionist?" she asked, almost primly.

He shook his head, smiling again. "Room 422," he said as though she'd dragged it out of him. "Has it occurred to you that you're ruining my reputation here? By morning, everybody in the county will know I let a woman pay for my dinner, like some yahoo who can't hold down a job. They might have me thrown out of the cowboys' union."

"Tough luck," she said lightly, picking up the accompanying pen, adding a tip and a total and scrawling her signature on the dotted line.

"You're one stubborn woman," Mace told her.

She smiled sweetly. "Keep that in mind," she answered.

Just then, Mace's cell phone rang. He glanced at the number and his mouth tightened. "Do me a favor?" he asked.

"What?"

"Answer this call."

Kelly frowned, confused, but she took the phone when he offered it, still ringing insistently, pressed the button and said, "Hello?"

There was a silence on the other end, followed by a female voice demanding, "Who the *hell* is this?"

Kelly looked at Mace. "Kelly Wright," she said. "Who's this?"

The only response was a muttered curse and the sound of a flip-phone snapping shut.

Slowly, Kelly handed Mace's phone back to him. "What was that all about?"

"Thanks," Mace said grimly, accepting the phone. He'd just screwed up, big-time, and all because he didn't want to deal with Felicity Donovan, then or ever. Considering that he'd drawn Kelly into the drama by asking her to take the call, he owed her an explanation.

Kelly merely raised an eyebrow and waited.

Mace sighed. He'd met Felicity at a conference several months before and they'd gotten a little carried away, after a full day of wine-tasting, followed by a rubber-chicken dinner with more wine, and ended up in Felicity's room, sharing a bed.

With the morning came stone-cold sobriety, the hangover to end all hangovers and a whole lot of regret. Politely, because he knew he was responsible for his part of what had been a truly lousy decision, he'd tried to play down his hasty departure even as he scrambled back into his clothes and practically bolted for the door.

Felicity's fury had surprised him. She'd yelled, and yelled plenty, and Mace had stopped and listened, shocked to discover that what he saw as the end of something that shouldn't have happened in the first place, Felicity had interpreted as a *beginning*.

He'd said he was sorry she'd misunderstood, and fled.

For the rest of the conference, Felicity had turned up everywhere he went, alternately sniffling into a cocktail napkin and scorching his hide with the stink-eye. He'd tried to be diplomatic; that hadn't worked, either. He supposed he should've left the conference early, but there were still meetings he wanted to attend, people he wanted to talk with, and besides, it just wasn't in him to run. So he'd stuck it out to the end. Surely, he'd thought, an intelligent, successful woman like Felicity would see reason once she got home, if not before.

Except she hadn't.

She'd sent emails until he finally blocked her.

She'd raged at him on every available social media site.

And she'd called and called, and called again, relentlessly. Mace had considered changing his number, which would be a huge hassle and, ultimately, a temporary fix. They were in the same industry, with a lot of the same contacts, and she'd manage to charm the new information out of one of them.

He couldn't bring himself to say all that to Kelly. They hardly knew each other.

So he said some of it. "There's a woman," he told her.

"So I gathered," Kelly said flippantly.

"She wanted a relationship, and I didn't. Still don't." God, this was hard. He should've ignored the call when he recognized Felicity's number, let it go to voice mail to delete later, the way he usually did. What had given him the harebrained idea to involve Kelly?

"And you thought if she called, and a woman answered, she'd leave you alone?" Kelly's tone told him nothing, but there might have been a spark of something in her eyes; he couldn't really tell.

Mace nodded. "I'm sorry."

She absorbed the inadequate apology. Nodded.

Silence.

"Say something," he said when he couldn't stand it anymore.

"Fine," Kelly responded coolly. "You don't know much about women if you thought a lame trick like that was going to work."

Mace felt heat rise up his neck and pulse under his jawline. "Not that one, anyhow," he said. Here he was, sitting across a restaurant table from the first woman who'd interested him in a couple of years, and he'd already blown his chances.

Nice work.

Kelly pushed back her chair and stood, leaving Mace with no choice but to do the same.

"Well," she said very quietly, "I guess maybe we're even."

Great. She was going to get a good night's sleep, collect her belongings from the rental car right after breakfast and hightail it back to the airport. He'd never see her again, and worst of all, it served him right.

He stood there, swamped by an emotion so unfamiliar that he couldn't quite put a name to it, taking in Kelly's honey-colored hair, elegantly cut, her delicate features and those incredible aquamarine eyes. He'd wanted to get to know her better, in so far as he could, considering the context. Besides being uncommonly beautiful, Kelly Wright was a representative of one of the largest wine and spirits distributors in the country, with the ability to put his winery in the black for years to come.

She was also the polar opposite of Felicity and women like her.

For the first time in his life, Mace wanted to say, "Don't go."

But he didn't. His tongue was stuck to the roof of his mouth.

Mercifully, she broke the silence. "This," she said, "has been a very, *very* long day. I think I'll turn in, provided my room is ready."

"Right," he said, still not moving.

Kelly walked out of the restaurant and into the lobby, going straight to the reception desk.

Mace followed. If he had half a brain, he'd cut his losses and run. The winery was doing well financially, he reminded himself, and there were other distributors in the world. The problem was, they didn't have Kelly Wright on their payrolls.

She waited at the desk, arms folded, then approached one of the clerks, not once looking back.

When she'd collected her key card, she finally made eye contact. He was only about six feet away, and he probably came off as some kind of weirdo, a stalker even, but it was too late to step back and give her more space. She was holding a small plastic bag filled with travel-size grooming supplies, and it rattled as she shook it at him and smiled.

She actually *smiled*.

"See you at tomorrow's meeting," she said, as if the whole Felicity fiasco hadn't happened at all.

A moment later, she was in one of the elevators, the doors closing in front of her.

SHE'D BEEN UPGRADED from a regular room to a suite, Kelly soon discovered. There was a living room, a spacious bedroom and an en suite bath with a jetted garden tub and one of those fancy shower stalls with strategically placed sprayers.

The space was furnished Western-style, expensively rustic, with a hand-hewn headboard on a king-size bed graced by an exquisite quilt in rich brown, crimson and gold, coordinating nicely with the drapes and the wall decor, which consisted of a few landscape prints and a collection of framed photographs of racing mustangs and snow-covered ski slopes. The desk, where she hoped she'd be drafting a hefty contract with Mountain Vineyards—if she ever got her laptop back—faced a window, promising a glorious view.

For tonight, she wasn't going to think. She'd give herself a break, enjoy the novelty of being unplugged, however temporarily.

She found a fluffy robe in the bedroom closet and hung it on the back of the bathroom door.

After tearing open the plastic package she'd been given at the desk, she brushed her teeth at one of the two sinks, and immediately felt a little less grubby than before.

Normally, Kelly liked to soak in a bath at night—she got some of her best ideas relaxing in the tub—but for now, she didn't want to linger in the waking world. She was not only exhausted, she was on physical and mental overload.

She kicked off her ruined shoes, stripped off her clothes and took a quick shower, using only one sprayer. Afterward, she dried off and bundled up in the hotel bathrobe, tightening the belt until she felt almost swaddled. Her favorite nightgown would have been less bulky and therefore a lot more comfortable, but the robe would do in a pinch, and this was definitely a pinch.

With luck, she'd have her suitcase and other things by morning.

Keeping her mind closed to thoughts of Mace Carson, the woman who'd called his cell phone at dinner and the disturbing parts of her past, Kelly switched off the lights. She threw back the quilt and top sheet, fluffed her pillow and sank gratefully into bed.

She didn't miss the games on her smartphone or the audiobook she'd nearly finished the night before.

A few seconds after she closed her eyes, she slid into a deep, dreamless sleep.